Forbidden Origins

book one apostasia

www.dkratcliffe.com

This book is a work of fiction. Names, characters, businesses, places, events and incidents are either the products of the author's imagination or used in a fictitious manner. Any resemblance to actual persons, living or dead, or actual events is purely coincidental.

Copyright © 2016 by Daniel Ratcliffe

All rights reserved. This book or any portion thereof may not be reproduced or used in any manner whatsoever without the express written permission of the publisher except for the use of brief quotations in a book review.

Cover designs by Krystal Dutkiewicz & Daniel Ratcliffe

ISBN 978-1539429890

Printed in the United States of America

Acknowledgements

We have been so blessed to have the support, advice, and guidance from our close family and friends throughout the process of writing this book. There are too many to name everyone individually, but you know who you are! As much as we'd like to say we won't lean on you as much for the remainder of the series...we can't, because we all know that would be a lie. So from the bottom of our hearts, thank you for all that you've done and everything that you will help us to do in the future.

Forbidden Origins

book one apostasia

CHAPTER ONE
The Big Announcement

"Welcome to the Lacey Evans show. Today I would like to dedicate this segment to a new shocking scientific breakthrough for the controversial topic of cloning. As most of you know the first major success was Dolly the sheep in the mid-90s. Years later the cloning of pets became popular; what owner of a beloved pet wouldn't want to be able to own an identical pet to replace the one they lost? But the biggest success is the human organ cloning for donating. There are matches for every size and blood type.

Donor lists are virtually obsolete. Although you may need to wait a month or so for all the matching and preparations for transplanting to take place, the wait time for an organ is almost nonexistent!

This method of donating saves countless lives, and also creates a massive employment opportunity. It helps veterans with missing limbs, children fighting cancer, and even victims of horrific car crashes who need multiple limb and organ replacements. No doubt cloning is a scientific miracle for many, but unfortunately not without a dark history due to its high failure rate. The extent of these failures across the globe are still unknown, but estimates range between hundreds to thousands, and even hundreds of thousands. Because of this, the process of cloning came to an abrupt halt. There had been too many organs that stopped working and cloned pets that unexpectedly keeled over.

This caused the government to intervene and not allow the production of cloning to take place anymore. It wasn't until a private laboratory made a huge breakthrough and gained government funding that the cloning research was allowed to continue. This organization is now called Federal Duplications. Able to produce more effectively and with consistency, cloning is now a practical and standard solution for patients undergoing almost any type of surgery, without any fear of sudden organ or limb failure. They even have perfected the replication of blood, eliminating the need for human blood donors. Starting to sound a little like science fiction, or something you would see in a movie, huh?" When Lacey paused dramatically, the audience chuckled.

Well, unlike the movies no real living breathing person has ever been cloned... until now. So far, Federal Duplications has been pretty tight lipped about this and has not allowed any of their employees to talk to the media about these phenomenal breakthroughs. But at long last they made the decision to allow the world in on the secret of their success and have agreed to do an exclusive interview on my show. So representing Federal Duplications is Dr. Timothy Phillips, who is here with us today to explain this revolutionary process. It is wonderful to have you on the show Doctor... this is a real honor."

Dr. Phillips:
"Thank you, it's good to be here Lacey."

Lacey:
"So Dr., you and your team have actually cloned a living human?"

Dr. Phillips:
"Yes Lacey, we certainly did."

Lacey:
"I read an article stating 'The attempt to make any living clone

has devastating results. Out of one hundred clones, three might live through birth. Those three might even die right after birth due to unknown complications. If the clone is born perfectly healthy, it doesn't mean it will even stay healthy.' So have you developed a way for greater success as well, or was it a lucky one?"

Dr. Phillips:
"The kind of article you are talking about is behind on cloning facts Lacey, because until now no legitimate organization has ever come out with full details. I'm here after years of painstaking research to say not only did we accomplish this, we've done it several times and with impressive results."

Lacey:
"This is quite the news and I would like to stop for a moment and tell the viewers. This is no hoax, it's been verified, and is being shared for the first time on my show."

Dr. Phillips:
"That's right Lacey; I am able to share with you today only because so much time and research has passed we are at a point where the progress needs to be revealed to the public."

Lacey:
"So if you could Dr. Phillips, please explain the process or what

your team did differently."

Dr. Phillips:

"To prevent the defects you were reading about in the article; we originally couldn't make a clone without major alterations. By maintaining the 'empty egg', we eradicate harmful genetic diseases, isolate a problematic genome, destroy it and replace it with perfect versions of the defective ones. We then chose the perfect DNA strand we wanted to use, and altered that strand. This provided a greater chance of clones surviving through birth as well as their overall longevity. There was one major drawback, though: no one would be able to afford them. As complicated and time consuming as the process is, you can imagine the prohibitive expenses involved."

Lacey:

"I can see how that would be a problem."

Dr. Phillips:

"Very problematic indeed. We decided to make a work force like no other, profitable and helpful. What better way to offset these exorbitant costs than by making it so the clones can basically pay for themselves? With that in mind we would make a whole new breed of workers. However, this also meant we needed a whole new method of cloning. We would need to supply the buyers

Forbidden Origins-apostasia

faster as well as having a clone who wants the job."

Lacey:
"I suppose a business wouldn't want to wait years, just to end up with a clone not wanting to do the job."

Dr. Phillips:
"Precisely, so we had to be creative. We found you could speed up the process by using stop and go cells. These cells determine when your growth spurt happens as a child and when it stops as an adult. Using the smallest amount of electrodes, we could alter the growth speed. We could then use a neural-computer to program the clone for the specific job. This was all done without a surrogate mother by the way."

Lacey:
"Okay, I think we should talk about this more in depth, because these are beginning to sound more like robots, rather than humans. So could you explain to us what a clone is, is it a direct copy of an individual? Also what do you mean by neural-computer? "

Dr. Phillips:
"Everything we do is what nature does already. When a baby is born, the path has been decided; your talents, mindset, personality, etc. In the case of cloning, instead of nature

choosing these certain paths, we did. A clone can technically be anything identical; take identical twins, for instance. These are nature's clones. They share remarkable similarities, yet they are separate people. So like nature, we can clone an exact look alike, but it's not like the movies where it's the same person. Federal Duplications clones are not identical physically to anyone in particular; rather they are a copy of many elements. You can use the term 'designer baby' if you want, but you start splitting hairs because we do duplicate a variety of different attributes.

To answer your other question, Lacey, we do our programming through our neural-computers. We use this technology to download the job task into the clones. By cloning human brains, we learned how to make neural-computers. These contain physical software that has the capability to grow as they learn. For instance, the computer feeds the neurons information constantly. This makes the neurons expand and make several stronger connections with each other. It's like memorizing a speech. When you recite it over and over the memory gets stronger...uh oh, it looks like maybe I am losing you now, Lacey."

Lacey: (laughing a little awkwardly)
"I'm sorry Dr., but I think you may have lost my audience with that as well. Could you break this concept down for us in a little bit simpler terms?"

Dr. Phillips:

"Of course. Let me put it like this: during the first six years of life, your brain is in a fully hypnotic state. And then for years six through twelve your brain is in a semi-hypnotic state. This is why children are so impressionable. They learn things much easier than an adult can, and even have the capacity to believe in fictional characters as being real. The reason being that the brain is naturally programmed to form lots of neural connections during the early phases of life, so that you can grow and develop at a rapid rate. The brain is also very plastic, meaning it has the ability to form new neural connections and pathways anytime during your life. So you can analyze and decipher new things.

Let me give you an example of the magnitude of what this allows. Our brains have the capacity to form hundreds of trillion of neural connections with each other. To understand how immense that is, this number of connections adds up to more than the grains of sand on all the beaches in the entire world. Tapping into that power with technology is what allowed us to develop neural-computers, which led us to the programming. It works by mapping the entire brain activity of individuals carrying out specific jobs and tasks then download that information into the clones. Any bad thoughts that occur during the mapping are edited out, so that the clones don't have any emotional or psychological 'baggage' to deal with."

Lacey:

"Obviously you don't want theses clones starting out with bad behaviors."

(AUDIENCE LAUGHS)

Dr. Philips:

"Exactly!"

Lacey:

"So is it possible with your programmer to transfer all my thoughts and memory's into one of your clones?"

Dr. Phillips:

Another good question. We have the capability to map and download all your memories, thoughts, experiences, etc. But here's the problem. If you and I go to the same amusement park, ride the same rides, eat the same foods, and see the same people, we may have the same memories and possibly even the same thoughts. Yet we are still two separate people. Transferring just your memory into a clone, would be like giving your diary to your twin sibling. They may be able to access your inner most thoughts and feelings, but they are still going to process it all and react differently than you would. So if you are looking to completely transfer consciousness Lacey, cryonics as of now looks like the best way to do so."

Forbidden Origins-apostasia

Lacey:

"Cryonics is the science of preserving your body in a dormant stage, right?"

Dr. Phillips:

"In simple terms yes, all we need is the brain and we can transfer it into a clone. We believe that with your original brain we can achieve a full transfer of consciousness, not just the ability to pass down information and memories. Of course like anything else, it's all up for debate, but it is the way of the future.

Lacey:

"This is so exciting to hear and to think about. But let's back up to the specific subject of cloning. We now know that these clones are programmed to fulfill a certain roll in the work force. So what if for some reason they have the path and mindset, but they don't want the job, or find something else they might want to do?"

Dr. Phillips:

"That's exactly the same question we asked ourselves. This brought us to the instinct conclusion. Animals live on instinct without any question. Humans are also born with many instincts we rarely think about. For instance, when a baby is born it will search for the mother's breast for milk. What we did is replace those types of instincts with the DNA of our closest ancestor, the primate. This proved to be difficult, but it was worth it. No longer would there be a need to question life, what does it all mean, or what you are or aren't good at, you would just know."

Lacey:
"Are the clones allowed any free choice outside of work?"

Dr. Phillips:
"The only choice they don't receive is where they work. I want to express that that they don't view it that way, though. It's just a major part of who they are."

Lacey:
"Alright, so now we have some knowledge on how the cloning starts. But how do you raise a clone?"

Dr. Phillips:
"Excellent question, Lacey. As we all know, a typical human baby is born after nine months. The clone's gestation takes place inside an 8' by 4' capsule; something that almost looks like it's out of a sci-fi movie. We don't use surrogate mothers because the clone is kept dormant fourteen years. It is during this time that they are programmed for their specific job, and with skills for day to day living. Once the fourteen-year developmental period is over, the appearance and maturity of the clone is almost double, so its age would look to be around late twenty's early

thirty's. This is all possible because of the manipulation of those stop and go cells I mentioned earlier. The clone then undergoes several tests, mentally and physically for about ten months to make sure they are up to speed."

Lacey:

"So the simple things are taught as well, like brushing your teeth."

Dr. Phillips:

"Yes, and after all tests and exercises to strengthen the body and mind, the clone is then ready for the buyer."

Lacey:

"Truly a wonderful discovery, but wouldn't these super human clones put people who are conceived in the 'normal' fashion out of a job? Aren't there enough people as it is? Wouldn't clones be better for parents who can't have kids of their own?"

Dr. Phillips:

"Great point Lacey, but remember, at the start of all this, no average family could afford a clone. At the time this had to be aimed towards business corporations. But now that the clones do not need to be so advanced we are able to make clones simpler and cheaper for families.

However, to your other point, these clones are not popping off an assembly line. They are created for different purposes. Such as where there is a major need for a specific economic job. Doctors in third world countries, for example. After they complete so many years of college to become what they are today, most doctors don't want to move to a third world country where they would make quite a bit less money than they would in a more developed, advanced country. Which is not a judgment on doctors, but it doesn't decrease the need. They would also need to accept significantly less wages, due to the economic standing of where they would be going. We don't want to bankrupt these countries further; we just wish to give them people they need. While volunteers are great, they don't stay. They need a person who will live with them and stay there on a more permanent basis."

Lacey:
"This is so exciting to learn because these scientific breakthroughs have many implications. We are talking about world changing stuff here, or am I wrong Dr.?"
Dr. Phillips:
"You couldn't be more right Lacey. The possibilities are almost endless. In addition to these clone creations, we possess the capability to not only defeat diseases, but also to give you a new body that would never get sick! With our neural-computer programming, you can learn almost anything. This could also

Forbidden Origins-apostasia

mean no more crime or poverty."

Lacey:

"What a wonderful thought to look forward to!"

Dr. Phillips:

"It is, and if we can get the legislation to pass, you may be able to start on your new body sometime in the next couple of years. We are looking to get set up in as many hospitals around the U.S. as we can. This important piece of legislation would put a mandate in place to allow any human who can obtain the funds (or the insurance) that needs/wants a new body to be able to get one."

Lacey:

"Dr. Phillips, this all sounds incredible; I wish we could talk about this more, but unfortunately we are almost out of time. But before we go Dr., I hear you have one last bit of important information you would like to share with our audience?"

Dr. Phillips:

"Yes Lacey, and thank you for bringing that up. I have been one of the leading geneticist's for cloning now for just over seven years. I do my absolute best to serve Federal Duplications in any way I can, and for the longest time I was required to keep all my research and successes in the field top secret. It is with great pride and relief to finally be able to share those things with everyone today. In saying that, there's another revelation I need to share. Up until now this was one more thing I had to keep classified. I appear to be in my late thirties, however I'm actually only twenty-one years old. And you are probably wondering how I possibly accomplished so much in such a short period of time on this earth, and there is a simple explanation. And no, I was not a child genius or even a prodigy. The truth is ladies and gentlemen, I am not just Dr. Timothy Phillips, an employed scientist by Federal Duplications; I am also one of their first creations.

Lacey:
(Gasps) "Dr. Phillips...are you saying...?"

Dr. Phillips:
"Yes Lacey. I am a clone."

CHAPTER TWO
Dr. Tim's New Life

"Dr. Phillips!" (FLASH) (FLASH) The cameras lit up the night sky while reporters yelled Tim's name as he walked by. Today was an important and special day for him; the legislation for hospitals to have cloning stations for people who needed new bodies was approved. He was eager to get inside to the celebration party and away from the media, and perhaps finally have a chance to relax and enjoy himself now that the bill had passed.

"Dr. Phillips, please, just a few questions!" Tim sighed as he reluctantly turned back toward the cameras. Ever since his appearance on The Lacey Evans Show he felt as though he could not get a moment of peace. Like all clones, he was happy to do his job and do it well, but he never realized that there would be so much fame and notoriety involved to go along with it. His superiors at Federal Duplications shrewdly guessed that the best way to promote cloning and all its potential success was to show off one of their own cloning success stories. Tim was the embodiment for all that they wanted to prove to the world that they could do, so he became their official spokesman for cloning and other related scientific breakthroughs. Despite this, Tim himself was never quite comfortable with all the attention.

"Dr., could you please tell us how you feel about the passing of the Cloning Bill?"

Tim cleared his throat and answered, "Of course I am pleased, as I am sure the rest of you are as well. Everyone is looking forward to when the cloning stations will be functional, however, because this legislation has only just passed, these stations will not be fully operational for some time yet."

After his answer to the first question, one of the reporters that stood closest to Tim then asked, "Despite this win for Federal Duplications and other key supporters of the bill, there has been quite a bit of bad press and push-back by the

Christians and hard core conservatives. What do you have to say to those groups now that the bill has been approved?"

"Well, I can understand their concerns and I have answered too many of these during my debates that I participated in throughout this last year. We are not trying to play 'God' and are not trying to mess with the natural order of things as they claim, our goal is simply to enhance that which already exists. Science has allowed us to understand more and more about evolution and genetic code, so why shouldn't we try to perfect the human body if we have the means to do so? To be perfectly honest, the majority of voters want this opportunity to live longer and in healthier bodies. Otherwise the motion would not have been voted for and passed by such a substantial margin. And to those that claim that it is 'unbiblical' or immoral to mess with God's creation, I'm convinced that God himself promotes cloning. From the very beginning, he cloned Eve by the rib of Adam. Need I say more?"

"But Dr. Phillips, don't you think that -"

Tim held his hand up to put a stop to the barrage of questions and stated "Please, no more questions. Goodnight everyone."

And with that he smiled politely and walked away, turning back towards the party. While walking up the long carpeted stairs, he couldn't help but to think of how successful he'd become. Certainly it came at a price, but there was no denying that he enjoyed the glory to a degree. Yet something had his stomach turning, but not from nerves about the media or the party. He had every reason to be proud of himself and all his accomplishments, yet something seemed off that he couldn't quite put a finger on. After reaching the top of the stairs and leaving the fans and paparazzi behind, he decided to not worry about it just now, not when there was so much to celebrate. As he drew closer to the massive double doors to the governor of Colorado's mansion, they opened before he could even knock. Once entering the grand entry hall, he saw incredible jade antique vases, a spiraling staircase, and impressive ornate glass chandeliers.

As Governor Martin Weston walked over personally to greet this special guest, he noticed Tim admiring the chandeliers. "Did you know that in the 1800's one of these beauties used to hang in the ballroom of the White House?"

Tim was a bit startled to realize the Governor had approached without his realizing. "Hello sir. You have a beautiful home."

As Tim said this the governor shook his head in dismissal and replied, "Aw, come on now Tim, no need for such formality! You must call me Marty." He placed his arm around Tim and began escorting him over towards a group of men. "I have some friends over here that are dying to meet you," he said.

Tim could smell the alcohol sweating through the governor's pores. This disturbed Tim a little at first, but then he quickly got over the smell. It was a day to celebrate, after all. As

20

Forbidden Origins-apostasia

they joined the rest of the party guests in the Palm Room, Tim noticed more beautiful and unique décor, such as a hand-carved baroque credenza and lavish tapestries. With his arm still around Tim's shoulders like they were the best of friends, the governor made the introductions. After a little bit of generic questioning like what he had received from the reporters outside, eventually the questions from the group turned a bit more personal. They asked him what it was like to wake up as a fully grown man, did he know how lucky he was to have never experienced puberty, whether he got to keep his full paychecks or did Federal Duplications get a percentage of it, etc. Tim was used to such questions from the many people he dealt with on a day to day basis, so he answered them all in good humor. But as is the case in any party there is always the one guy that cannot handle his liquor very well and takes his questions too far.

"They sure knew what they were doing when they designed you, eh Tim? I suppose it was no accident that they gave you such a baby face. Being the first famous clone and all, I'm sure that you've got the ladies just throwing themselves and drooling at your feet!" one of the friends blurted out with drunken lips.

"So spill it, Clone Dr.! How many have you had at one time? Or would you rather clone yourself some perfect females for a perfectly good time?!" The group chuckled, except for Tim.

"Huh, now that's an intriguing idea...Percy, right? But like you said, since I already don't have any issues with the ladies, I think if I was going to clone women, I would clone them for men like you. And to make certain you are happy with their performance Percy, I would have to program these 'perfect' clones to be satisfied with your disappointingly small...er, package, if you will."

Shocked silence invaded the group until one of the men starting giggling, at which point the whole group began laughing, except the man who became the brunt of Tim's joke, of course. His face got beet red and he started to sputter.

"Look here, you worthless clone...!"

Before he could say anything else, one of the most sober in the group cut in.

"So Tim, tell us, with this new legislation, will this enable people like Mr. Walt Disney be able to be put into a new body?"

This abrupt change of subject did the trick of distracting from the drunken man's rudeness.

Tim let out a slight smile and answered, "This question actually comes up quite a bit in all the interviews I do. Although our current technology is getting to the point that we could possibly revive people who have had their bodies preserved (frozen) after death, there is no documented evidence to suggest that Walt Disney was interested in, or had even heard of, cryonics before he died. As a matter of fact, he was cremated. So, the rumors about his frozen body being stashed beneath the Pirates of the Caribbean ride at Disneyland are also untrue. I know that many want to believe that the much beloved Disney

Forbidden Origins-apostasia

will be rejoining the living, but I'm afraid that isn't likely to happen."

He paused for a moment after everyone absorbed that tidbit, and just to yank their chains a little he added, "Now Elvis, on the other hand..."

The men stood up a little straighter at hearing this and leaned in closer to hang on whatever Tim was about to say, but he just shook his head and laughed, causing the rest to follow suit once they realized he got them. After a little bit more chit chat on the subject, Tim excused himself and left the group.

As he circled around the room and socialized, other famous people and important government figures would stumble across him and make similar small talk. Although most were polite and not as drunk as Percy, he quickly grew tired of this and wanted nothing more than to find a quiet corner somewhere by himself and have a few moments of peace.

But before he could accomplish this, he heard another voice cry out "Tim! Over here!" Tim tried to pretend he couldn't hear him by ducking his head and hastily making his way through the crowd in the opposite direction.

Despite his best efforts to avoid being detained again, the man caught up with him. "Geez, Tim, is that how you treat your oldest and best friend!?" the man inquired.

Tim lifted his head and saw that it was his best friend, Dr. Paul Sullivan. "Paul!" Tim replied, slapping him on the back in a familiar greeting.

23

"Well, I can see that you're having a wonderful time, rubbing elbows with the rich and famous. Word of advice...take advantage of the free booze!" Paul nodded towards his own drink.

Tim shook his head at Paul's attempt to tease him, because he knew good and well that Tim never touched the stuff. As any good friend would do, Paul continued to try and lighten Tim's mood.

"Come on Tim, if ever there was a time to celebrate, that time is today! You have been working enough overtime for two people, spreading yourself too thin. Between you working at the lab and then playing patty-cake with the press in your 'spare' time, you need to learn how to relax and enjoy life! Take a minute to stop and smell the roses, my friend." At the end of his playful scolding Paul held out his drink to Tim and looked at him in a 'come on, I dare you' type of way.

Tim said, "Nice try, but I'm high on life...can't you tell?"

Paul laughed at this and then finally conceded the battle of the wills to Tim. "Ok, so if you aren't going to loosen up by having a drink then at least do me a favor and take one of these gorgeous women home with you tonight. You might as well put your infamous lady killer skills to good use."

Tim genuinely laughed out loud for the first time that evening, glad that Paul was there to help him feel more like himself. "Well, I think I certainly have a better chance at that than you, old timer."

Forbidden Origins-apostasia

Paul rolled his eyes. "Is that so? Just because you are technically only fifteen years old, fifty years my junior, and have a body of a cage fighter that doesn't mean that I can't kick your butt. Especially once it's my turn to get a new body! There will be no stopping me at that point. Then we'll see who's the one charming the wits off of all the ladies!" At this Paul sighed in mock defeat. "But, I suppose in the meantime I will just have to gracefully step aside and let you have the crème of the crop. Which reminds me...I have a friend here that very much would like to see you."

Pulling a stunning brunette beauty out of the crowd and in front of himself he stated "Tim, this is my dear friend Aavah. In between your time cavorting around the country and making television appearances, you may have seen her from time to time at the lab. She's becoming a rising star in our field."

Paul said this with a hint of pride, as if he had a hand in her progress. Which very well was the case, as Paul was one of the top researchers in the cloning industry, and was one of the first to be on the human cloning project.

"Good evening," Tim said. In a gentleman-like fashion Tim reached for Aavah's hand and brought it to his mouth for a soft kiss.

She gave an amused laugh and said to Paul "Oh my, I can see I am going to have my hands full with this one."

"I'm afraid you are on your own with that, sweetheart; I still have the rest of my rounds to make. Tim, I expect you to

25

show Aavah a good time and don't do anything to embarrass me." And with that Paul walked away from them and continued to mingle with the other party guests.

Tim stared after him, feeling a little bit envious at how easily Paul seemed to fit in at events like this, whereas he felt like a rara avis.

Trying to gain Tim's attention back, the woman said, "Did you know your name has been on just about everyone's lips at this party Dr. Phillips? And I think just about every man and woman in the place has tried to steal you away to pick your brain and to be able to say they talked to that famous guy. You must think your pretty big stuff, huh?" the attractive woman said while putting a strand of her long curly hair behind her ear.

"That's what everyone tells me, but honestly how can idiots call me anything?" As Tim said that he saw her face turn red with embarrassment. "Oh, no, darlin! I didn't mean you!" He tried to recover himself. "I'm sorry, I don't know what it is today, I just haven't been myself. Please let me make it up to you. I see that you don't have a drink in hand, so why don't we go up to the bar and fix that problem?"

Seeing that Tim was being sincere and hadn't meant that jab to be towards her, Aavah replied good naturedly with, "Well neither do you, but I get the feeling that you aren't much of a drinker."

Forbidden Origins-apostasia

Blushing, he responded, "You caught me on that one, beautiful. But that's no reason that you shouldn't be able to enjoy one. A glass of red wine, perhaps?"

Appearing to think this over, she looked like she was about to say something and then stopped. Finally, she said, "Well the music has just started, maybe we should dance instead?"

Tim smiled. "Yes, I think that's the best thing I've heard all night." Tim led her to the dance floor located in the middle of the Palm Room, and began to dance slowly to the music. Her long blue dress flowed perfectly to the rhythm. Her blue eyes sparkled like the glass chandeliers above, and as they swayed together Tim could smell a seductive mixture of vanilla and something else that he couldn't quite identify. Tim was completely mesmerized and couldn't take his eyes off of her.

"You're a fine dancer," she said.

"Well, I have taken some classes, but don't tell anybody...it's a secret," Tim replied with a smile.

She moved closer to Tim's body and whispered in his ear, "I'll keep all your secrets safe." Then she rested her head on his shoulder.

Tim's stress seemed to melt away in that moment. All that gossip about him being a 'lady's man' aside, he couldn't believe how lucky he was to be holding this woman in his arms. He couldn't help but be disappointed when the song ended, wanting just a little bit longer for the magic to continue. A faster, more upbeat song began, and so regretfully Tim said, "I'm afraid

27

I have already shown you all that my dance lessons have to offer. But if you're ready now for a drink and want to wait until the next slow song begins...?" He trailed off at the end, wondering what her answer would be.

"I'd like that, as long as you're sure that you don't have to run off and continue circulating among the other party guests like our friend Dr. Paul?" she asked with a raised eyebrow.

"Ha ha, definitely not! Paul is the king of networking, but I'm going to let you in on another little secret: that sort of thing has never been my forte," Tim said.

"Oh really? With you being Federal Duplications poster child for cloning and with all the interviews and appearances I have seen you do, I would have guessed you to be a natural," she told him in surprise.

Tim sighed and said, "You are correct that I'm a natural at it in the sense that I have been programmed to be intelligent, articulate, and able to speak with impact, but despite all that I still find that I don't always enjoy being put on display and pretend to delight in constantly answering questions and grease the wheels of politics.

"Paul mentioned that you are becoming a 'rising star' in the field (coming from him not a small compliment by the way, but I'm sure you know that). So with your background and experience I'm sure you have an understanding about how the programming of clones works."

Forbidden Origins-apostasia

She answered, even if his statement was meant to be more rhetorical than an actual question. "Yes, you could say I know my way around a programming chip, and particularly around a clone's development."

He smiled and said, "Ok good, then you must know that although the neural chip downloads all the software it needs for day to day functions and initial knowledge, it has absolutely nothing to do with personality?"

She replied simply with, "Of course."

"Then knowing that, is it so hard to believe that I do not love the part of my job that takes me away from home, away from the work I am really passionate about, and away from those that I care about?"

He looked at her so intently when he said this she could only hold his gaze for a couple seconds before she lowered her eyes rather than let him see them well up in empathy for him. "I'm so sorry, I had no idea it was like that for you. If I said anything insensitive to suggest that-"

Tim cut her off with, "Please, no apologies. Enough about work; what do you say we go have that drink and really get this party started?"

A bit taken aback by his sudden shift from serious to playful, but wanting to keep the evening light-hearted she eagerly agreed. Tim escorted her up to the bar and to his surprise she only ordered a water with a splash of cranberry. That was his favorite drink as well, so he ordered the same. "I guess neither one of us really knows how to let our hair down, huh?" he said jokingly as they both took their drinks and went to sit down.

She chuckled and said, "Maybe I just think it's best if I'm able to keep my wits about me when you're around."

Tim gave an injured look and replied, "Well why in the world would you want to go and do a thing like that? It just so happens that I think tonight would be the perfect evening for the two of us to abandon our wits and just enjoy our time together."

This made her blush and smile coyly, and he couldn't believe how her smile had the ability to take his breath away. As they continued conversation he did his best to try and make her smile every opportunity that he had, and every single time it happened was well worth the effort. In Aavah's presence Tim felt as though the rest of the party faded away to the point where it seemed as if they were the only two people there.

He heard another slow song start up and asked her to dance with him again.

'Any excuse to hold her is a good one,' he thought to himself.

The feeling of being in Tim's arms was like no other. When she had been invited to this party Aavah was certain it was going to

Forbidden Origins-apostasia

be a dull time, even though she had Paul to escort her. Paul had a special way of making just about anything entertaining and fun, but with the stresses of work and personal life weighing on her lately, she just didn't have high hopes for it turning out the way that it had. Having had this special time with this man has been almost like a dream.

Tim was a very important figure for the company they both worked for, so she had not hoped for more than a few minutes of his time at this special event that was practically in his honor. There are so many important and famous people at this party, but he seemed to want to be with her more than anyone else there. This realization made her indescribably touched, as she knew that he could have easily used the time to network and further his career by promoting the next phases of the cloning bill.

Even though they essentially worked at the same place, it had become almost impossible to even to catch a glimpse of him there, he was always so busy lately. There was something she wanted to share with him and now that she finally had him alone she thought about telling him, but just as she was about to, he pulled her in a little bit closer as they danced, and all logical thoughts flew from her mind.

'Oh well,' she thought to herself. 'There will be time for that later.' Instead of ruining the moment with words she decided to just let the music run through her and relish the enchanted time she was having with him.

Tim was thrilled that the evening was going so much better than he imagined that it ever could have gone. He and Aavah continued to have deep conversations throughout the night, along with carefree teasing back and forth. Between that and the dancing, the chemistry was heating up to almost a boiling point. After the last slow dance, Tim asked her if she would like to have one last drink.

"I have a better idea. How about we sneak out of here?" she offered.

A bit surprised at her answer but not wanting her to change her mind, Tim did not say a word but quickly took her by the hand. They rushed off the dance floor and strode past the Greek style columns that lined the room, but stopped short when Paul moved into their path. He had a somewhat sloppy grin on his face and spoke to them in loud, slurred tones.

"Now where are you two kidss going in sucha hurry? You weren't thinkin' about leaving little ole' me here on my own without at leascht offering me a ride home first, were ya?" Tim glanced over at Aavah and as he opened his mouth to respond. Paul waved a hand dismissively and said "Nevermind, I think I'd rather not know the answer to that." Just then another colleague of theirs strolled by and Paul grabbed him by his arm before he could walk past. "Grayson!"

Forbidden Origins-apostasia

The man turned around and said "Oh, hey Paul! Great party, huh?"

"Yeah, the best I've been to in a while. Guess what, buddy?"

Just as Grayson was about to take a sip of his drink, Paul slapped it out of his hand and it clattered to the floor. Grayson looked at Paul in amazement and Paul happily announced, "You're the lucky winner that gets to drive me home tonight!"

The stunned man just stood there gaping at Paul as he continued blathering on about how fortunate it was that he found a new designated driver, and seeing as Grayson couldn't drink anymore, the least he could do was go and grab Paul a new drink.

Before Grayson could pull his wits about him to tell Paul off, Tim decided now would be a good time to make their exit before he ended up being their responsibility again. Tugging on her hand in the opposite direction, this time they headed for the kitchen to leave through the back so they wouldn't get stopped again; both of them giggling like two teenagers trying to avoid getting caught by their parents.

As Tim drove Aavah home he struggled to keep his eyes on the road because he kept looking at her, anticipating what was to come. Amazingly they made it there without incident, and they eagerly rushed inside. Tim finally felt like he was celebrating his accomplishment properly, and for him what started out as a second-rate night ended quite perfectly.

33

The next morning Tim woke up to the smell of breakfast being made; the tempting aromas of coffee and bacon. Rubbing the sleep from his eyes he walked down the steps to the kitchen.

"Well good morning, handsome! I'm glad to see you're up just in time for breakfast," Aavah said cheerfully as Tim came in.

"Honey, you never cease to amaze me with how good you treat me," Tim replied as he sat down and started eating. Feeling exhilarated from the exciting 'stranger' role playing they did the night before, and thoroughly satisfied from the great time at home that resulted from their romantic interlude at the party, he attacked his French toast and bacon with gusto. Thinking back to the night before, Tim still couldn't believe how blah the party started and ended up being one of the best times he could ever remember having. Due to his introspective thoughts, it took him a few minutes to realize that his normally talkative wife wasn't saying anything, and when he looked up at her he could tell instantly that something was wrong.

"Hey now, what's the matter? Just a few minutes ago you looked happy as could be, and now all of a sudden you've grown quiet. What did I do now?"

Aavah twisted her wedding band around her finger in a familiar nervous gesture, and then finally responded. "Tim, do you remember when you said we could start a family once the cloning proposal passed?"

Not expecting this conversation so soon, Tim replied slowly. "I do, but it's only been a day. Can't it wait a little longer?" Immediately after finishing his sentence he could tell that he had said the wrong thing and she was displeased with his answer.

"Tim we've been married for seven months. We would have been married sooner but for political and media reasons, so the company made us wait until after your announcement to the world that you're a clone. Please, Tim, can we stop basing how we live our lives according to everyone else's agenda?" Aavah tried to keep her composure, but it was no use, the tears started streaming down her face.

Aghast at this reaction from his normally poised wife, Tim stopped eating and stood up to hold her. "Sweetie, I'm sorry if I haven't been sensitive to your needs lately. As you know, I have been working so hard to prepare the materials needed once this proposal passed, and I guess I didn't realize how badly you wanted to start a family."

Aavah's crying finally subsided, and she took a few calming breaths. "I know, Tim, and normally I wouldn't fall to pieces like this, except that I just haven't been feeling myself lately."

Tim shook his head in confusion. "Not yourself? I know that you've had a touch of the flu lately, but if it wasn't for that I would say that you have been even happier than usual. That's why I am so surprised to find out now that something is wrong."

"Well, that's just it. In my opinion, everything is just right," Aavah said.

Puzzled, Tim looked at her strangely and said, "Ok honey, now I'm totally lost - "

Aavah quickly placed her fingers over his lips and interrupted him. "Tim, ready or not, you are going to be a daddy. I'm pregnant."

CHAPTER THREE
Life Is Full of Surprises

"Pregnant?" Tim mumbled.

"Yes Tim, we are going to have a baby. Please tell me that you're okay, because I just need you to -"

Tim pulled Aavah's body away from his own and looked into her eyes. "Do you remember the first time we met?"

Aavah wiped her tears with her sleeve letting out a light laugh. "How could I forget? It was Paul and I who watched you wake up from your dormant stage. Paul loved you so much; he was always talking about how you were going to be his finest creation. He chose me to be your nurse because I was the only one he trusted. I was to tend to your every need. And you weren't exactly my easiest patient...quite demanding, if I recall," they both chuckled at the memory.

"I finally figured out you were just coming up with excuses to see me any chance you could. And my insistence of having a boyfriend at the time hardly deterred you from pursuing me. I thought Paul would be angry that I was starting to have feelings for you, so I tried to transfer. When he asked me why, I told him the truth. All he could do was laugh. He said, 'This does not exactly come as a shock to me, Aavah. I've seen the two of you together. Don't leave on my account because you think I might disapprove. Of course I want you both to be happy! You are the two people I care most about on this planet.'

So I stayed, and after many, many of your pitiful attempts at flirting, I fell in love with you."

Tim smiled at her version of the story and said, "Aavah, it's my turn to take care of your every need, and now the needs of our new little one on the way. How about we go out tonight? Somewhere special to celebrate, just the two of us. What do you say?"

Feeling relieved and becoming more joyful now that her secret was out in the open, Aavah replied, "Yes, that's sounds amazing. But for now, I guess I better leave for work if I don't want to be late. Paul called before you got up and he is dropping by in an hour. He wants to show you something at the lab, but he didn't say what. I don't know what to do with the two of you sometimes...even on your days off you still want to be at work!"

Tim did not say anything but just pulled her back into his arms once again, kissing her silent and breathless.

Forbidden Origins-apostasia

"Alright, my darling. I suppose one of us had better get moving at least," she said. Reluctantly she pulled away so that she could finish up getting ready and she could head out the door.

As Tim showered and got dressed he couldn't stop thinking about the fact he was going to be a father. Being a clone, Tim never had a family life experience. Even though he had the programming for all life's possibilities, he still couldn't grasp the enormity of this change. Let alone deal with the unfamiliar emotions he was beginning to have.

Before Tim could think any deeper on the situation, he heard the doorbell ring. Taking a quick look at his watch, he realized that his contemplative mood had put him behind schedule. He shook his head at himself in the mirror, because he has never once been late to anything. Whether it had been part of his original programming or not, being punctual was important to Tim. After hearing the doorbell go off yet again he left the bathroom and then hurried down the stairs to get to the door.

"Took you long enough! You want me to die of old age before I can even get you out the door?!" Paul teased.

39

Tim let a smile out with a slight laugh. "Old or not, it would seem that your charming sarcasm is as intact as ever."

"Touché. Seriously though, Tim, I've never had to wait for you before...I was about to break the door down and see if Aavah had tied you up in the house somewhere."

Paul gazed at his friend with curiosity and when Tim didn't explain he followed that up with, "Hey, is everything ok? Did you two have a fight or something?"

Not ready to confide his terrifying (terrific?) bit of news yet, Tim quickly responded, "Oh no, nothing like that. Let's just get on the road, shall we? I promise to tell you about it another time."

As they walked to Paul's car, Tim studied his surroundings and tried to picture what it would be like to raise a child here. He and Aavah lived in a nice, peaceful suburb where crime was virtually unheard of, and most of the people never locked their doors. He glanced over at Paul and thought to himself that Aavah would want to make Paul the unborn baby's godfather, and of course so would he. Paul was not just his creator, but his closest friend and confidante.

Paul lived in the same neighborhood, and being best friends he was an often visitor. And since all three of them worked at the same place, it was pretty common for them to carpool into work. Tim and Paul also had some mutual friends that they would go golfing, bowling and play cards with. Paul was always the life of the party; joking about anything and

Forbidden Origins-apostasia

everything. While Tim is usually quieter, he had smart comebacks and knew how to use Paul's jokes against him.

Besides being off the charts intelligent, Tim and Paul made for quite the comedic pair. Which truly made them a great team; in both their professional and personal lives.

Pulling out of the driveway Paul asked, "So did you and Aavah have a good time last night? In my more lucid moments I saw you guys dancing like you were the only two people in the world. Then you both ditched me at the end of the night, as if you couldn't wait the extra two minutes it would have taken to drop me off at my place."

Tim was still drifting away in thought about fatherhood, but managed to reply, "Yeah, it was good."

Seeing that something was a little off about Tim, Paul asked "What's going on Tim? First you weren't right at the door when I arrived like you always are, and now you look like you're off in never-never land. The last time you were this distracted, you wanted to ask me if it was okay to marry Aavah."

At this comment Tim finally snapped back into reality from his musings. "I'm sorry Paul, I'm not trying to be distracted. I sort of had a bomb dropped on me this morning and I'm still trying to process it."

Paul glanced over at Tim and said, "Ok, then out with it."

Tim was quiet for a minute, trying to decide if he was ready to say it out loud so soon. Finally, he took a deep breath and told him.

"I just found out this morning that Aavah is pregnant."

Paul pounded the steering wheel in glee. "You're going to be a father Tim?! I was wondering why you haven't even asked me what we are doing going to the lab on the weekend. You're always so curious about everything; it was really out of character for you. But now I completely understand."

Pleased to see Paul was so happy for him, Tim said, "I'm glad you're taking the news so well, Paul. I've been having a hard time grappling with everything I'm going to need to know about parenting. That wasn't exactly part of my programming."

Paul could only smile and chuckle. "Oh, Tim. Being a parent has nothing to do with 'programming'. Every father has to figure that stuff out as he goes along. There are self-help books you can read, of course, but it is just one of those things that you have to experience for yourself before you know what to do. I'm sure you will find you have all the natural paternal instincts kick in from the moment you hold that baby for the first time."

Tim leaned his head back on the seat of the car and sighed. "I want to be able to spend time with my family, Paul. I've been with Aavah for how long now, but we barely see each other. Last night at the party and this morning has been the longest time period that we have been able to spend with one another for weeks. The kind of crazy schedule I have right now just won't do, you know?

Forbidden Origins-apostasia

I want to be able to be there for her, help her around the house more, go with her to her prenatal appointments. All the things that a good husband and father would do. There's just no way that I can keep up with all the traveling, seminars, interviews, and political speeches that I've been doing and be able to be there for her like I should be. But at the same time, all those things are part of my programming...it is everything that my life was meant for. Plus, how would the company act to my absence?"

Paul could hear the concern and confusion in Tim's voice. "Tim, you are my creation. After many years of research, the company allowed me to make my own clone. Yes, the company did have stipulations, and one of those stipulations was that you would work for them. But you have accomplished everything they wanted and then some! They knew what would happen when you got married. You're not out of a job, you're obviously going to need to provide for your family still.

I think what I am about to show you today will help ease your mind. Your assignment for this project is going to require you to start working in the lab more. Not on the road promoting clones and all the nonsense that went along with that.

That stuff isn't everything you were made for; it was just an important piece of it. Now your new family is going to be the next important part, and also the reward you deserve. You were designed to have it all Tim, because that is what I wanted for you."

Not used to hearing Paul talk so seriously without even a trace of sarcasm, Tim felt overcome with emotion. Trying not to tear up, he said, "Thank you Paul, you have always been there for me." Paul glancing at the road and back at Tim replied finally with, "Tim, you are like a son to me, and my best friend. I will always be here for you."

Pulling into the driveway of the laboratory building, Paul and Tim met Ernie the security guard at his post.

"Hey guys! What's so important to bring you here on the weekend?" he asked. "Well, we could tell you that Ernie, but then we'd have to kill you." After that response from Paul, Ernie looked hard at the two men as if he were about to pull out his Taser, but instead he started laughing hysterically.

"A simple 'that's confidential Ernie, mind your own business' would have been sufficient fellas. But I suppose I should expect nothing less from this wise guy," he finished as he nodded towards Paul.

"Oh Ernie, you know my day wouldn't be complete without pulling your leg a little. I'll tell you what, though, Tim here has some great news that *he* can share with you." Paul emphasized.

"OH?! What's this big news?" Ernie exclaimed.

Blushing a little as it was hard enough to tell his best friend the news, taking a deep breath Tim responded.

"Aavah is pregnant; we're going to have a baby."

Forbidden Origins-apostasia

"Really?! That is exciting news. Congratulations Tim! Well try to not work too hard in there today...get plenty of sleep while you still can!"

All three men laughed at this, although Tim's laugh had hints of nervousness. Ernie waved them through and said, "Alright, you guys have a great day; and best of luck to you Tim!"

Paul and Tim both responded with "Thanks, Ernie!"

After leaving Ernie and parking the car, Paul and Tim began to walk through the various secured doors. Going down through several levels of the building, they entered a holding chamber in a very specific part of the facility.

"I know our lab is upstairs and pretty much on the other side of the building and so you rarely have had any need to come this way. Do you know what section we are in right now?" Paul asked.

"This is the section that requires the highest security clearance, so I have never been here before. I knew that you were working on something big, but I didn't realize that it was this big. Even if you have the authority to come in this section, how is it that I am allowed in here?" Tim asked.

"I've been working on a couple new projects, and one of them is for some of our elite military special forces. Right now it is still considered a top secret project, but I've convinced the company to allow you some access. Let me show you why."

Paul went up to the retinal scanner in the holding cell that they had been waiting in. After being scanned, a heavy steel

45

door unlocked and opened to reveal the next room. As they walked in, Paul began to explain further.

"Tim, imagine a military that didn't have to die. Whether the soldiers are clones or standard individuals, death doesn't have to be an expected result of war; at least not for the U.S."

Despite having worked on quite prestigious projects himself, Tim couldn't help but be impressed.

"Paul, are you serious? This is a real possibility?"

At that Paul led Tim over to a glass chamber. Inside appeared to be a strange formation of a hollow person.

"This is what I've been waiting to show you. This shell is a living armor. It can identify with any person, matching your DNA structure exactly. Just by wearing it, it well self-replicate your DNA into the armor. The armor acts like a thick second skin, except better. It can massively reduce the impact of lethal objects, as well as heal injuries in a fraction of the time it would take normally."

"Whoa...Paul, it looks like you have been hard at work. I had no idea that we were able to put something together this advanced with where we are with our current technology. But why are you showing me this now?"

Paul smiled and said, "I'm glad you asked. Eventually the armor will be able to save the lives of millions of civilians. But in order to do that, it has to be concealed. The technology cannot get into the hands of the enemy. The company has given you this job opportunity...a promotion. To work in this department to

Forbidden Origins-apostasia

help figure out how to develop this particular part of the project."

Paul paused for a moment to let that sink in for Tim. "Well, what do you say?"

"Honestly, I'm not sure what to say, Paul. This sounds like a great opportunity, but I do have some concerns. What kind of concealing are we talking about? Making it into a machine, heavy bandage or type of vaccine?"

"Whoa, slow down there buddy! That's for you to decide and test once you're on the project. But my aim is not to overwhelm you with this, just introduce you to the idea. This is the weekend, so don't think too hard about it until Monday, when you start. Sound good?"

"Okay Paul, but let me sleep on it before I say yes. Aavah and I are going out tonight, so I would also like to talk with her about it first." Tim answered. "Of course, I'll take you home now. Just remember Tim, everything in this room is top secret. You cannot share any of the details with her," Paul told him ominously.

CHAPTER FOUR
A Night to Remember

Tim was intrigued with everything Paul revealed to him at the lab, but his main focus was still on Aavah's announcement from that morning. He could not wait for her to get home so that he could take her on a night out on the town to celebrate. He had heard that a great new restaurant had opened up recently, so he called and made reservations there. After that, Tim putzed around the house trying to kill time until Aavah got home.

Not very accustom to having time off, Tim quickly grew bored with watching TV and reading magazines. At last he decided to at least make himself useful and started cleaning up the morning's breakfast mess in the kitchen. He was humming to himself while finishing the last of the dishes when he felt someone press up against him from behind and wrap their arms around his chest.

Forbidden Origins-apostasia

"Mmmm.... there is nothing sexier than a man doing dishes," his wife said.

"Oh, is that so?" Tim responded. "If I had known that, I would have been offering to do the dishes every night!"

Aavah laughed at that. "I appreciate the thought, but I'm sure that would change after the first week."

"I wouldn't be so sure about that. Never underestimate a man when he is trying to get lay- Umm, I mean, when he is trying to make his wife happy," he quickly corrected with a wink.

Eager to get their special night started, he told her, "Sweetie, why don't you go ahead and get changed? I want to take you to that new little restaurant that opened up in town. I hear that it's unique, but good."

"Really? That's wonderful! I've been curious about that place since it was first under construction."

Tim waited in the living room while Aavah freshened up. As she came in through the doorway, he glanced up from the magazine he had been idly thumbing through.

"Tim, while I was getting ready I had the best idea. I've been cooped up in the lab all day, so how about we go for a walk? The restaurant is only a few blocks from here, so that way I can stretch my legs and we can think of baby names...hopefully ones that we can both live with!" she said with a smile and a laugh.

Tim smiled back indulgently. "Alright, a walk it is."

Grabbing their jackets, they set off. Hand in hand, they began to immerse themselves with playful banter back and forth about the names. Barely aware of their surroundings and of how much time had passed, Tim finally looked up and realized they were just about to town. Just a short way ahead of them he could see the neon sign of the Jungle Paradise restaurant.

"Welcome to Jungle Paradise! Do you have a reservation?" the greeter from the restaurant asked.

"Yes I do; it should be under Dr. Phillips." Tim replied.

"Dr. Phillips! It is so good to have you with us! Please, follow me and I will show you to your table," the greeter said with sincere excitement.

As they walked to their seats, Tim pointed out all the unusual décor to Aavah, who seemed to be loving it. The name of the restaurant wasn't called Jungle Paradise for nothing. Exotic animals filled the building. Some of them, such as the panthers, monkeys, and parrots were stuffed, but there were actual living creatures, as well. Impressive aquariums lined the walls that had all types of marine life, and there was even a cage with a gigantic snake in it. The floor tiles had fossils in them, and the booths were set up like primitive huts. As they took their seats they observed that even all the silverware was made to look like ivory.

"The owner of the restaurant was so pleased to hear you were coming, Dr., he wanted to come out to greet you himself. So just relax for a moment and I will go grab him," the greeter said while handing Tim and Aavah their menus.

Forbidden Origins-apostasia

"This is such a nice restaurant; I sure hope the food is as good as what people say it is." Aavah said as her eyes roamed the room and pointed out neat decorative details.

Tim gazed at her lovingly and was just speechless at how stunning she appeared to him just now. He always thought she was beautiful, but now the effects of pregnancy seemed to make her glow. She was still as slim as ever, although with round, beautiful curves in all the right places. Tonight she was wearing a black spaghetti strap dress that sparkled when the light hit it just right. Her brown curly hair reached to the top of her back and her blue-green eyes seemed luminous with elation.

And now she was carrying his child, a special bond and seed between them. Tim never struggled with the thought of being a clone, he was created not to. In fact, most of the time he thought himself superior to others. Aavah was different though; he found himself weak next to her. Sometimes it was hard for him to think straight at all when they were together. Tonight was even worse than usual; the thought of having a family seemed almost too good to be true for a clone. Tim and his team have made clones for certain purposes around the world, and besides him, none of them have married, let alone had children.

"Dr. Phillips!" A man walked up and greeted them with a brilliant smile. "My name is Al. I'm the owner of this restaurant. I was so excited when I heard you made a reservation this morning. For a while I thought one of my employees was just playing a prank, but obviously that's not the case. Because here you are! So, I would like to wait on you both personally. And whatever you want, it's on the house. Could I start you off with a drink?"

Once they had placed their orders, Tim was eager to question Aavah about her pregnancy.

"So how long have you known? How far along are you? When is the due date? What all did the doctor tell you?" Not even taking a breath between each question, Aavah had to laugh at her husband's almost childlike exuberance.

"How about we tackle one at a time and go from there? Ok, now let's see...how long have I known? Well, don't be mad, but I have known for a few weeks now." Tim looked like he was about to give her the third degree, so she quickly added, "You have to understand, darling, that I wanted to tell you in person. We talked on the phone every night while you were away for the promotion of the cloning bill, and believe me it was so difficult to not spill the beans as soon as I knew for sure. But as we were so close to the election and I knew you would be home shortly after, I thought that it would be less stressful for you to learn about it then."

"Ok, ok, fair enough. I guess instead of giving you a hard time about that I should be thanking you. Those last few weeks leading up to the voting of the bill were brutal for me," Tim told her.

"Yes, I know that, sweetheart. I could hear it in your voice every time we talked. The last thing I wanted to do was add

Forbidden Origins-apostasia

more to your plate. I thought about telling you at the party last night, but finally having you back I selfishly didn't want to say anything that could spoil it."

Looking a little hurt at hearing this last part, Tim said "Now why in the world would telling me you were pregnant spoil it? Do you have such little faith in me?"

Aavah took a sip of her cranberry water before responding. "Of course not. But I also know that whenever I would talk about having a family with you before, you would turn as white as a ghost and start sweating as if you were in a sauna."

Tim looked down at hearing this, knowing he was guilty. "I'll admit to having a bad case of the jitters when the topic has come up in the past, but once faced with the reality of it I have to say the idea has grown on me, Aavah. I hope you don't mind, but I talked to Paul about it this morning after he picked me up, and he surprisingly had some good advice." He wasn't sure how she was going to feel about that little bit of news, but to his surprise she appeared relieved.

"I'm glad you told him. It was almost as hard to keep the secret from him as it was to keep it from you. He is so astute and notices everything, so I thought for sure he was going to figure it out before you even got home. He takes his duties of looking out for me very serious, you know."

Tim nodded in agreement at hearing this and replied, "Yes I know, and I am grateful. There is no way I would feel comfortable to leave you home alone for such long time periods

53

while I have to travel for work if I didn't know he was there to check in on you. I was thinking to myself today that we would ask him to be the baby's godfather, if you were amenable to the idea."

"Oh yes, of course! I hadn't thought about that yet, but I think that is a perfect plan." Aavah looked and sounded so pleased about it that Tim was glad to have brought it up.

Just then their food arrived, and it looked every bit as delicious as it had sounded from the recommendations they had received from Al earlier. After a few minutes of companionable silence as they savored the meal, Tim finally broached the topic of work.

"Since we were just on the subject of Paul, I guess I should tell you why he dragged me in this morning on my first day off in ages." Aavah raised her eyebrows in interest, as she had been wondering all day about that herself.

"As you know, Paul has been working on some top secret assignments for a little while now. Stuff that he hasn't even been able to share with us, his closest friends. Well, I guess the company is requesting my help for one part of the main project. The good news is, this would enable me to stay home from now on rather than have to do the type of traveling I've been doing since we've been together."

"Oh Tim, that would be fantastic!" Aavah exclaimed happily. "What will you be doing?"

Forbidden Origins-apostasia

Tim finished the bite he was working on and then answered, "That's the tough part. I can't share much about it with you, unfortunately. All I can say is that it is definitely different from the cloning work I have done in the past, and it has something to do with advancing our military."

Aavah looked intrigued, but she knew better than to attempt to pry more information from him. She knew that Tim loved her more than anything on earth, but his loyalty to the company always came first. It would have hurt more if she didn't know that it was a part of his programming, so she just accepted it for what it was.

"As long as it is something you are happy to be doing my darling, and it will allow you to spend more time at home, then I think it is a great thing. I just have one very important question for you, and I need your complete candor and honesty with me."

Tim shifted a little uncomfortably in his seat as he did not want to hurt Aavah's feelings if he couldn't answer her question. "Okay...what is it?"

Aavah smiled seductively and asked him, "How do you feel about dessert?"

55

Aavah started giggling after walking out of the bamboo doors of the restaurant.

"I can't believe after that incredible service and meal that we had, a bus boy randomly walks by and sneezes all over you."

"I know! Then he kept trying to clean me up." That started Aavah's giggles all over again.

"Hey! It's *snot* funny!" Rolling his eyes, Tim laughed at his own terrible pun. After a minute Aavah's giggles subsided and they linked arms and began the walk back home.

"I can't believe how late it is. Maybe I shouldn't have suggested that we walk. I hadn't considered it might be dark by the time we got done eating," Aavah said anxiously, while clenching Tim tighter.

Kissing her forehead, he reassured her that things would be fine, and that home wasn't far. However, Tim had his own concerns; he had the uneasy feeling that someone was watching them, although he didn't see anyone else around. Picking up the pace a bit, he pulled Aavah along wanting to get back to the safety of their home as soon as possible.

As they approached an empty intersection, a white van suddenly pulled up right in front of the startled couple. Four men from the shadows behind them appeared out of nowhere. Pushing and shoving, they took Tim and Aavah by surprise

Forbidden Origins-apostasia

and covered their faces and bound their hands and feet with zip ties. The men proceeded to open the van's sliding door and threw the couple inside.

"Move! Move! Move!" one man yelled after jumping inside and closing the door. Aavah screamed in terror, and Tim tried demanding answers. Lifting the sacks off their heads, the men tied some kind of thick material around their mouths. After that, they started going through Tim and Aavah's personal items.

"Look what we have here! He was right! It's Dr. Clone and his wife!" One of the men snickered while sifting through the contents of Tim's wallet.

After about a half an hour the van turned into a small abandoned building and then came to a stop. The thugs opened the side door of the van, pulling Tim and Aavah out, then they proceeded to tie them up to a couple of chairs. The man that had been going through their belongings walked up to another man that seemed to be waiting for them.

"Here is what I found on them, Nero. Looks like the intel we received was good."

"Nice work, Rahm," the man replied. Tim watched as the man referred to as Nero grabbed his wallet from the other man, and then pulled out his driver's license.

"Well, well, well. It's none other than Dr. Timothy Phillips!" he said with sarcasm. Tim kept trying to mutter words through the cloth tied around his mouth.

"I think this greasy clone wants to say something. I've got to say, I am a bit curious to what that is. How about we let him talk for a minute, and see if the freak has anything interesting to say? But if you try anything stupid, I will blow the head off of your little Mrs." While aiming his pistol at Aavah, he signaled for the one of the others to take off Tim's gag.

"Please, I can give you whatever you want, just don't hurt her. If you let her go, I can get you whatever amount of money you need. I'm sure this is all just a big misunderstanding, anyways, so there is no reason to get the police involved. All you have to do is let her go." Tim pleaded.

"That's a nice offer Doc, but I'm just a simple delivery man. I kidnap people of extreme value and then let the big boys do the ransoming. It's actually not all bad, the money you bring in funds important causes to our organization. Just think, your ransom could end up financing a small terrorist group, sex trafficking, or maybe even children soldiers." Nero chuckled at the look of horror on the Phillips's faces, and then proceeded with his monologue.

"I couldn't believe my ears when my informant told me the news that *the* Dr. Timothy Phillips had made reservations to the Jungle Paradise." Reaching over, Nero grabbed a tiny tracking device off of Tim's shirt.

"You know; I would have thought that a doctor would have better manners. You ought to offer someone a hanky if they sneeze."

Forbidden Origins-apostasia

Tim's eyes lit up in rage, but before he could do or say anything, Nero gestured to have the gag to go back on.

"But I guess you're not really a doctor, are you? Pretty much just a walking, talking monkey in a suit...or better yet, more like a Frankenstein monster, if you ask me."

Just after saying that Nero's phone beeped at him, so he picked it up and look at the screen.

"Well, as much as I've enjoyed our little conversation, I have to step out for a bit. I need to go and confirm the highest bidder for you, I hope you don't mind. But don't worry, you won't be too lonely. I'm leaving you with plenty of company." Nero stated in good cheer as he left with a couple other men, which left three men remaining to guard Tim and Aavah.

The group's energy had changed right as Nero left. The man that Nero had referred to as Rahm walked up to Tim.

"So this is what a clone looks like up close, huh? Disgusting! I think that Nero had it right saying that you were some kind of Frankenstein, but it's creepy how human-like you appear...but of course we all know you aren't human at all. There are just some things you shouldn't tamper with, and making slimy clone people is one of them. It's too bad really. If we didn't need you in one piece for the ransom, I would have loved the opportunity to beat the unnatural right out of you."

Having stayed silent up until that point, Aavah could not stand any more of their harassment. She tried to break free of

59

her bondage, straining desperately against the ropes, but it was futile. And it unfortunately gained the attention of Rahm.

"My, aren't you a feisty one? And awfully pretty, now that I take a good look at you. All this attention on your husband, I hadn't realized the gem right in front of us." He walked over to her and lightly stroked her cheek. Looking at her more intently, and hovering over her body he became aroused.

"What a shame that this tight little package has been wasted on the freak show doctor over there." At that he quit stroking her cheek and then pulled her head back hard by her hair. "Or maybe I could take you to the next room and show you how a real man does things."

Tim was trying his best to calm down, because he knew he needed to keep his cool in order to figure out what he was going to do. Because Aavah was sitting to his left, he was able to see a snake shaped tattoo on the creep's inner right wrist as he raised his hand to reach for her face. He tried not to listen to the vile things that Rahm was saying to Aavah, but he almost lost it completely when he saw him touch her.

"I don't think we should do that. Let's just stick to the plan." One of the other guards pointed out.

Annoyed with that statement Rahm snapped back with, "Mind your own business, Keith! I am sticking with the plan! I just need a little bit of entertainment to help pass the time. Besides, I can't let this beauty go to waste."

60

Forbidden Origins-apostasia

Aavah tried struggling even harder when Rahm let her out of her bonds, but he was too strong for her and ready for any desperate move she may try. After pushing her in front of him a few steps, she tried to turn around and kick him. Pinning both of her hands with one of his own, he used his other to squeeze the back of her neck. As she let out an enraged shriek through her gag Rahm could also hear shouts from the two other thugs.

"What now!?" he said with extreme annoyance. Looking back to see what the fuss was all about, and WHAP! He didn't even register the blow that hit him, but suddenly found himself on the ground.

The whole time Rahm and the other guards had their focus on Aavah, Tim was hard at work escaping his ropes. First he tilted his chair back, and freed up his feet by sliding them down the chair legs. Then he stood up smashing the chair against the wall bending it out of shape. Using the chair fragments as weapons he quickly beat Keith and the other guard, and then took Rahm out when he turned around to see what all the commotion was.

Shaking off the daze he was in, Rahm could see Tim ripping off the cloth around the woman's mouth and then take her by the hand and run towards the van they all arrived in. All he could think was 'Oh man, Nero is going to kill me for this!'

After jumping in Tim turned the key that was still in the ignition and slammed the gear from park to drive.

61

The three guards recovered enough to draw their guns and start shooting at the van.

"Aim low, we need the clone alive." Keith yelled out. Emptying their clips, they blew out the rear tires. Riding on the rims, Tim lost control not more than a hundred feet away from the building.

"We got them!" Rahm cried out.

As the van came to a complete stop, Tim checked the glove compartment. A pistol was lying inside, and fully loaded.

"Aavah, keep down, I'm going to draw their fire away from the van. When it looks clear, run as fast as you can to safety. I love you," Tim said all this frantically while grabbing the gun and getting ready to exit the van. Already somewhat injured from the first attempt at escape, Tim slid out of the driver's seat and moved with stealth along the side the van. Then, making a dash for cover, he ran while trying to dodge the gun fire.

Approaching an outbuilding, he felt two bone shattering hits. Almost falling down once he reached the back of the building, he tried blocking out the pain. All that mattered was his wife and unborn child's safety, so he would do whatever it took to protect them. Quickly assessing the damage, he found that he had was shot in the left shoulder and leg, but nothing serious enough to prevent him from the task at hand...survival.

"Hold your fire! He's down! He's down!" Keith ordered the men without realizing Tim had a weapon.

Forbidden Origins-apostasia

Hearing the command, Tim decided to play along until they came close enough to where he can pick them off easier. Once the approaching footsteps were within earshot, Tim began timing his moment to come out of hiding and surprise them. Taking one last deep breath, Tim aimed the gun around the corner of the small building.

(BAM) (BAM) (BAM) The deafening shots were all Tim could hear as he emptied his clip into the armed guards.

Not realizing what hit them, the men fell almost instantly to their deaths. Too late Tim realized that there were only two guards; one was missing. Tim's heart dropped into his stomach, as at that moment he started hearing the anguished screams of Aavah.

"Hey Frankenstein! I have your wife! Surrender now and I will let her go!" Rahm yelled out. "She's not the one that we want, anyways. So give yourself up or this is going to get bloody!"

Tim checked one of the guards he killed, looking for ammo. 'Only a few rounds left,' he sighed to himself, then stuffed the gun in the back of his pants. Keeping his empty gun in his hand, he proceeded to limp towards the enemy. Coming into view of each other, Tim lifted his hands up in surrender.

"Throw your weapon towards me, or she dies," Rahm said while tightening his grip, and pointing his gun at Aavah's head.

"Don't do it Tim, it's too late for me!" Aavah cried out.

Irritated with her talking, Rahm slapped her hard across the face. Not wanting to put Aavah in any more danger, Tim threw his empty gun towards her captor.

"Okay, I did what you asked! Let her go, and I'll come quietly." Tim said while holding back every desire for instant gratification to hurt and kill this man. He had to make sure that Aavah was out of the equation first.

Laughing, Rahm pushed then kicked Aavah towards Tim, while keeping his gun aimed at the couple.

Stumbling she walked towards Tim, going limp as she clutched onto him.

Kissing her face and wiping her tears he told her, "It's okay now, everything is going to be alright."

"Awe! Well isn't this the pretty picture?" Rahm said sarcastically.

Before he knew what Tim was doing, Tim put his body in front of Aavah's. But as he reached in the back his pants and tried to pull out his hidden pistol, Rahm threw the knife that was in his hand straight for Tim's chest.

Tim's other arm lifted up to deflect the blow, which protected his chest but caused the knife to stick right into his forearm. Tim yelled out in fury and pain, and slumped to his knees as the thug smirked and started approaching him. Tim was afraid to pull out the knife as he didn't want to bleed out before having killed this man and saving Aavah from the immediate danger.

Forbidden Origins-apostasia

He tried to continue to reach behind himself with his good arm to grab the gun, but just as Rahm almost got to him Tim felt the gun being pressed into his hand. This gave him just enough time to bring it around in front of himself and shoot Rahm three times in the chest almost at point blank range.

As the gangster fell to the ground, Tim crawled over to him. Only after he was certain that the creep was dead did he return back to Aavah, who was on her knees. Tim assumed that she got into that position when he had been stabbed by the knife and fell to the ground, in order to help him reach for the gun.

"Darling, we did it! They are dead and we are safe!" To his surprise she slumped the rest of the way to the ground and stared at him with glassy eyes.
Afraid that she was in a state of shock, he asked her, "What's wrong Aavah?" But it was much worse than he imagined.

After asking, Tim noticed all the blood on the ground around her. Looking down on Aavah's back he could see multiple stab wounds. Finally, he realized that the screams that he had heard earlier were not just screams of terror, but of pain. After capturing her from the van, Rahm had stabbed her into submission and used her screams to reel Tim in. That was why Aavah tried telling Tim to not give up his gun. Cradling her as gently as he could manage in his arms, he could see her life draining out fast.

Finding a cell phone in Rahm's jacket pocket, he called 911.

65

"You're going to be okay sweetie, just stay awake," Tim said with tears dripping down his face.

Trying her best to keep her eyes open and on Tim, she weakly replied "I love you…" It seemed she had more to say and was struggling to get it out without choking.

"Hush, baby, don't try to talk. Just stay with me!"

Despite Tim's attempts to shush her, she rasped out, "12-77-92-8A."

Tim's heart stopped; he knew what those numbers meant. Those are clone serial numbers, but they were not his. Before he could think any more on the situation, he starting hearing sirens in the distance. Tim felt a mixture of surprise and relief that the help was arriving so soon. He was afraid that they may have been in such a remote area that it would take a while for anyone to respond and find them. But even as the sounds became louder, approaching closer towards them, Aavah stopped breathing.

Pulling up next to Tim the first responders jumped out of their vehicle to evaluate the situation. The paramedics rushed to Aavah and started checking for vitals.

"Help her please!" Tim cried out in panic, while clutching Aavah's lifeless form to him.

The first paramedic turned to the second. "Give that man a sedative and assess his condition. Tell Joy I'm going to need all the help I can get for this one: Oxygen, blood, plasma, right now. Radio in to the hospital that we have a critical on the way and for

Forbidden Origins-apostasia

surgeons to be prepped and ready to go. She can't afford to lose any more time. From the looks of it, she's lucky to have held on this long. Go-go-go!"

Hearing the last part of what the medic said, Tim insisted that they call Dr. Paul Sullivan, and gave them the phone number.

"No matter what happens, do not put me under. Understand? I am a doctor and I need to talk with Paul."

The medics listened to Tim but warned him not to give them any trouble or they would sedate him. As Tim was being lifted into the ambulance, he could see Aavah lying in the other. There were so many tubes and wires; she just looked so small and fragile. As he watched in painful silence, the door closed and he could see his wife no longer.

CHAPTER FIVE
Surviving

Reaching the hospital in record time, with speed and precision the medics unloaded Aavah's body from the ambulance. As they put up the gurney she was on, they were joined by hospital staff. The ambulance that Tim was in was a close second and he was immediately brought in to be examined.

Over the next hour, he received x-rays and pain killers for his leg and arm, but no one could tell him what was going on with his wife. All they kept telling him was that "She's still in surgery." By the time a doctor came in and was ready to go over the x-ray results, Tim had had enough of not getting any answers.

Forbidden Origins-apostasia

"Hello Dr. Phillips, I am Dr. – "

"How's my wife!? Is Paul here?" Tim interrupted.

The doctor sighed and said, "I'm sorry but I haven't been given any new information about your wife and I haven't seen Dr. Sullivan."

Enraged by the lack of information he was receiving Tim slammed his fist in the metallic tray beside his bed.

"I don't care what's going on with my results right now. The only results I want are updates about my wife until she comes out. Until then, everything else can wait."

"I'm sorry about everything that you've been through this evening Dr. Phillips, truly I am. I understand that you are under a lot of stress right now, but unfortunately this can't wait. If we don't operate within the next hour or so, you may lose your leg. Your bone shattered into so many pieces, if we don't start retrieving them out of the muscle tissue soon, it will cause irreparable damage.

Also, we need to make sure that none of them work their way any closer to your nerves, veins, or arteries. If we don't get a move on this now, it is unlikely that we will be able to save your leg. Dr. Phillips, are you listening to me?"

"Doc, I'm a clone and so getting another leg for me would be as easy as getting my teeth cleaned, but I can't get my wife back! I'm not cooperating with any more tests or agreeing to any surgeries until I'm certain that Aavah is going to be alright.

Now leave me the hell alone, or get me some answers!"

The doctor shook his head in frustration and said, "Please, let's not make any rash decisions. Why don't I just give you a moment alone?"

The doctor briskly left Tim's room, only to walk right into a gentleman in the hall.

"Hello, my name is Dr. Sullivan, and I am a friend of Tim's. Can you tell me what's going on?"

"Dr. Sullivan, I'm so glad you are here; Dr. Phillips has been asking for you. But to be honest, it is not looking good. Dr. Phillips has a shattered tibia; if we don't operate on it within the hour, he could risk losing his leg or even death. I informed him of the situation, but until I get him answers on his wife's surgery he won't let us do anything for him. And I'm afraid if it's bad news at all, he won't let us do anything anyways."

Paul hung his head. "You'd be right on that account. He's not going to let you do anything at all. Fortunately, he doesn't get to make that call. I do. You will accompany me with a few orderlies who can sedate him. Once he's under, my own team will take him into surgery."

The doctor looked confused. "I'm glad he has such a good friend, but the only person who can make that call is Dr. Phillips. What you are talking about doing would be unethical. Without his consent, there is nothing we can do..."

"Under normal circumstances, yes, that would be true. Yet he is a company asset, not a person. Even though he is given leeway to make many freewill choices, ultimately he is our

Forbidden Origins-apostasia

product. We made him, and if he makes decisions that put our investors' money or our hard work in jeopardy, we have the right to go over his head. I have the power of attorney over him; not even his wife is able to have that privilege." Paul handed over paperwork signed by high level government officials.

"You can call whomever you'd like to verify the validity of this documentation."

Recognizing one of the signatures at the bottom as belonging to the Chief of Medicine for the hospital, the doctor shook his head and said, "No, that won't be necessary."

"Alright then, Doctor, I suggest we don't waste any more valuable time."

Paul waited for the doctor to gather a few orderlies, and once they joined him, he walked into Tim's room. When the door opened, Paul saw Tim's face light up.

"Paul, thank God! Where have you been? The doctors here won't tell me anything..." Tim paused when he saw the doctor walking in with his support staff.

"Paul, you can save her," Tim pleaded.

An orderly looked at him with sympathy, but continued to inject a sedative into Tim's IV.

When Paul still said nothing, Tim started yelling frantically.

"Paul, why are you doing this? Save her Paul! You better save her!"

"Now Dr. Phillips, I need you to relax, you'll be out in a couple minutes," the orderly said in a soothing voice.

Tim looked at her in disbelief. Looking down at his arm, he could already feel the medicine kicking into effect.

"Paul! What have you done? You can't do this! Paul!!" While starting his rant, he reached over to pull the IV out of his arm, his adrenaline working its way back into high gear.

The orderlies pounced, struggling to keep him restrained. After holding him down for a minute, they realized that the sedative wasn't kicking in fast enough.

Tim was screaming in fury and pain. The doctor yelled at a passing nurse to bring in Fentanyl, hoping that the stronger sedative would do the trick.

Meanwhile, Tim was still struggling on the bed and the doctor wasn't sure how much longer his orderlies were going to be able to hold onto him. A minute later, the nurse was back and began to inject the additional medicine into Tim's IV.

Twenty minutes, two more high doses, and some Nitrous Oxide later, Tim was finally under. The doctor turned to Paul as the nurses wheeled him away.

"Well that was highly unusual. Keep me updated," he said with concern.

Forbidden Origins-apostasia

Tim woke up a few hours later to find Paul sleeping in a chair by the side of his bed. Picking up a book from the night stand, he threw it at Paul to wake him up. Startled awake by the book, Paul rubbed his eyes.

"Good to see you up and ornery-"

Tim cut him off. "This is not the time for jokes, Paul. I need to know... did you save her?" Tim could hardly hold back his emotions, because deep down inside he already knew the answer. Adjusting and lifting his body using his arms, he noticed something. Paul remained silent as Tim uncovered his gown.

There it was on his body, the new armor that Paul showed him just the other day. Tim started to whimper as he felt the armor attached to his skin.

"Please Paul, tell me that Aavah is okay. Tell me she's alive!"

Paul hung his head down because he couldn't look Tim in the face.

"Tim... I'm sorry... there was nothing I could do..." Paul mumbled in shame.

There was a dead silence in the room for nearly a full minute, and finally Tim rasped out, "I need you to leave... Get out." He didn't raise his voice when he said this, but Paul still flinched.

Knowing that saying anything else to Tim right then would be pointless, Paul grabbed his jacket and headed for the door.

Not satisfied enough with Paul leaving, he shouted at his retreating back. "You could have saved her! I know more than what you think! You should have saved her! You pathetic coward!" Paul did not respond but continued walking out into the hall and was met by a nurse.

"Is everything okay in there?" she said with a worried look.

"Tim is under severe stress; he needs to be on suicide watch. Until he's able to calm down, sedate him as needed. His wounds are almost healed, but don't let him touch or pick at his new skin plate, it's still fusing to his body. I'll be back for him when he's ready to go home." Immediately after giving the nurse these instructions, he left the hospital.

The nurse gathered her cart of medicines and rolled it towards Tim's room.

"ID please," demanded one of the two guards standing outside of Tim's room, because only approved personnel were allowed in. The nurse showed her credentials, and they stepped aside so she could enter.

Forbidden Origins-apostasia

As he suspected they would, the police came to visit Tim in the hospital to get his statement as soon as his doctor would allow it.

"First off, Dr. Phillips, we would like to offer you our condolences for what happened two nights ago. We know this must be a hard time for you, but we were wondering if you were up to talking us through what happened that night. Can you tell us what you remember?" one of the two cops standing by Tim's bedside asked.

Tim's emotions had turned from deep sorrow into silent rage. The only reason why he would talk to anyone was to be able to get out sooner. The goal was to play dumb, yet cooperative. Tim wanted his own revenge; the rest of those thugs involved in that night would pay in blood. And on top of that, he wanted to get to the bottom of his suspicions that Aavah was a clone. He hadn't even told Paul that he suspected this. Tim knew that you just don't ask questions without arousing the interest of those that want it to remain secret. Since it was a secret, he wanted answers why.

"I don't remember much, everything happened so fast. It was like a dream you can't wake up from and every day that passes makes it harder to remember the day before. It could also be all the medication I have been on," Tim said.

The second cop chimed in, hoping that sharing some of what they knew with Tim would trigger some memories. "From the bodies we have, we suspect that they're part of the underground organization called the Pitoni."

At Tim's blank look the cop explained that this is Italian for python. "...we could really use your help to catch these low lives. But the only chance we have at getting these guys is for you to tell us everything you can remember. Is there anything at all that you can tell us?"

Incredible, Tim thought to himself. The cops just gave him vital information he needed on who he would be exacting his revenge on. 'The Pitoni huh? I wonder if I can get them to tell me anything else I can use?' he wondered. Then proceeded to dangle the bait by telling them just enough to where they may end up giving him more information to help him try to remember.

"I'm sorry officers, but everything is a little hazy and I can't remember too many of the little details. I recall that we were kidnapped during our walk home from the restaurant and then they brought us to a strange abandoned building. They started harassing my wife and I lost it. I broke free and knocked out the thugs. I grabbed my wife and we tried escaping in the same van that brought us to the building we were taken to. They shot out the tires before we could get away, and so we fought for our lives...I wish I could have fought more to save hers. Adrenaline is an amazing thing to have on your side, and it helped me completely block out the pain. Unfortunately, it seems to have created tunnel vision for my memory," Tim said, giving them a fair measure of truth and part of a lie. In reality he remembered every detail.

"Even though we don't have records for the three men you shot, they each have tattoos that seem to be affiliated with the Pitoni," the cop stated. Opening a manila envelope full of pictures, he went through them one by one and showed Tim the tattoos on the bodies, as well other members with similar tattoos. At seeing the pictures Tim recalled that he saw a snake tattoo on the one called Rahm's wrist.

"As you can see the tattoos are not uniform, but have a parallel theme with a snake in a circle. You can see the differences between them all; some are cartoon-like, while others are more realistic. They can be anywhere visible on the body, as well as different items/themes part of the tattoo itself. We don't know why they are different, probably to make our job harder, which is working. Or it could be the different types represent what level they are at within the organization, which we believe has direct ties to the Mafia. So far we have been able to identify that the group has about twelve ranking men, and who knows how many pawns. Nero Lombardi seems to be the leader, and his son Nikki Lombardi might be following in his father's footsteps."

The cop handed Tim the pictures of Nero and Nikki. He instantly recognized that tanned pitted face, and he found that the son's face was familiar, too. Tim now had names to go with the faces, as well the gang's name, and the knowledge about the tattoos. He could hardly keep his heart rate down; he wanted his revenge immediately. Something new and dark starting to creep into his soul.

"I'm sorry officers, but I only recognize the three men I shot," Tim said in apology, and handed the photos back to the cops.

"Thank you for your time, Dr. It may not seem like it now, but you are very lucky to be alive. What happened to your wife was a tragedy and we will do everything we can to keep those criminals off the streets. Here is my card; give us a call if you remember anything else.

This appears to be a cut and dry case of self-defense, so I don't see anything coming back on you at all. So rest up and try to take it easy," the cop told Tim with sincerity as they left.

Tim sighed in relief when the cops closed the door behind them. He was confident that he hadn't given them enough information to help them get closer to catching the Pitoni. Vengeance would be *his* and his alone. Prison would not be a good enough punishment for them. They would pay for taking Aavah from him, and pay dearly.

Forbidden Origins-apostasia

It had been three days since waking up in the hospital. His wife and unborn baby were gone forever, and he was still here to pick up the pieces. Something inside him was gone too. The hospital psychiatrist said it was just the tragic loss, the violence and brutality of the whole ordeal, but Tim knew differently. The darkness that was spreading went way beyond the "normal" pain and anger that someone would feel at the cruel loss of a loved one. Something felt wrong inside of him, but he couldn't waste time thinking about it now.

On the outside, he needed to pretend that other than the grief everyone expected from him, nothing was wrong. He needed to be allowed to go back to his home, and only when he was there would he start plotting his retaliation. Because anytime he would get wrapped up in his own vengeful plot, his anticipation rose, along with his blood pressure; setting off his heart monitor in the process.

Even planning the most minor details would raise suspicion, so Tim decided to just meditate until his release. Tim's anticipation to leave soon grew more and more intense with each passing hour. Meanwhile, something else was harboring and growing in strength; something sinister that was patiently waiting to escape into the world.

CHAPTER SIX
Planning the Reprisal

Early the next morning, Tim had the approval to go home. Even though he knew he was not Tim's favorite person in the world right now, Paul came to pick him up from the hospital. Once they were underway Paul decided to try to address the elephant in the car and explain his actions and decisions for that night.

"Tim, I can't begin to tell you how sorry I am about what happened. As crappy as the situation was, the bottom line is that Federal Duplications owns you. As your creator and best friend I wanted to do everything in my power to honor your wishes, but the company didn't give me the option to make any calls on your or Aavah's treatment. I was just following orders."

Forbidden Origins-apostasia

"Don't worry about it Paul, I've come to peace about what happened. One of the requirements of my release was to have a few sessions with the hospital shrink, and believe it or not, I think it actually helped. I'm glad to still be alive, even if I have to learn to live a life without her. You made the right call by following orders.

I wouldn't want you to get in trouble with the company or lose your job over something that was out of your control. None of this is anyone's fault besides those good-for-nothing thugs. I just need a little more time to grieve and get back into the rhythm of life." Tim forced himself to say all of this, while at the same time trying to appear calm. If he let Paul see any emotion out of place, he'd take him back for evaluation for sure. He just couldn't take that kind of risk, so he masked his true feelings.

Paul nodded his head, at a loss for anything more he could say to help his friend. He knew that Tim was sugar-coating what he was saying and had more anger towards him than he was letting on, but didn't want to force the issue when it was clear his friend was trying to be forgiving.

As he pulled into the driveway, Paul said, "Remember, don't pick at the new skin plate, it still has a little more fusing left to do. It's permanent, so you don't want it to heal funny." Attempting to lighten the mood in his usual way, he added "You don't want that...you would never be able to look right in a bathing suit again!"

Forcing himself to crack a small smile, Tim replied with, "Yeah, yeah, I got it; thanks for the ride."

Paul stared in sadness at Tim's back as he made his way up to the house and let himself in. Sighing and shaking his head, he put the car in reverse and pulled back onto the street to head for home. "Just some more time Paul, that's all he needs," he said to himself as he drove away from Tim's house.

With the door locked behind him, Tim went around the house closing the blinds. And in the comfort of total darkness, he made his way to the kitchen to sit at the table. Relishing the quiet solitude of his familiar surroundings, he finally allowed himself the long awaited pleasure to begin his plotting.

The underlings of the gang would go first. As many he could find, they'll be the ones to squeal and give away more Intel on the higher ups. Tim realized that this would involve some physical and psychological torture. His old self would have been disgusted and horrified at the thought, but now he was looking forward to it. He would start with the bus boy at the restaurant, the one who planted the small tracking device on him to begin with. He should be able to lead Tim to some more of the inferiors, and then from there he would go for the leader Nero, and his son Nikki. He didn't want to kill them right away though, as that would be too easy of a death for them. He would use them to help him to gather the rest of the higher ups one by one, and perhaps kill them in front of their leader.

Forbidden Origins-apostasia

Tim felt a dark pleasure rise up in himself as he started to formulate ways to kill; savoring every single concept he could think of, each one more twisted than the last. After he had dispatched the Pitoni scum, he would turn his attention to Federal Duplications and all who worked there.

Paul was beyond stupid if he thought that Tim would buy the lies he spewed in the car. He was obviously just trying to placate him and make him believe there was nothing that he could do to help Aavah or his unborn child to survive. Well, they were all going to regret the calls that had been made. Whatever they might think, he wasn't anyone's property. And if they all wanted to play God, then they would feel the wrath of the devil. They were all going to suffer, and he planned on prolonging that suffering for as long as possible. None of them would walk away from his vengeance. They would all go in a fiery inferno, burned to death beyond recognition.

Satisfied that everything was going to fall into place, he got up and started the grueling task of getting into shape – mentally and physically. He was far from healed yet, and he couldn't let anything hold him back.

In the midst of all his plotting, the day that Tim was dreading finally arrived; Aavah's funeral. Not in a mood to try and play nice and deal with Paul's clumsy attempts at repairing their friendship, Tim adamantly refused to ride with him to the funeral home for the service. It seemed as though the second he entered the building everything was happening in tortuous slow motion, which did nothing to improve his mood.

As well-meaning friends and co-workers came over to him to relay their deepest sympathies, it was all he could do to not scream at them that he did not care they were sympathetic, that was not going to bring his Aavah back. Most of these people also worked at Federal Duplications, so as far as he was concerned they were all the enemy. But of course none as much as Paul, who had the gall to look as bereaved as if Aavah had been his own flesh and blood. Although Paul did not stay right next to Tim throughout the day, he kept close at hand, as if to let Tim know he was still there for him.

During the graveside service Tim watched Paul as he stood across from him, staring down at the coffin as it descended into the cold, hard ground. Tim had never seen Paul cry before, but at that moment his face was streaked with tears. There was something about seeing Paul in such a rare vulnerable moment that cracked a tiny portion of the ice that was now Tim's

Forbidden Origins-apostasia

heart. It was then that the gravity of his deceased wife's and unborn child's body being lowered into the ground, hit Tim like a ton of bricks. As he started to feel his own eyes sting and burn from the buckets of tears that had been building up over the past week, he roughly swiped at them with his hands as though he could just as easily wipe away the emotions. Tim looked up and saw Paul staring at him with a mixture of remorse and pity, and suddenly he felt his heart restore back to solid ice. 'He has no right to grieve for Aavah, acting as if he didn't have anything at all to do with the fact she is being buried in the first place.' Tim thought to himself. 'I don't want his pity...but I will accept his guilt.'

For the next few days Tim tirelessly channeled his rage into his physical therapy, mental planning, and the building and gathering of materials. He already had a laboratory in his basement with some supplies he'd obtained from Federal Duplications. Sometimes he would take his work home with him when he was working on a particularly grueling project. This way he was able to have everything he needed in the event he woke up in the middle of the night with a brilliant idea. But now he needed a dungeon as well. So for hours he would labor in the basement, boarding up all the basement walls and windows in effort to soundproof the room. Once he completed that, he started breaking up the concrete in a section of the floor, and then dug a pit for a holding cell. Not wanting to arouse the suspicions of his neighbors, he just stored all the dirt and debris in another room in the basement.

After finishing the construction, he decided it was time to decorate. A couple of cots with car straps for gurneys and shackles in the pit should be a nice touch. Next, plastic on the wall and floor where the gurney would be to help with clean-up for spilled body fluids. And finally some extra tables for store bought chemicals and tools to round everything out. He would use his little storage room for what would be his weapons and explosives area.

When he would shop for supplies he would take all the necessary precautions; he never wanted to buy too much at one store at a time. He figured that by using prepaid credit cards and mapping out the same type of stores in different locations it should prevent anyone from taking notice. He would need tactical gear from military surplus stores, chemicals and containers at general stores, lumber, tools, and fasteners from hardware stores. He also ordered extra stock from Federal Duplications for his grand finale. Everything had to be perfect. He ignored nearly all phone calls, unless they were from Paul or one of the detectives, as he wanted to keep them satisfied that all was well. It was while he was cleaning his two matching 9mm

Forbidden Origins-apostasia

pistols that he noticed his hand turn dark and blotchy. As he examined his hand he felt angry and slammed his fist on the table. Tim felt less human every day; his skin was already blotchy around his chest and stomach, and now it seemed to have progressed to his hand.

In his frustration, he saw Aavah's initials engraved on one of the pistols. Running his finger over the engraving he remembered the times they would go and do target practice together. He had been so focused on his revenge that he hadn't had time to give her a thought since the funeral. He spent most his time in either the basement or the kitchen, and he never went into the bedroom they once shared. It seemed as though he didn't need much sleep, but when he did take naps he would use one of the cots or the couch in the living room. Deep down he knew that his plot to avenge her was his way of avoiding dealing with her loss, but just then he felt unable to cope with all the emotions that have been trying to break their way to the surface. He almost had tears escape from his eyes when he heard a knock at the door.

Quickly throwing a towel over the weapons, he went to go see who it was. Looking through the peep hole in the door he saw that it was Paul, stopping by unannounced. Taking a few deep breaths to try and regain some calm, Tim opened the door.

"Hello, Paul, I wasn't expecting you. I just spoke with you this morning and you didn't say anything about coming by..."

"Tim, there's no other way to say this; I'm not an idiot and neither are you. The B.S. small talk over the phone is driving me insane. I know you hate my guts right now, and the sight and sound of me probably kills you inside. You know that Aavah was like a daughter to me, so this has been hard for me, too. I can't believe that she's gone, or of the senseless of it all. She was so young, kind, and beautiful, and didn't deserve to have this happen. And none of us deserve to have lost her... but please don't make me lose you too!

I know how bad this all looks and how difficult it must be to believe me, but from the depths of my soul I am sorry, Tim."

Seeing the raw pain and emotion in Paul's eyes, Tim felt immense relief that he didn't seem to suspect any of his plans, so he decided to cut him a little slack. He'd still have to pay for the aftermath of that night, but it was obvious that the events of everything that had happened since then were taking a toll on him as well.

"To be perfectly honest with you Paul, I don't think things will ever be the same between us. Our discussions we've had on the phone might only be stupid small talk, but I'm still trying to figure all this out. You're right, just hearing your voice makes me want to go through the phone and throttle you. But I know that Aavah wouldn't want me to blame you, and for the sake of the friendship you and I once shared I am still making the effort. Perhaps not as much effort as you would like, but as much as I'm

Forbidden Origins-apostasia

willing to give right now. I can't promise I'll ever forgive you, but I will try."

Paul looked Tim hard in the eye as if to see if he was telling the truth, and finally just sighed.

"I suppose that sounds fair enough. You're right, I should be grateful that you even talk to me at all, so I guess I will take what I can get. I know that there is nothing I can do to make it up to you, but I want you to know I am here for you, for whatever you need. Whether it is for a cup of sugar or a trip to Paris, I am here for you, man." Paul gave a little sheepish smile at the end of his speech. But then he furrowed his brow as if a thought just occurred to him, "Hey, do you worry about that gang tracking you down? I could get you some protection, you know."

Tim shook his head. "As you know, I have this armor fused to my body, which makes me practically bulletproof, right? Plus, it's virtually impossible for the gang to find me here. No card or ID known to man has my real information on it, except my name. I believe that was part of the Clone Safety Act, which is to prevent clones from being tracked down from those fanatics that believe that we're unnatural and immoral. It's also a backup plan in case a clone should run into trouble or become injured. Vital supplies and replacement parts are available *to all clones.*"

Paul either missed or ignored the implications of what Tim said and replied, "Yes, I believe I know the Clone Safety Act quite well. I'll leave you be, I suppose I have worn out my welcome for now. I don't know about you, but I feel better already."

Tim did too, but not for the same reasons. It seemed as though Paul's concern about their broken friendship was genuine, so Tim felt confident he was free from any suspicion.

By the time Paul left, Tim had completely forgotten his earlier moment of vulnerability and nostalgia. His obsession with punishing those that had wronged him and taken away his wife and child was in full force again, and he was feeling liberated. In fact, it seemed like a good day to go and get his first victim.

CHAPTER SEVEN
Let the Games Begin

As the bus boy was the first person on his "hit" list, Tim called the restaurant where he and Aavah had been to the night they were kidnapped.

"Hello thank you for calling Jungle Paradise my name is Jenny how can I be of service?" All of this spoken in what seemed like a single breath.

"Uh, hey Jenny, my name is John, and I'm looking for a co-worker of yours. He's a bus boy, tall and gangly, blonde hair, young twenties..."

"Oh, you must be talking about Cody. He's here if you would like to speak with him."

"Yes, please." Now that he had the kid's name, Tim quickly hung up the phone after Jenny went to find Cody.

'This is perfect, I have the name of the kid who planted the tracking device on me, and he's at the restaurant right now,' Tim thought to himself. Wasting no time, he grabbed his jacket and keys and then rushed to the car.

As he neared his destination, he could feel the rush of adrenaline starting to pump through his body. Pulling into the back parking lot of the restaurant, he waited. His body shivering from anticipation, he felt unusually cold and sweaty.

Two hours later, there he was. Cody- the tall blonde bus boy who seemed to be the one that started the tragic chain of events leading up to his wife's death- had come out the back entrance to have a smoke break. Tim could hardly keep himself in his car; it took every ounce of all the self-control he had in his body to not to attack him right then and there. But logic won out as he knew he needed the cover of darkness and stealth to pull this off. So he watched Cody savor his cigarette and thought to himself, 'That's right kid, enjoy every last drag...it very well may be your last.'

After a few minutes the boy finished up and went back inside. Aware that closing time was still a few hours away, Tim settled back in his seat. Might as well get more comfortable while he waited for the bus boy to finish for the night.

Forbidden Origins-apostasia

But the time passed and before he knew it, it was only twenty minutes until closing. Tim was on high alert at that point and was more than ready for what was next. A half hour later Cody finally came out the back door again, jumping into a faded yellow Dodge Neon and pulled away from the restaurant. Tim pulled out behind, and stalked him carefully for the rest of the drive. Going through town, then to the outskirts of the county, he pulled into a run-down trailer park.

Parking a safe distance away where he was sure Cody would not be suspicious, Tim watched him walk into his trailer. Sneaking out of the car, he then scouted the area, making sure no one else was home.

"Looks like today might be the day," Tim whispered to himself while grabbing some bags out of his car. From there, Tim went up right to the trailer door and knocked.

"Who's there!?" Cody said with frustration, already running behind for his second job.

"Nero sent me; he has a job for you." The door began to unlock and started opening slowly. Once the door cracked enough to see Cody's face, Tim pulled up a pepper-spray canister that he mixed with some special ingredients.

Cody, startled by the spray and then the sting, tried running backwards, but ended up falling to the ground

93

while choking. It didn't take long for him to lose control of his muscles, and shortly after that he blacked out.

Waking up, Cody found himself on the floor tied up and with tape around his mouth. Tim was setting all sorts of sharp, shiny objects on the table. He noticed that Cody had awoken. Tim walked over to him.

"Remember me?" Finally Cody got a good look at Tim's face and instantly recognized him, and it was like seeing a ghost.

"You look surprised to see me Cody, must be the Pitoni didn't tell you what happened? Now that I think about it, why would they? You're just a small piece of gristle among those meat heads. I'm sure they could care less if I killed you right now;
your life has no value to these people.

But you are in luck; I do care, and at this moment I value your life very much. So let me fill you in on what you might have missed. You planted a tracking device on me, and shortly after my pregnant wife and I were kidnapped. And then while we tried to escape, she was killed.

So this is where you come in: You are going to help me find Nero and his son and whomever else I can get my hands on. As I'm sure you are figuring out by now, I have dedicated my life to the rightful punishment of these men. That's why I value your life; for my revenge. But if you prefer to look at it as also doing society a favor by getting this scum off the streets, then that's your prerogative.

Of course, if you choose not to cooperate, I can just kill you now. And if you try to double cross me in any way because you have a change of heart later, I will hunt you down and kill you very, very slowly."

Cody looked at Tim with round, terrified eyes, but because of the tape that had been put over his mouth while he was knocked out, he couldn't utter a sound, let alone agree to help Tim with anything.

Lifting Cody over his shoulder, Tim placed him at the only chair at the table.

"Now, as you can see, I have an assortment of interesting supplies on your table. As a scientist – a *clone* scientist, at that – I have access to technology you couldn't even dream of. My job is to help people survive, and as you can imagine, that also means I know many different ways to destroy and kill. See how that adds up? Just so you know I'm not lying, and deadly serious about needing your full cooperation, I will have to use some of these items on you. It will also help you to realize that this little slap on the wrist is nothing compared to what I will do if you don't do exactly what I say."

Tim grabbed some sharp metal objects and started assembling them. At that point Cody's fear was a primal thing, almost tangible enough to grab onto; he tried to talk and scream through the tape wrapped around his mouth.

"You want to talk? How about I make you a deal? I'll take the tape off your mouth, and you won't scream. If you do, I'll kill you... slowly."

Cody shook his head in agreement. In one fast yank, Tim pulled off the tape covering his face.
Cody winced, but stuck to the agreement and did not scream.

"I'm only an informant; I don't know much; they just tell me what I need to do. I've never even been allowed to contact Nero directly, I'm way too unimportant for that. I have a number that I call to reach the Pitoni, and that's how I relayed the message about you making reservations at the restaurant. From there, they gave me instructions about the tracking device.

I didn't even want to work for them, but you have to believe me that I had no other choice. I don't know what happens to the people that they have interest in and put tracking devices on. I try not to think about, to be honest with you. I'll do anything you want to help you get to them, but please don't hurt me." Cody cried throughout his explanation.

Showing no mercy whatsoever Tim looked at him square in the eye and stated, "You're mine now; you do and say exactly what I want. Understand?" Cody nodded his head and whimpered what sounded like a "yes".

Tim took some more tape and wrapped it around Cody's face. Showing him a tiny metal object with even smaller wires attached, Tim said in an offhand manner, "I decided that I won't torture you; yet I still need to do one more thing that will hurt...a

Forbidden Origins-apostasia

lot. I'm going to insert a tracking device/explosive inside of you. This way, if you think about running away from me, this little bomb will destroy the organ I attach it to, at which point you will bleed internally for a slow, agonizing death." Tim grabbed a scalpel and immediately proceeded to cut into Cody's chest. Seeing that Cody was nearly crazed from panic, Tim grabbed a syringe and injected him with it. He soon went into a deep sleep. Tim stopped cutting him, and began putting his stuff back into his bags.

"Kid doesn't know devices and bombs from crushed tin cans and car wiring." Tim gave a chuckle in satisfaction that his scare tactic worked.

Pulling his car closer to the door, he dragged Cody's limp body to his backseat, and then drove back to his house. Once inside, he carried Cody down the basement steps and then placed him on the cot. Even though Tim would be locking the door leading out of that room and the door at the top of the basement stairs, he handcuffed Cody to a support pole next to the cot, not wanting to take any chances that he could escape.

The next morning Tim went downstairs to check up on Cody and to bring him some food.

"Good Morning! I brought you some breakfast. I don't feel like feeding you like an infant, though, so I'm going to uncuff your hands. But you better not do anything stupid or you will die. Got it?" Cody nodded yes and so Tim took off the handcuffs.

97

As a precautionary measure, however, he used some rope to tie one of his legs to the pole.

Once Tim handed him the food, it was like the guy had never eaten, scarfing down everything nearly faster than he could chew. When he finally slowed down enough to take a drink of the bottle of water that Tim had brought along with the breakfast food, he said in an off-hand manner, "So, your surgery went well last night; be sure that you don't pick at the stitches."

Cody looked down at his chest and saw the bandage. "If I'm going to be working for you, the Pitoni leaders all need to die. I also want total freedom after this is over."

"I'm sure I can arrange that, but why do you want them all dead?"

"I only signed up with them because I was so desperate for cash. I had been having some bad rotten luck at the casino this past year, to the point that I had to sell pretty much everything I owned and move out of my apartment and into that dilapidated trailer you found me in. But even that wasn't enough, so I started to get some heat from some extremely scary people. That is when one of them told me about the Pitoni. In exchange for the loan they gave me, I would have to work for them until they said I had done enough to pay it all off. The catch was that if I didn't do my part in a certain amount of time, they would kill me.

I had three conditions. One: find a higher end place to work in, and they would provide a reference. Two: 50% of what I earned would go to them. Three: after they had decided a special task for me to carry out, they would set me free completely of my debt if I was successful. At that time, I would then go through a certain initiation to be hired in; a full time crew member of the Pitoni.

I was running out of time, and I was running out of options. The third condition would allow me to be debt free and to live another day. When they told me to let them know when someone big would be coming to the restaurant, I knew that was my chance. I knew that whatever their plans were probably wouldn't be pleasant for whoever ended up on the wrong end of them, but I tried not to think about it. You can understand that man, right? I tried to think of it as just business, and that it was the only way to survive. So since their pick up attempt of you and your wife was a failure, then that means what I did for them isn't going to matter. They're going to end up killing me anyways. The way I see it, I'm better off working for you than them."

After listening to Cody's explanation, Tim appeared deep in thought. Finally, he said, "You will be free and never bothered by me again after this is over, but try anything..."

Cody quickly cut in with. "I will die a horrible slow death, I know. I just want out of this mess."

Tim had to fight back a serious urge to smile at Cody's response. "Well, I'm glad we are on the same page."

"So, do you have a plan?"

"My first priority is to capture Nero and his son, then make one of them squeal. He'll have no choice but organize his men in my trap. I can't afford to spook him away by failing or attacking anyone else first."

"From what I understand Nero rarely visits anyone, and he always has his favorite guards around. How do you plan on getting to him?"

This time Tim let the smile come, but it was anything but reassuring to Cody. "Well my boy, that is where you come in."

A short while later and a couple hundred miles away, Nero's personal cell rings.

Nero: "This better be good, I'm in the middle of something."

Francis: "I'm sorry boss, but this sounds important."

Nero: "Go on."

Francis: "That kid we gave the tracking device to place on that clone doctor..."

Nero: "Yeah. What about him?
Francis: "Well he says cops have been snooping around the restaurant he works at and have been asking him questions. He

Forbidden Origins-apostasia

wants our protection so he doesn't end up in jail. He sounds pretty paranoid."

Nero: "Hmmm...I don't know how in all the chaos of that massive screw up I forgot all about that kid. Should have known that freak of nature clone would tell the cops about having the tracking device put on him while at the Jungle Paradise. Well, he doesn't need to worry about going to jail, and we don't need to worry that he's going to talk. Set up a meeting with him and send some of our guys."

Francis: "Sir?"

Nero: "Serious? Do I really need to spell it out for you over the phone? He's a problem, and the Pitoni doesn't mess around with problems. We take care of it."

Twenty minutes later and back in Tim's basement Cody hangs up the phone.

"Okay, the meeting is all set up. They want me to meet them at one of their properties just outside of town at eight tonight.

"Good, that gives us some more time to go over the details."

Trying his best to not sound as scared as he felt, Cody stammered out, "Uh...I was hoping that my part was done. I

101

think it would be better for you if I stayed here as your hostage until this passes. I'd just end up getting in the way."

Tim stared at him hard until Cody had to look away. "I think you are forgetting that you got me in this mess; now I'm giving you the chance to make it up to me. Or call it justice if you'd like."

At about 7:45, Tim pulled over to the side of the road, a couple miles away from their destination.

"Okay kid, this is where you drive," Tim said with a cough. He had been in agony the whole trip. Something was severely wrong, but none of that mattered as long as he could live long enough to get his revenge. Holding his stomach, he left the driver's seat and then laid down in the back so he wouldn't be seen.

"Are you sure this is going to work? You don't look so good."

"I'm fine, just drive!" Tim said in a pained, raspy shout. Pulling next to an old barn, Cody looked back at a sweating, miserable Tim.

"This must be the place." Cody told Tim. Tim nodded his head and Cody left the car and walked into the barn.

"Hello!?" Cody yelled when inside.

"Stop right there!" a voice came from across the other side. "Take your clothes off, and throw them into the barrel to your left."

"My clothes?" Cody hesitated.

"Yes." The man in the shadows replied. Cody nervously took them off and threw them in the barrel as instructed, then covered himself with his hands. The man walked towards him.

"Here, throw this on." The man said while throwing a burlap coat to Cody. He then proceeded to soak the clothes with lighter fluid and then set them on fire with a match. He waited a few moments, watching the fire burn, to ensure that there was nothing much left.

"Sorry kid, but we can't afford anyone listening in, or you talking for that matter." The man said, while lifting his gun and pulling the hammer back on his revolver.

(BANG) (BANG) Two shots rang out. Emerging from the side of the barn door came Tim, shooting the man twice, once in the arm that was holding the gun and once in his leg.

"GET THEM!" The injured man screamed in misery. Hearing footsteps from up above, Cody stood frozen.

"Come on, over here!" Tim yelled, but the kid just stood there, unable to move. Seeing that Cody was frozen in fear and hearing the sound of feet from above shuffling and running closer towards them, Tim ran to Cody and pulled him to a stall in the side of the barn. Both of them toppled to the ground as they dove in. Shots were being fired in their general direction.

Tim's heart was racing so fast, he felt like either he was going to have a heart attack, or that it may simply explode. He tried pulling himself up to fight, but couldn't. His hands and body were weak with tremors. He couldn't even grip his gun his body was shaking so hard. His body was experiencing the worst pain he had ever felt, like an alien being was killing him from the inside and taking over. He felt that his life was fading out rapidly.

Cody saw what was happening and in terror he shuffled himself away from Tim, trying to hide in the farthest corner of the stall. Cody closed his eyes and tried waking himself up from this nightmare, but every time he opened them back up nothing had changed. Closing his eyes one last time he prayed. "Oh God, please help me." Once he opened them that time, Tim was gone.

The gunmen proceeded with caution to check the area where they had seen Tim and Cody run for cover. To their surprise, he was not there; only Cody, who was cowering in the far corner. Before they could do anything about him, they heard a scream coming from behind them, along with gun fire. Turning around there was one of the men ripped apart into pieces. Then in the shadows they could just barely glimpse a mysterious object that moved like lightning. They started shooting at everything that appeared to move, and then out from the dark the monstrosity appeared.

Forbidden Origins-apostasia

Chasing the men, the creature ripped them limb by limb. Moving faster than their eyes could keep up, they couldn't get a good shot.

Finally, a man lying on the ground was able to empty his clip into the beast. It was the man that Tim shot before running for cover.

Turning around and dropping a man he was in process of dismembering, the creature prowled towards the gunman.

The man became panicked and tried half crawling and pushing himself along the ground as fast as he could to scramble away from the beast. Although the creature had many injuries from all the gunshots, he persisted after him. At this point the beast seemed to be struggling to stay on two feet. Yet he relentlessly made his way towards the final gunman as he frantically tried to reload his revolver. The beast was now having problems holding himself up in any kind of way. After crawling along on all fours he finally just crashed to the ground and stopped moving completely.

This helped reassure the man and calmed him down enough to finally get his gun loaded. When he looked back down at the unmoving body he was startled to realize it was now in human form. Not taking any chances, he took careful aim at the man's head. Unaware of another presence, out from behind him Cody suddenly sprang out with a shovel, hitting the man in the head and knocking him unconscious.

CHAPTER EIGHT
Surprises Around Every Corner

Tim started waking up a couple hours after his incident. Everything was blurry at first, and then once his eyes finally cleared he saw Cody sitting there, watching him. Trying to pull himself up, an immobilizing headache stopped him. Cody noticed his struggle and came to his aid.

"Tim, I can't believe what you did! It was incredible! I mean, I'm not gonna lie, you petrified me, but at the same time I was amazed at how bad a**-"

Tim interrupted Cody with, "Kid, I have the worst headache, please keep it down. But wait, what did I do that petrified you and was so incredible? What happened?"

Forbidden Origins-apostasia

"You don't remember? I thought that was all part of your plan, and you just didn't fill me in on all of it. Oh man, I can't believe you don't remember! You changed into a half man/half animal beast thing like a comic book hero come to life, and then you went through the Pitoni garbage as easily as a hot knife goes through butter!"

Tim dropped his face into his hands. "Trust me kid, whatever happened was not part of the plan or any type of hero." He looked back up from his hands and asked worriedly, "Did I kill them all?"

"Nope; one is still alive, I knocked him out and tied him up for you."

Tim looked at the kid in amazement, and then started to stand again. He noticed his clothes were ripped and stretched, and then saw bullet holes in his shirt. He checked himself all over for wounds but there were none; just a few faint scars that appeared to be growing fainter even as he watched.

Cody noticed Tim checking himself. "Dude, it was seriously amazing! After you passed out I was sure you were dead, but your body was hard at work healing itself. I was so relieved, because I want you to take this bomb out of me ASAP."

Tim responded with, "First off, don't call me 'dude'. Second, take me to the guy you tied up and then I'll get that explosive device out."

"Okay, but there's one thing I need to show you before I do that."

107

With that, Cody led Tim to what appeared to be a hidden hatch that opened up in the floor and had a passageway that continued under the barn.

"I found this when the last Pitoni guy was getting ready to shoot you after you passed out. I was digging around through the hay on the ground to find some kind of weapon to hit him with, and I tripped on the latch for the door."

Following Cody down a steep narrow stairway he showed Tim a room at the bottom that had a door with a small window.

"Take a look inside; I couldn't do anything about it until after you woke up because I'm going to need your help to get the door open."

Tim cautiously looked into the small peep hole not knowing what to expect, and what he did see made his heart drop.

"I already knew that Nero is one evil man, but I was hoping to stop his activities, not run into them."

Cody nodded his head in agreement. "Do you think you can open this door?"

"I need an ax and the Pitoni member you tied up."

Together they sought out an ax and from there drug the lone surviving gunman to the scene they had discovered. Chopping away at the thick wooden door, Tim was finally able to dislodge the handle and lock so that they could go in. After walking into the room they both felt the overwhelming presence of fear and sickness.

Forbidden Origins-apostasia

In the room was a group of maltreated girls, ranging from 8 to 15 or 16 years old.

"They're so young..." Cody breathed.

His remark retriggered Tim's anger. Picking the injured man up, he yelled into his face.

"Do you get off on this, kidnapping little girls?! How many of them did you and your boys touch!? Need to feel like you're a bigger man than you really are??" Choking the man and slamming him against the wall, Tim continued his rant. "How about after I free these girls, I let each and every one of them stab you, huh? But don't worry about dying; I have something much better than that in store for you. I'll inform Nero where you are and let him and the rest of your buddies finish you off."

As the man was bound and gagged he couldn't respond to anything with much more than a strained gurgling, at which point Tim dragged him out of the room and threw him in the tiny passageway. Tim needed him alive for the time being, so he didn't want to risk losing his control and end up killing him in his outrage.

"What are we going to do?" Cody asked about the girls. Timothy rubbed his eyes and face in frustration and tried thinking of a plan. As he was discovering, he wasn't completely heartless yet. He couldn't just leave these poor girls here. At the same time, though, he couldn't have this discovery get in the way of his revenge. If anything, it only strengthened his resolve to follow through with the elimination of every single Pitoni

109

member. But after a few more minutes of thought, he was able to come up with the easiest solution to be able to do the right thing and not have it interfere any more than it already had.

"It's possible they might have a vehicle somewhere on these grounds they use to transport these girls. Take a look around and if you find one, bring it in."

Cody went outside and found another little barn in the back. Heading inside, sure enough he found a mini bus with the keys inside. So he started it up and then pulled it into the barn, just like Tim had asked.

Between the two of them, Tim and Cody were able to get all the girls loaded onto the bus in under ten minutes. They didn't have too much trouble with them as they all seemed very weak from malnutrition and in quite a state of shock. It was possible they had been drugged at some point during their captivity, which would also explain their extreme lethargy. Despite their non-resistance as they were placed on the bus, Tim didn't want to take the chance that any of the girls get spooked and try to escape before they were brought to safety. Since the vehicle had been modified with belts to strap them in, Tim and Cody grudgingly used the straps to help ensure this.

"Ok kid, so what you're going to do is drive these girls near a police station. Buy a prepaid phone, call 911, and then inform them where the bus is at and what is on it. Don't stay on the phone after that. Throw it away and run. Don't go home and don't visit family."

Forbidden Origins-apostasia

Tim then pulled some cash out of his pocket and gave it to Cody. "And this is important: don't tell them anything about me, the Pitoni, or this barn. I'm going to burn it down anyways. It'll be the easiest way to clean up my mess."

"Uh, ok...and then what?" Cody asked.

"Then what, what?" was Tim's response.

"Well, is that it? I'm done after that?"

"Yes; you are officially free of them...and me."

"After everything I've seen last night and today I want to kill all the Pitoni too, I'm sure almost as much as you do. And what about the bomb you put inside of me?"

Tim finally did have to laugh at the kid's reminder of the "bomb". "There is no bomb or any explosives inside your body, kid. After I knocked you out, I cut your skin with a dull blade. Then rubbed the blunt end up and down several times to make it look a lot worse than it was and then slapped a bandage on it. I figured I would keep you too occupied to really pay too much attention to it."

At this, Cody removed the pitiful sack he had been wearing so that he could rip his bandage off and examine his wound. "Aha! I knew you didn't hate me! After I take care of the girls we can meet up somewhere and I can help you with whatever you're planning next."

Tim glared at him and stated point blank, "I do hate you, and I don't need or want any more of your help. Not ever! Just

111

forget about me, forget about what you saw and just do what you're told. Now go! I have business to take care of."

Crestfallen, Cody's shoulders slumped and then he turned away and started to get aboard the bus. At the last second, Tim called out, "Hey kid!"

Quickly he turned back around with hope in his eyes. "Just one more thing...stay away from those casinos!"

After watching Cody leave with a bus full of girls, Tim decided it was time to have some fun.

He walked down the hidden stairway back to the Pitoni member.

"Well scumbag, it's your lucky day; like I mentioned earlier, I wanted each of those girls to take their turn at cutting you. But it would seem that they have experienced enough violence. Another reason you're lucky is because I want to know how I can get to Nero and Nikki. So I'm going to take this gag off of you and we are going to talk." As Tim does this he told the man to start with his name.

"Strigoi..." the man gasped as the gag came off.

"Ok, Strigoi, let's talk about Nero and where he's at right now."

Forbidden Origins-apostasia

"No, no, you misunderstand; I am Vinnex. Strigoi is man that is also demon. You are Strigoi; Vinnex has seen with his own two eyes, da? Please Strigoi, do not take me to Iad. I'm not ready for hell."

Tim answered with, "The way I see it Vinnex, you work for me and help me get Nero and Nikki, and you can escape hell a little longer."

"How can I trust you, Strigoi? Demons do much to deceive."

"I just let the kid go that you were going to kill without any mercy or regrets, along with a bus full of young girls that you may or may not have had a hand in kidnapping and torturing. If I was going to, I could have killed you several times over by now...or even could have done some torturing of my own."

"Yes, I see your point Strigoi. Promise me that you kill all (the Pitoni), because if you don't I might as well be dead now."

"Once I am through, there will be no survivors. You can rest assured of that, Vinnex."

"I'm also in an extreme amount of pain, so I need some help before I can do anything for you. I know that you're that clone doctor, and with your powers you can heal me."

Tim noticed how bad Vinnex wounds looked, and decided if he wanted his help, he'd better try to fix him up some. "I'll see what I can do."

"Thank you, Strigoi."

Tim went to his car and pulled out his duffel bags that held his supplies. Included in one of them was a medical kit, right next to some of his torture devices. He knew that he was going to have to do some healing along with the hurting to get the most out of his prey. After returning to Vinnex, he told him, "Looks like only two of your wounds are semi-serious, and even those aren't terrible. But you do have a bullet lodged in your leg, so I'll need to get that out. I don't have anything here with me stronger than Vicodin to give you for the pain, so you are just going to have to grin and bear it. Telling me how to get to Nero and Nikki might help distract you."

Vinnex didn't say anything at first, but once Tim started working on getting the bullet out he sucked in a deep breath and said in a strained voice, "Da, Strigoi, perhaps talking would be a distraction. Nikki loves the ladies; he even has his own harem kept at a place called the Pitoni Nido D'Amore. They are beautiful and paid very well. And like Nikki, most of them are also heavy drug addicts. Sometimes Nikki will get so messed up, that whoever he's with will have to call his dad to have him come and take care of him."

"What kind of man needs that close of supervision from daddy? I thought the Pitoni is supposed to be made up of pretty hard core gangsters?"

Even though Tim hadn't meant that as a compliment, Vinnex puffed up a bit with some pride at that remark and then continued.

Forbidden Origins-apostasia

"Nikki is the apple of Nero's eye. No matter how much of a liability he is or how often he screws up, nobody has the guts to call him out on it. Nero won't tolerate anyone speaking against him. The ironic thing is that the idiotule repays this loyalty from his father by basically robbing him.

But I stray from the point that I am trying to make...get Nikki in distress, and Nero will come. I think this is your best option, Strigoi."

"Ok, so we use the drugs and put Nikki in distress." Tim responded.

"Da, but remember, he's a heavy hitter, so just drugs won't always do it. He's emotionally unstable, so a little kick to his self-esteem while using drugs usually does the trick."

Tim looked at Vinnex in question. "What do you mean that 'usually does the trick?' You seem to know a lot about this?"

"I have worked for Nero loyally for years with no raises or any other type of reward. So, sometimes to get a well-earned bonus, me and some of the other guys would create a situation to separate him from his stash. Using the method I just told you about with his son was always the most effective way. We'd get paid what we figure is already owed to us and he and his son would get some bonding time together." Vinnex snickered.

"Well let's give them the chance to bond one last time."

Finally done with the quick patch up job he performed on him, Tim helped Vinnex to the car. Then he brought out a gasoline container out from his trunk and started pouring it in

115

random areas around the barn, enough to be sure it would all burn. Throwing a lit match on the gasoline trail he had made leading out of the barn, he stood and watched it all go up in flames for a few minutes before turning away and walking back to the car.

Vinnex whistled low between his teeth as Tim got in. "Wow, Strigoi. Perhaps your last name is 'distrugător'; for not only are you the demon man, but you are also the destroyer."

An hour later, Tim pulled them into a truck stop, and told Vinnex, "We need to clean up. Pick out a set of clothes and we'll hit the showers."

"Da Strigoi, very good."

Walking into the store section of the truck stop they went straight for the clothes, and then took them up to the register. After setting the clothes on the counter the lady at the register asked, "Is everything alright?" She looked concerned over the two men's bloody and torn clothes.

Tim started to answer with "Yes, actually –" but then Vinnex cut him off.

"My friend and I just came back from tryouts for a zombie movie, ma'am. We didn't realize they were going to have us in

Forbidden Origins-apostasia

full costume for the first round of auditions, so we didn't pack a change of clothes. As you can imagine we have been getting quite a few funny looks from people, so we are eager to get cleaned up." Vinnex smiled and winked at the woman as he said this.

Completely charmed, the lady gushed, "Oh, how exciting! I sure hope you guys get the part!"

"Maybe if we do, I'll invite you to the party..." Tim paid as fast as he could and rushed Vinnex to the showers before he could ask for the woman's phone number.

Sitting in the car near Nikki's house, Tim and Vinnex went over some details while waiting for night to fall.

"Okay, so what I am going to do is give my Lily some special directions and she'll be the one to get Nikki unstable." Vinnex suggested.

"Your Lily?"

"Yeah, well technically she's Nikki's, but we –"

"I get it, you guys have a thing," Tim interrupted. "I'm sorry I asked. So then what?"

"Well, Lily is going to mix the drugs with something special. She'll beg to be with him tonight and start taunting him. Works every time."

"Nikki hasn't caught on to this?" Tim asked.

"We do it a little different each time, but he gets so spaced out he doesn't remember much when his dad arrives, anyway. He's just there to comfort him and calm him down, I guess. Once Nero arrives, you'll know it's time to move in."

"Okay, give your lady a call." Tim gave his phone to Vinnex.

After dialing the number, the call picked up after the second or third ring. "Hey sugar puss, it's your Vinnie binnie bear. Want to pull a money grab tonight? Then maybe later we can find waldo?"

Tim rolled his eyes in disbelief.

"Yeah, meet me at our usual spot on the corner of Silver and 9th street." Vinnex listened to her response and then smiled and gave Tim a thumbs up. "Alright, I'll see you in a bit, lolly lips."

When he hung up the phone Tim shook his head and said "I hope that went better than it sounded. I think you'll have to excuse me while I go hurl in those bushes over there."

Vinnex shrugged and replied with, "I can't help my charm, I'm a dirty boy and she's my cherry pie. But don't worry, she'll be here soon." Sure enough, not more than twenty minutes later a scantily clad woman appeared at the street intersection that

Forbidden Origins-apostasia

Vinnex mentioned that was a short distance away from the harem.

"Okay, I have to go talk with her alone; I don't want her thinking you're a cop."

Tim watched Vinnex leave the car and walk towards the infamous Lily. It was an appalling sight of what looked like instructions made with sweet talk, mixed with fondling. The Vicodin he gave Vinnex earlier was doing its job; you almost couldn't tell he was injured. Watching them giggle one last time with a quick grab here and there, Vinnex finally made his way back to the car.

"Go well?" Tim asked.

"Yeah, and you want to know something? I think that once the golden boy is out of the picture I should take over his harem. I mean, someone has to look out for those girls and take care of their needs." Vinnex said as though deep in thought.

Tim looked at him with surprise, but then Vinnex ruined the moment when he continued with, "And I'm pretty sure I have the right 'tool' for the job."

"If you don't mind, please don't think out loud. I just want to get this mission over with." Tim was getting anxious, and was popping muscle relaxers and Xanax almost like candy. He couldn't afford to lose control at a time like this.

It was then that Vinnex could see that something was wrong. "Hey Strigoi, you don't look so good; are you sure you can do this?"

"Yes, and it would be great if you could stop talking. You're really starting to get on my nerves... and that's not a good idea for either of us."

"Hey, it's all good. Look, here's Nikki now; the magic will happen soon."

"Not soon enough," Tim whispered to himself.

Giving Nikki time to get inside the house, Tim then followed and parked a few buildings down from the Nido D'Amore. Some time passed and then finally lights began to flicker on and off in one of the rooms on the second floor of the house.

Vinnex sat up in his seat and announced, "That's the signal. Nikki lost control and they are calling Nero. When he arrives, wait a few minutes so you can be sure that he's with Nikki. You'll get both in one clean shot."

Fifteen minutes later and there was Nero, just as Vinnex said he would be.

"Okay Strigoi, this is it."

Pulling in the driveway and then exiting the car, Tim made his way inside. Although the lights were dim throughout and loud music was playing, it was clear that Nikki's harem was having all sorts of illegal fun. Making his way through the sea of intoxicated women, he eventually came to the stairs. It wasn't difficult to find his way to the right room, as he could hear yelling the closer he got. Nikki was screaming so loud that no one even noticed Tim walking into the room.

Forbidden Origins-apostasia

"Hands up where I can see them." Tim said calmly while he aimed his gun."

Nero stared at him like a ghost. "Dr. Clone?"

Ignoring the question, Tim ordered, "You and your son, down to your skivvies...well, it appears your son is already there. So I guess that means just you, Nero. Start stripping."

"I'm sure we can work something out..."

"My patience is wearing out by the second; now I said undress!"

Nero started taking his shirt and pants off while Nikki just stood there glassy eyed and red-faced. Once Nero was down to his underwear, Tim walked over and handed Nero a zip tie. Pointing his gun at Nikki's head, he instructed Nero to tie his son's hands behind his back. After he complied, then Tim did the same with Nero's hands and then he led them both downstairs.

"Get in," Tim said while opening the back door to his car. As they scooted in, Tim injected both of them with a strong sedative. Before they fell asleep they noticed Vinnex in the front passenger seat. Nero just about went ballistic.

"I'm going to kill you! Worthless Romanian!" he tried to yell and throw a fit, but the sedative took effect quickly.

Vinnex, taken by surprise and with a look of shock on his face screeched out, "I thought you were going to kill them, Strigoi!"

"I am, but not yet. Now get out! Before I change my mind and kill you too!"

Vinnex jumped out of the car and ran off.

As Tim started thinking on his drive home, he couldn't believe how everything was coming together. Vengeance was going to be his, and he was going to have fun doing it. Looking down to check his speed, he noticed his skin had gotten worse. Yet it no longer bothered him like it did before. In fact, he was starting to love it. The old Tim was dead, having passed away with Aavah and their child. Whatever was happening inside him, he had chosen to accept. The bottom line was it had helped him in his quest to capture Nero and Nikki, after all, and that's all the reason he needed to embrace the beast from within.

CHAPTER NINE
Mysterious Ways

"911, please state your emergency."

"Yes, I'd like to report a suspicious bus I saw on South Wilkes Street. It looks like there are some captives inside."

"Okay sir, please stay on the line..."

Cody hung up the phone on the emergency operator, and then threw it away just as Tim had told him to do. Within a few short minutes he could hear emergency sirens about a mile away, likely headed towards the bus. A half hour later as he was walking past a shop with TV screens in the window, he saw news reports about what was found on Wilkes street. Satisfied that the young girls were now in good hands, he continued on his way.

Once reaching the outskirts of the city, he stopped. 'What now?' he asked himself. Going home wasn't an option; or visiting any friends or family he had. Until he knew for sure that the Pitoni was no longer in the picture, he didn't want to risk putting any of his loved ones in danger. And it was also possible the cops may be looking for him, as well. He didn't think the girls that he helped to save were with it enough to be able to describe him to the police, but stranger things have happened. All the action he'd experienced in such a short time led to a climax that left him with nothing and nowhere to go.

Glancing over across the street he saw a pawn shop that advertised all comic books 50% off. Checking his pocket, he found that he still had the small ball of money that Tim had given him. He knew that it wasn't going to get him very far, but at the same time thought to himself, 'Might as well get some entertainment to help pass the time until I can figure out what to do.'

Walking into the store, he saw old guitars, televisions, tools, etc. The sight of all the old neglected items made a twisting knot in his stomach he couldn't explain. Continuing to the back corner of the store, he finally found what he was searching for, the comics that were on sale. Scanning through the various colorful heroes, there was one that struck his interest more so than any of the others. It was called *Forbidden Origins*. Flipping through the pages it was like no other comic he had read before, and yet at the same time seemed familiar. Stories of young and old heroes, mighty giants, demons, and evil aliens, as well as plots thick with greed for power, lust and betrayal. Engulfed with the story, Cody was startled out of his reading when a voice suddenly spoke from behind him.

"Do you like that comic?"

Dropping the said comic book and then turning around to see who was speaking to him, he saw that it was an older man, perhaps in his sixties.

The man knelt down and picked the book up off the floor and handed it back to Cody. "I'm sorry, son, I didn't mean to scare you. I just wanted to tell you that if you're interested in these comics, I'll show you where there are more," the man said helpfully.

"Um, thank you. Where did these comics come from? I've never seen any like these."

"Well, that's because the comics I have here never made it big. In fact, this is probably the only place you can get them. I even have a hard time giving them away. My sign outside used to say 'free comics', but I got more customers looking at them by advertising 50% off all comics. I still give them away, though, as I like sharing these stories and have plenty of them," the man said with a mixture of kindness and sorrow.

"You said this is the only place I can find these comics?" Cody asked puzzled.

"Yes, I'm actually the writer. You see, I was a pastor for my church, but I struggled with grabbing the attention of the young people of my parish. Several years ago, I saw kids running around in my church pretending to be super heroes. These same heroes are the ones that are now featured in most of those big Hollywood movies, and it seems that people of all ages enjoy them. I thought it would be great if I could incorporate biblical stories into comic books and try to use popular media to teach important messages. While it worked for a short time in the church, it never made it far outside my store walls," he said with a sigh.

"I'm sorry to hear that, sir. I went to church when I was younger, but to be honest, I hated it. Maybe if I went to yours and had a pastor that cared about gaining the interest of the young people, it would have been cool," Cody said trying to cheer the man up.

"If there's one thing I learned, no church can be 'cool', just like parents can't be, but I appreciate you saying so," the pastor said with a smile. "What's your name?" he asked as he went to shake Cody's hand.

Cody panicked, not wanting to give out his real name, so he quickly thought of one. "Silas Zadok," he said, stumbling a bit on his new name as he shook the reverend's hand. Silas was his middle name and Zadok was his maternal grandmother's last name.

Not giving any sign that he noticed how long it took the boy to answer the question, the reverend shook his hand with enthusiasm and responded with,

Forbidden Origins-apostasia

"My name is Shelemiah, but my friends call me Shem; it's good to meet you Silas Zadok."

"Thank you for the comics, it's not every day you run into a preacher that writes them." Cody said.

"As well as owning a pawnshop," Shem chuckled and winked.

"That's no joke!" Cody burst out laughing and shook his head in irony. Then added more seriously, "You are a busy man, sir."

"Yes, but as you can see by the dust I'm not staying busy enough. I just keep running out of time to do everything..." Shem trailed off a little as he glanced around his neglected shop. Then he turned back to 'Silas' and stared at him as if deep in thought for a moment.

"You know; I've been thinking about hiring some help around here. Would you be at all interested? I have a lot of work that needs to be done, and I could pay you a decent wage. Maybe you could also help me restart those comics and make them more interesting?" Shem looked like he had a new spark of life when he asked the question.

A bit taken aback at the unexpected offer, Cody wasn't sure how to let the old man down gently. "Umm...gee...I'm really grateful for the offer sir, but to be honest I wasn't planning on sticking around this area. I'm looking to find a fresh start for myself, as I've made more mistakes than I care to think about. Truth be told, if you knew all there was to know about me and

127

what I've been a part of, I don't think you would really want me around," Cody said while shrugging his shoulders.

"Well, can I at least leave you with a couple thoughts?" the pastor asked and led Cody over to a guitar. "See this old beauty right here? Well, believe it or not, I found her in the trash. It looked like this guitar had been played and beaten by Satan himself. I don't know exactly what lured me into grabbing the guitar, maybe I just couldn't watch it rot. I had plenty of new instruments at the time, so it's not like I needed it. I spent hours working on it every day; I spent more time and money on it than what it was actually worth. But after I got her all fixed up, I didn't have the heart to sell her, because I couldn't stand the thought of her being beaten down and broken all over again. As it turns out, now she's worth more than my entire store.

All new things become old, and a lot of old things become new. Just because you are searching for something new doesn't mean it'll stay new. Let me know if you change your mind." With that said, Shem sat down with the guitar and started playing a melody.

Cody walked away from the old man, confused about what in the world he was talking about. He stepped out of the pawn shop and proceeded down the block. Every step he took felt heavier than the last with the realization he had nothing, and the further he got from the store the further he felt from a new opportunity.

Forbidden Origins-apostasia

Stopping to gather his thoughts, he glanced at the cover of one of the comic books the kind pastor had given him. One of the pictures on the cover was of a beast, and it reminded him of Dr. Philips. As Cody stared into the picture he replayed the events of the previous day. For some reason he kept remembering the fact that he had asked help from God while in the midst of all the chaos. Maybe if there is a God, this was an opportunity he was meant to accept, but instead he'd just walked away from it.

Dr. Philips has a new power and is set on revenge, and the Pitoni might still have other victims in need of saving. What if no one ever finds them? Or what if Dr. Phillips himself is in need of saving? Thinking about these things helped Cody to make the decision he knew was the right thing to do. Just maybe he could be a hero after all, and working for the reverend wouldn't be such a bad idea.

When Nero woke up, he found himself gagged and tied to some type of rigid surface in a darkly lit room. He attempted to look around but found that he couldn't turn his head very far too either side. He tried as hard as he could to remember how he'd gotten to where he currently was, but his mind drew a total blank. He closed his eyes, striving with all his might to focus all his concentration on recalling how in the world he came to be where he was.

As he was trying to assemble his thoughts, he heard someone else breathing in the room. The memories came flooding back to him, that he and his son had been kidnapped by that clone doctor freak. Nero tried to get his son's attention and see if there was any chance that they could escape, but the gag muffled any sound he could make, and the bonds restraining him made it difficult to move any part of his body. Curling his fingers, he tried feeling if he could somehow loosen his restraints, but it was useless. Frustrated from not being able to move or talk, he jerked his body from side to side, throwing his weight around. The cot he was strapped to tipped precariously on one side and then the next until...BAM! He hit the floor hard after the cot was finally knocked over. The pain and shock of the fall knocked the wind out of him.

Nervous he might have caught the doctor's attention, he listened for footsteps. Not hearing any, he tried scooting himself on his belly over to where his son was strapped down. Looking like an awkward turtle with the cot still strapped to him, he gained inch by precious inch as he painfully made his way across the hard floor.

He was able to make it over to his son's cot after a while, but then he couldn't figure out what to do next. Not having the use of his hands, he thought that maybe if he knocked this cot over the way he did with his own cot, they might be able to figure out a way to untie each other. Using his body weight again, he brought the top of the cot on his back to the bottom of Nikki's cot and tried lifting himself up off the ground as hard as he could. During his pitiful attempt a light came on, blinding him.

"Look at what we have here: an escape artist! Perhaps you've been in captivity before. Well, no matter, because you're not leaving here; not alive anyway." Tim said this with a sort of crazed merriment. Grabbing the cot, he dragged Nero back to his spot and put him back upright. Then he pulled a rope attached to a pulley, attached it to the cot and pulled Nero up to eye level. Locking it in place Tim went on.

"I must have fallen asleep in the other room finishing some surprises I have in store. You'll see some of them soon enough, but in the meantime let me go over some rules and expectations. You are mine now, and your son over there is also mine. You both are going to work for me, giving me information so I can wipe out the rest of your Pitoni crew.

So before you tune me out and stop listening, let me share a couple things with you. Remember when you slid in the back seat of my car? Well do you remember who was in the front passenger seat?"

Nero's eyes lit up in answer as he remembered seeing one of his own men in Tim's car.

"That's right, your own man ratted you out; Vinnex, I believe his name was. Does that sound familiar? At any rate, he set you up. Without his help, I never would have been able to capture you. In fact, he and some other members of your little group have been stealing from you. They have been finding assorted ways to provoke your unbalanced son into having one of his notorious fits. Seems to work effectively in getting you to come running and separate you from your stash. They have been executing this plan for quite some time now, but last night's performance was specifically so I could capture you.

Vinnex has been sleeping with your son's harem and winning the trust and loyalty of all the girls. In exchange for his cooperation I told him I would get the two of you out of the way so that he could have them all to himself. He didn't say it, but I'm pretty sure his plan is to take control of the Pitoni. Who would have thought snakes weren't very trustworthy?"

This was rhetorical, as Nero wasn't able to answer with the gag in his mouth. So he just glared at Tim with an intense hatred.

Not fazed in the slightest, Tim continued. "Ok, so back to the 'rules and regulations' part of our little chat. You help me set up a situation where I can kill the rest of the Pitoni and I'll let your son live, unharmed. If you try to escape again, I will kill your son. If you refuse to cooperate, I will kill your son. If you give me any false or misleading information, I will kill your son. If you even look at me funny...well, I think you understand. So just like you told me before my wife and unborn baby died, I'm

132

Forbidden Origins-apostasia

going to take the gag off, but try screaming or anything else stupid, I will kill your son. Understand?"

Due to the restraints there was not much that Nero could do to respond, so he just continued to glower until Tim released the strap on Nero's head and then removed the gag in his mouth.

"You are a crazy bastardo that belongs in hell! No, I take that back, even Hell is too good for you...a freak of nature that was never even meant to exist. I knew that ransoming a Frankenstein monster and his wench was going to be a mistake, but against my better judgment –" before Nero could finish his rant Tim slapped him hard across the face.

"I think it would be in your – and more importantly – your son's best interests to not ever speak of my wife again."

Nero could taste blood in his mouth and guessed that his nose had been broken. His instinct was to bring his hand to his face to assess the damage but all he could do was struggle against his bonds.

Tim ignored the other man's struggle and told him, "Now that we have all the rules established, I need you to tell me how we can orchestrate all your men to come together in one place."

At this Nero spit in Tim's face and answered, "I will tell you nothing, you filthy clone!"

Wiping the mixture of saliva and blood from his face, Tim calmly walked over to his table of tools. After picking up a sledgehammer, he then approached Nero's son, who still lay unconscious on his cot.

"I feel a little bad that Nikki is not awake and able to contribute to this discussion. Do you think I should wake him up?"

Nero remained silent as Tim positioned the hammer over Nikki's hand. Tim then shrugged as if to say 'Ok, you asked for it' and raised the sledgehammer up and started to bring it down...

"Wait! Stop! You don't need to do that!"

Tim stopped just in time before smashing Nikki's fingers into a fleshy mess. "Oh really? I think that I do. After all, doesn't he have a right to know that his father would rather sacrifice his life than set up one tiny little meeting with his co-workers? Co-workers that have already proven their 'loyalty' by ratting out their leader at the drop of a hat?"

Nero dropped his head down as far as the restraint would let him go. "Do you swear on all that is holy that you will release my boy unharmed if I do what you say?" Nero asked in defeat.

"I swear it," Tim replied.

Nero was silent for a few long moments, and then finally spoke again. "I can't say that I wasn't suspicious of my crew before, but I had no idea it would go this far. I'll give you any information you need, but I want you to kill Vinnex very slowly and painfully."

"Done. But I need you to organize your gang before they realize that you're missing; I want them all, and I want them all in one place."

Forbidden Origins-apostasia

Nero looked thoughtful for a second and then replied, "To do that I would need to call a serpente uova; it means snake eggs. It's a code name for a meeting at a certain place where we hatch ideas. It is the only meeting that requires all ranking Pitoni.

"Make the call." Tim said with an excited shiver in his voice and fire in his eyes.

"I want the job," Cody said while charging back through the pawn shop's doors. The reverend looked up expectantly and laid his guitar down.

"I'm glad. Out of curiosity, what made you change your mind?" Shem asked.

"I have a lot of questions, and I get the idea that maybe you would be the person that can answer them. Just please, don't get preachy on me," Cody said.

"Well, grab the two guitars that are over in that corner, any two will do." The pastor pointed towards the far wall.

Cody walked over and picked out two guitars and brought them to him.

"I'll try to answer your questions while we clean these guitars."

"Well I guess to start with, how does a preacher become an owner of a pawn shop?"

Shem laughed at this. "Well that's a good question. When I was young, my father used to own this place and we lived on the upper floor. I used to help him after school and on weekends. There is a little room in the back where I would do homework and fiddle with broken items to get them working again. I also used that room to write; I loved to write stories. We never had enough money to go anywhere exotic or special, so I used my imagination and wrote of adventures I would take.

My mother died in a car accident when I was just thirteen and then my older brother died a couple years later of cancer. My father never remarried, so it was just him and I for a long time. I never went to college, but I had a desire to be a pastor. The church my dad and I attended saw how much I wanted to be in the ministry and was very supportive; they helped put me through seminary school. Then I became a student of our reverend. I studied and wrote sermons in that back office where I did school and wrote stories as a child.

When the head pastor retired I took his place. My father got to see me preach for one year before he died of a heart attack. I was left with the pawn shop, but it's also my home." Lifting the guitar he cleaned, and then the one that Silas had done to inspect them for any more dust, Shem declared them good and asked Silas to grab a couple more to clean.

Forbidden Origins-apostasia

"You mentioned earlier of things you had done that made you feel that I wouldn't want you around. If you don't mind me asking Silas, what happened in your past that has made you feel so guilty?"

"That's a long story sir, and quite personal. Plus, I don't think you would believe me even if I told you," Cody said trying to avoid the subject.

"I think I would surprise you, Silas. I like unbelievable personal stories. I am after all an old reverend that writes comics in a pawn shop, remember? But if you aren't ready to talk about it, that's fine. I am, however, trustworthy and when you're ready, my ears are open."

Looking down at the tired looking and beaten up guitar he was working on, Cody was silent for a couple of minutes. "Actually Shem, there is something I should tell you."

CHAPTER TEN
Shedding of the Pitoni

L ooking about as beaten as a man could look, Nero hung up the phone.

"There, I made the call. Your meeting is set up for tonight at 8pm. The address is 605 Riverview Road; it used to be a bank a long time ago but has been vacant for a while.

I have a sign that says 'Restaurant coming soon' on the door. There isn't going to be, but that's how I keep anyone from getting too suspicious about the people coming in and out of there at all hours." That was as much as Nero was willing to tell Tim, as he was hoping that even without being able to warn his fellow gang members, perhaps Tim going in blind would allow for them to have the advantage and take him down.

Forbidden Origins-apostasia

Although there was no love lost between the members of the Pitoni, they were still brothers in crime. Despite his fury at the thought of his so-called brothers stealing from him at the expense of his son's sanity, Nero never thought he would be reduced to the lowly level of rat and serve them up to an enemy on a silver platter. So his goal was to tell Tim as little as possible and hope that their sheer numbers would overwhelm this worthless piece of clone trash that threatened the only thing he ever really cared about. He only wished he could be there to see it.

While Nero had all these thoughts running through his mind, Tim just stood there staring at him expectantly, as if waiting to hear more. But Nero also continued his silence, his belligerence clear in his empty, cold-blooded eyes.

Finally, Tim broke the silence with "I see.... can you tell me a little more about this place, and what all a 'serpent uova' meeting entails? About how many men will be in the building? Where is the location of the meeting room? What type of weapons will they have?"

Not wanting to anger the loco doctor while he and his son were still vulnerable, Nero thought that he would give a little bit of truth mixed with lies to give his team at least somewhat of an advantage.

"Well, typically each member of the team carries their own automatic weapon, along with at least one other weapon of personal choice, such as a blade or brass knuckles. Because everyone is already so well armed, there is little need to have additional guards at ready, particularly since the meeting room is strategically placed at a middle floor of the building with windows that go all the way around. This creates a view of all sides of the building to be able to watch for activity going on outside or potential threats. Because of that, I'm not sure what your best opportunity for entry will be, besides to try and appear to be a local delivery guy of some sort, and try to get in through the entrance to the basement when one of the lookouts may not be paying close attention." Nero was silently congratulating himself with thinking so fast on his feet, as he knew that if Tim tried to enter in through the basement entrance, he would likely be apprehended immediately as that is the actual location of the meeting, and so had the highest concentration of guards.

But instead of responding to Nero's information and suggestion, Tim just stood and walked over to Nikki once again. This time he nonchalantly grabbed a rusty saw and positioned it over one of Nikki's fingers. Although Nikki had yet to awaken from the sedation drugs he had been given, the contact of having his hand lifted and re-positioned made him moan and try to move against his restraints.

Nero began to sweat profusely and struggled against his own bindings. Not wanting Nikki to wake up in such a predicament he refrained from shouting and instead whispered "Wait – Stop! What are you doing?! I'm cooperating, telling you everything you want to know! Please don't hurt him!"

Forbidden Origins-apostasia

Tim responded with, "Why not? I'm not going to kill him...if you are truly cooperating, then I will stick to my word, but as I suspect you may not be telling me the whole truth, I figured it was fair to at least take a finger or two. It won't kill him, and he will even be able to do most things...he's right handed, right?" As he asks this he puts some pressure of the blade down on Nikki's left hand causing some bright red blood to rush to the surface of his skin.

Starting to moan more loudly now and his eyes began to flutter, Nero is no longer able to control his panicked voice from rising and he yells out, "NO! Please, I will tell you everything I swear, just PLEASE, JUST DON'T HURT HIM!"

Tim removed the blade from Nikki's hand and turned to grab a syringe, injecting him at the base of his neck where it meets the shoulder just as Nikki seemed to be coming awake. So before he even had time to ask "Where am I?" he succumbed to deep sleep once again. It wouldn't do to have him awake and distracting his father while Tim was trying to get more information from him. Tim took a rag and cleaned the tiny bit of blood off the blade, but allowed the blood on Nikki's hand to remain as incentive for Nero to keep talking.

"Ok then, now that you know I am serious about wanting to know more about this building, why don't you try again?"

Knowing he had lost once again, Nero turned his head away to the side for almost a full minute. Exhausted from the adrenaline rush that he just experienced due to the fear he felt

141

for his son, he eventually turned his head back towards Tim and began to speak.

"The serpente uova meetings always take place in the basement vault. The walls are so thick that if anyone was wired there would be no reception. There's just one door to go in or out, so you don't have to worry about anyone sneaking away. Expect a couple of armed guards, but if you are able to take them out quietly the rest will be like lambs for the slaughter. Weapons aren't ever allowed into the meeting room, in the event a topic gets too heated and somebody decides to lose their cool." While giving Tim all this information he spat every word out like it was poison in his mouth. He was disgusted with himself as much as he was for the clone doctor putting him in the position he was in. But he would sell his soul to protect Nikki, and that is where Tim holds the trump card.

"There, I told you everything. Now will you release my son?" Nero grudgingly asked.

Before answering Tim strapped the gag around Nero's mouth again.

"He's only free if what you are saying is true. After all that, you didn't really think I was still going to take your word for it, did you? If I run into a trap, then you are both dead. By the time anyone finds your bodies down here you will have long expired from a painful, slow death of dehydration."

With that said, Tim hooked Nero and Nikki's cots to a pulley system he had built just for this occasion. After lowering

Forbidden Origins-apostasia

them down into a hidden holding cell beneath the floor, he chained them up right against the wall. He wasn't taking any chances that they would escape while he was gone. Once that was out of the way, Tim grabbed some supplies from his little armory room. Some homemade explosives, knives, ropes, and two pistols.

Although he was feeling confident about his plans for the evening, Tim was a little concerned about losing control again. He needed things to go smoothly, and not only that, he wanted to remember killing the Pitoni. Tim wasn't sure what was happening to him; he just figured things got so crazy at the barn that his rage and adrenaline spiraled out of control. Whatever the case, Tim wasn't willing to risk it happening again, so he planned on taking some muscle relaxers to try and control his reactions. One thing was for sure, he still has plenty of rage and adrenaline to spare.

As a precaution, Tim parked his car down the street from the old bank; he wanted to be sure that he caught the Pitoni by surprise. As he sat motionless in his car, the cold and flu like symptoms he had felt before the barn incident started to envelop his body. With each passing day his body seemed to be getting progressively worse. Even with medication it almost seemed that any excitement would bring him to a sickly state. The power of his hate and propensity for brutality also grew within him each day, in sync with his symptoms. But he couldn't focus on his pain and get to the bottom of his illness just yet; he needed to keep a level head and get through this last stage for the Pitoni.

Grabbing his gear out of the car, he circled around the building to find the easiest way in, without alerting his victims inside to his presence. He located a window on the second floor that was already partially open and led out to a fire escape. With all the cigarette butts nearby, it looked like the Pitoni guards might be using that window and fire escape platform for smoke breaks. This meant he could sneak in without breaking a window, alerting the guards to his presence and giving away his position. Yet it also meant he had to figure out a way to climb up to the platform in his weakened condition. Grabbing a hook and some rope from his bag, he threw it onto the rusty steel fire escape. He tested his weight first and then decided it was time to climb. Using his whole body, he shimmied up the rope. As he made his ascent, the rusty fire escape started making creaking and grinding noises. Afraid of making too much noise, he moved at a slower pace to try and remain silent. Once he approached the platform he grabbed the side railing and started to pull himself up. But the rusty railing gave a screeching grind and broke, causing Tim to slip. Catching himself by the bottom ledge of the platform, he dangled in the air. He knew that this last

Forbidden Origins-apostasia

commotion was bound to grab someone's attention. Sliding over to a corner post on the platform, he grabbed it and threw his feet up, rolling his body beside the window.

Sure enough, he heard someone coming; laying down beneath the windowsill he tried to remain calm and keep his breathing quiet. The footsteps stopped on the other side of the wall where he laid motionless. Then a figure opened the window the rest of the way up and rested his palms on the sill. The man poked his head out the window to see what the commotion was.

Tim had his knife clenched tightly in his hands. 'One, two, three,' he counted in his head. Springing up, Tim jabbed the knife deep into the man's throat. Then he pulled the man's body through the window and rolled it onto the fire escape platform, finishing him off.

Once he stepped inside, he took a moment to stop and listen for any sign of movement. Hearing footsteps in the distance, he decided to take refuge in an office across the hall before anyone saw him.

"Tommy?" A man called out from the hallway. "Is that you smoking outside?" Tim could hear the footsteps approaching the open window. Tim opened the office door a crack and could see the man about to poke his head out the window to investigate. After hearing a loud curse Tim saw the man start to pull out his two-way radio to report what he found. But while the man was distracted, Tim took the opportunity to rush behind him.

Before the guard even realized anyone else was there, Tim was upon him. He again chose to go for the throat, slicing the man's neck wide open, making it impossible for the man to yell or scream for help. The man held his neck in shock and pain, and then slowly slumped down to the floor.

Tim grabbed the man by his feet and then dragged him to the office where he had been hiding to finish him off. Even after stabbing the man multiple times and it became obvious that the man was dead, Tim continued to stab him. It wasn't until Tim was close to being out of breath before he stopped. Moving away from the bloody corpse he realized how out of control he was becoming. He had to keep it together to finish the mission he set for himself.

Taking a minute for a breather he stared at the mutilated form that was seconds ago a living and breathing person. It reminded him of Aavah's body the last time he had seen her. It was getting harder and harder to remember the good times they had. And it seemed like the only memory he had left of her was her lifeless body in his hands and the blood surrounding her...so much blood. Tim's stomach began to tighten while his heart started to beat uncontrollably.

'The rest of the Pitoni are downstairs; I can't stop now when I'm so close,' Tim thought to himself. Forcing his body to rise up, he stumbled out the door and through the hallway. The pain in his gut was a fearsome thing, feeling like blades and fire cutting and burning him up on the inside. Holding his stomach,

Forbidden Origins-apostasia

he walked down the steps to the main floor. Leaning on the wall for support, he continued until he heard a couple more voices walking nearby. Finding cover behind some fake plants, Tim crouched down and waited for them to come around the corner. By now his entire body felt like it was being torn inside out and he had to bite down on his arm as he tried to keep calm and quiet.

"As you all know a serpente uova has been initiated. We are just waiting for Nero and Nikki to arrive," one of the Pitoni men stated to the rest of the group.

A different member spoke up and asked, "Has anyone gotten a hold of Vinnex? I've tried, but couldn't reach him. Also I've tried calling the crew he was with and no answers from them, either."

Another Pitoni chimed in with the answer, "That actually might be why we are having this meeting. Vinnex and his crew were taking care of some business dealing with that famous clone, Dr. Phillips. Maybe they botched the job."

"You mean Vinnex screwed up *another* assignment? No way!" All the men laughed.

Then another member spoke up. "Haven't you guys seen the news? I assumed we were here because of the girls that were found. It sounds like our latest shipment was discovered, and somehow got away." This last comment drew everyone up short and the laughter came to an abrupt halt.

"How can that be?! That location was so well hidden there is no way anyone could have found it," someone stammered out.

And then another member added, "If they are with the police, then how can we know they can't lead them back to the barn? What if this is able to be traced back to us??"

One of the men tried to regain order as the mutterings grew more and more anxious. "Hold on everyone, let's not lose our heads here. These girls were all drugged and blindfolded before being taken there, so there is nothing to worry about them remembering anything. But if it is true that they are gone now, what we need to address is our inability to fill orders. How are we going to get enough girls in an extremely shortened time frame to satisfy our customers?"

As everyone quieted to listen to this last member that spoke up, suddenly they heard shouts from outside the room.

"What was that?" one of the startled members asked, and then quickly after gun shots were heard followed by some more screaming.

Everyone scrambled to their feet and someone shouted, "We need to open the door and go get our guns!"

Forbidden Origins-apostasia

As a couple men went to the vault door, a light pound on the door came from the outside. The men stood frozen, not sure what to expect on the other side.

"Have we been found out? Is it the police?" someone asked the others. No one answered him, because of course they could not know who (or what) was on the other side.

(Pound Pound) Two more knocks, but more forceful this time. The two men by the door slowly stepped back. (POUND POUND) The knocks got heavier and heavier. The door shook and the frame seemed to weaken with each pound, then a blood curdling roar shrieked from the other side. At that point the pounding stopped, but then they heard scratching on the door; what sounded like fingernails scraping a blackboard.

The men flinched from the noise; whatever was on the other side of that door wasn't the police, or human for that matter. As all noise stopped, the men remained tense and on guard for several long minutes before they began to relax their stance or loosen their grip on any item they held.

After another minute or so one of the men asked, "Do you think it's safe to go out?" Cautiously the two men walked back up to the vault door and put their ears against it to listen for any sounds. Hearing nothing one of them stated, "I think that whatever was there is gone now."

The person who first spoke in the beginning responded, "Okay, but open it slowly and as quietly as you can. Make a single file line and we'll grab our guns that we checked at the door."

Turning the wheel for the vault door, the sound of screeching and grinding metal seemed deafening in the silent room. Shaking and sweating from his nerves, the man kept turning the wheel hearing every grind and screech until a loud (THUMP). It was the sound of the door unlocking.

"Okay, remember what I said, stay in a single file line." As the men finished lining up, the ones that were in the front had already made it out.

"Son of a –!" loud swears came from outside the vault.

"I told you to keep your voices down..."

"Well look what happened!" Two guards were lying on the floor and were torn apart so badly it wasn't even possible to identify who they were. Even more alarming to the men exiting the vault was the fact that all the guns that had been checked at the door were missing. Everyone's voices rose in pitch and nearing hysteria as they talked over one another trying to figure out a plan of what to do. "We need to get back in the vault where we have some type of protection..."

"No! We need to get up those stairs and out of here!"

"Well why don't we..."

While they were standing there in shock and panic, at a loss of what to do without their weapons, a rumbling, growling noise interrupted. By that time the fear had risen to an entirely new, primal level. Not a single man had dry palms or could quite

Forbidden Origins-apostasia

catch their breath, and the hairs on their arms stood straight up. Barely able to take their eyes off the carnage, but needing to see what was making such an inhuman sound, they looked up to see a dark silhouette appear at the top of the steps.

"What the...?" was the last coherent words anyone in that room said.

CHAPTER ELEVEN
Reflections

Waking up the next morning with a massive migraine, Tim realized he had lost control again. Removing his hand from his aching head he began to see the carnage as his eyes adjusted to the light. In that moment the piercing pain in his head became inconsequential compared to what he felt in his stomach. Feeling sick and nauseous from the sight and smell, he slowly picked himself up off the floor and took in the horrific scene around him.

Forbidden Origins-apostasia

The bodies strewn about were misshapen and dismembered; there would be no way to determine what parts went with which body. Being a scientist and having performed many dissections and experiments Tim had seen his fair share of the inside of bodies...but that knowledge did nothing to prepare him for the sights that his lost control had caused. Although he felt no regrets that so many of his enemies had been so brutally killed, for some reason seeing the evidence of the damage he had done did not sit well with his stomach. By this point there was no longer any denying the beast within, and that it was capable of just about anything.

Cautiously he moved around the carnage in the basement, and then moved on to the main and upper floors to make sure there were no stragglers. It appeared that the beast was thorough; he could find not even a shred of life.

After his check of the entire building he wasted no time grabbing several gallons of gasoline jugs out of his car. Time was of the essence as the dim light of the early morning still had plenty of shadows for him to move in, but they would soon be gone in the full light of day. So he drenched the bodies as well as the floor and walls as quickly as he could. Tim could have used more sophisticated substances that would have been more efficient but he wanted this to look like a rival mob or gang attack. Lighting his butane torch, he walked around the building setting everything on fire that looked flammable or that had been soaked in gas.

Once the fire seemed all consuming he rushed out of the building. As he hurried towards his car he could feel the intense heat emanating from the old building, but he didn't even glance back to watch it burn.

Driving home he couldn't stop looking at his hands and his face in the rearview mirror. He was checking to see if there was any sign of some type of monster, like Cody had described after the barn incident. Besides the scattered dark blotches on his skin getting bigger and darker, there was no sign of the beast. The longer he stared at himself in the mirror trying to detect a hint of something that would give it away (fangs, fur, scales...anything that would resemble a monster), the angrier he would get with himself. Not because he found something, but because all he saw staring back at him was the same face he has seen every day in the mirror since the day of his creation. For some reason Tim thought that if he could see some evidence of the beast on his face, it would be easier to deal with the weight of what he had done. He didn't want to associate the same face that Aavah had known and loved with the actions he was now capable of.

His bitterness knew no bounds as he realized that it didn't matter what she would think about his evil deeds. She would never see his face again regardless. Growing angrier and more disgusted with his reflection, he tore off the mirror and threw it out his window.

Forbidden Origins-apostasia

"Wow, I'm impressed. How long have you been up and cleaning?"

Cody had a broom and dust pan in hand and was just sweeping up a small pile of dirt and dust when the reverend had walked into the room.

"I wasn't able to sleep, so I thought I would clean up the shop."

Shem shook his head in regret. "I'm sorry to hear that Silas. I know that this is an old building and has a lot of moans and groans throughout the night. But I was hoping the room I gave you would be comfortable enough to -"

Cody quickly him off with, "No, no, it wasn't that. It's actually one of the best rooms I've spent the night in for years. It wasn't the noises of the building or my comfort that had anything to do with what was keeping me awake. I want you to know how much I appreciate you offering me a place to stay here...especially after what I told you about myself the other day."

Cody was being sincere, but he wondered if the reverend would be so nice and accommodating if he actually knew the whole story. When he opened up to him the day before, he only told him the bare minimum of details about himself. A little about his childhood, his rebellious youth, and how all of that led

155

to his eventual gambling problem. He didn't go too far in depth about the Pitoni, but just shared the fact that he got mixed in with the wrong type of people and how it caused him to do things he wasn't proud of.

He ended the story by stating that an unexpected savior came into his life and pulled him away from his dark deeds, but he still felt like he had dirtied his hands too much and would never be able to get away from what he had done. Shem did not press for more, but instead told him that there was no reason to keep holding onto the past and let it haunt him. Especially now that he had walked away from the bad influences of his life and made the choice to change. That may not right every wrong, but it is like starting over, with a clean slate. Cody wasn't exactly buying it, but is still was comforting to hear to some extent.

The good reverend would hear none of Cody's continued thanks. "It's my calling to help those in need; and besides, I love having the company. So I should be the one thanking you for humoring an old man and taking me up on my offer. So now tell me, what's been on your mind so bad that it would keep you up and resort to cleaning?"

Not sure exactly how to start, Cody began with hesitation. "Well, I have this friend. Well maybe not even a friend, but this person I wronged...probably the most out of anyone else I've come into contact with. And well, despite all that had happened he helped me escape from something awful. So I can't stop thinking how I wish I could help him in return."

Forbidden Origins-apostasia

The reverend looked thoughtful. "Hmmm...is this the 'savior' that you mentioned to me before that got you away from all the bad people you were hanging around with?"

"Uhh, yeah. I believe he may be in some kind of trouble, and I feel like I should be doing something..." Cody trailed off as the feeling of helplessness washed over him at the thought of what Tim may be doing at that moment. He had no idea how to find him or get in contact with him again, but he hated to think about him going up against the entire Pitoni by himself. He seemed to be so sickly and out of it when he saw him last, so Cody believed it wouldn't be long before the Pitoni captured him and tortured him. It just didn't seem right after what they had done to the poor guy's family. And if anyone knew how heartless and evil the Pitoni was, it was Cody.

After finding those poor girls locked away underneath that barn he was even more convinced of this, and it sickened him that he ever had any association with them at all. Shem waited patiently for Cody to finish while he was lost in thought.

In a moment of quick decision, somewhat out of desperation and partly because the pastor was such a good listener, Cody blurted out, "I know you are going to think this sounds crazy, and I hope that it doesn't make you want to throw me out on the street, but I was reading one of your comics last night before bed, and I read about your heroes fighting against the... Refferm?" Cody tried pronouncing.

157

Shem shook his head and corrected him. "You say it like Reph-eye-eem; the Rephaim. Now Silas, I will not think you are crazy and definitely will not send you away for this, but...are you trying to tell me that my comics scared you? That they are the reason why you had a hard time sleeping last night?"

Cody rolled his eyes at this in frustration and replied with, "No, of course not!" But not wanting to offend the reverend, he added, "Don't get me wrong, they are intense and even a little bit disturbing at times, but that is not what I am trying to tell you." Then Cody lifted up the magazine from his back pocket, and began to unroll it to the place where it showed one of the Rephaim characters blown up on the page, and showed it to the reverend.

"You see this guy right here? This is why I am worried about my friend."

Shem lifted up his glasses that were hanging around his neck, and studied the picture that he had drawn many years before. Trying to understand but quite at a loss at this point to figure out what in the world this young man was implying, he finally just admitted that.

"Silas, I'm not sure I understand what this comic book character has to do with your friend?"

Cody stated simply, "This is what my friend turned into a couple days ago."

Not expecting that as the answer, Shem sucked in air too fast and began coughing. Cody patted him hard on the back,

Forbidden Origins-apostasia

trying to help him to breathe normally again. Once he finally did catch his breath, he looked back at the comic in Cody's hand, and then back at Cody. All he managed to say was, "Ohh...I see."

Tim arrived home mid-morning. Although he felt completely drained of energy he couldn't help but go straight to the living room and turn on the TV to catch the local news broadcast. Sure enough, they were already reporting on the bank that he had turned into an inferno.

The reporter was stating that the police confirmed that the bodies found inside were thought to be notorious gang members, and the arson to be retaliation from a rival gang. The reporter went on to say that the police were not willing to speculate on the names of who may have been in there because the bodies were so badly burned that identification would be difficult.

Not being able to listen to any more of the story, Tim switched off the TV. All he wanted to know is if they took the bait, and it sounds like they did; hook, line and sinker.

Taking a minute to lounge back on his couch, he used the rare restful moment to muse over recent events, and on everything that has been happening to him physically. Placing his hand on his chest, he probed the protective armor that fused to his body. Finally, he accepted the fact that there was no more denying that all his physical and mental problems were stemming from the product. The armor was his new permanent skin, and along with it came the beast from within. He knew that time was running out, and that sooner rather than later his body and mind were turning into something evil. He could feel everything that was changing inside him, even if he was having trouble finding evidence of it on the outside.

But instead of feeling scared of what was happening to him, all he felt was desperation to finish the last of his plans before he was totally taken over. He had enough of his humanity left to not want to become a danger to society. The thought of hurting innocent women and children made him think of his Aavah, and their unborn child, and the pain he felt in his chest made it hard for him to breathe. It was becoming clear to him that Federal Duplications and Paul would not just be his last targets, but his last two missions on this earth. He would have to make sure that no one else got a hold of the armor technology, and as his own body was part of that, he knew that this was going to have to be a suicide mission as well.

The question that remained in his head was, 'How do I make sure that I eradicate all traces of the armor and the research?' Even though he would take out Federal Duplications headquarters, that didn't mean the process and production wouldn't start over somewhere else. Plus, he couldn't be sure how many people were involved in the project. So maybe the

Forbidden Origins-apostasia

answer was in leaking to the public what Federal Duplications was up to, and the horrors of the side effects of the armor. But what was the best way to warn them? Then suddenly the idea came to him like lightning: Nero and Nikki! He could perform a couple of tests. If they had a similar reaction to the armor like he had, he would have enough evidence to make it public. And if they didn't have a reaction, well then maybe he would not have to worry about whether or not he would be able to completely destroy the armor project. And the other good news would be that he would have longer to make Nero and Nikki suffer.

So the time had come for Tim to put his final mission in motion. Eagerly heading to his basement to start the experiments, Tim began by sterilizing all the lab tools. As impatient as he was to begin the testing on his two unwilling subjects, first things first, which was to extract some of his own armor skin.

It was not long for Tim to figure out that this was easier said than done. One of the characteristics about the armor that Tim quickly discovered was that when flexed or tightened, it was quite difficult for the skin to be cut or penetrated. And in the event that it was punctured somehow, the healing properties were amazing. This was going to make his job that much harder, as he was going to need to cut pretty deep for the experiment.

Taking some deep breaths to relax his body, he lined up the sharpened scissors to a piece of his stomach tissue, looked away and then – snip. His theory was that maybe the armor had

D.K. Ratcliffe

not become fully attached with his genetic code. This would mean his DNA would not have had the opportunity to be introduced to the outer layer of skin. The deeper layer of the armor would be the control test, to see if there was a difference between the inner and outer layers of skin/armor.

After some thorough analysis and testing it turned out that Tim's predictions were right. The inner layer of his armor was quite a bit more developed then the outer. In fact, it seemed like it was designed to grow from the inside. Building and copying more cells, then shed the outer layers that protected the armor during the development process.

Tim spent the rest of his day discovering new data and developing his tests; before he knew it, over twelve hours had passed. Deciding it was nearing time to finish up for the night, Tim removed a rug from his lab floor. Next he opened up the hidden cellar door that led into his homemade pit so he could check on his captives. Once he did this he met with the strong stench of foul body odor and excrement. Not wanting to have to work his experiments the next day in such an unpleasant environment, Tim decided it was definitely time for them to have a bath. Hooking up a hose to his laboratory sink, he thoroughly rinsed the prisoners off with cold water. Then he mixed up some water and dish soap in a five-gallon bucket and dumped it on the two men. Finally, he hosed them off again, making sure he washed all the little nasties down a drain he made in the pit. A lot less offensive than it was before, he felt the pit was now clean

162

Forbidden Origins-apostasia

enough for him to jump down in with them to get a closer look at their condition.

Since their capture Nero and Nikki had not had anything to eat or drink, so they were beginning to look rather gaunt and weak. Despite this, they both managed to lift their heads up a little bit to stare glossily at Tim as he came down. But even if they did not have their gags over their mouths, it was unlikely they would have the strength to say much. Not wanting them to croak in the middle of the night and also wanting to make sure they were strong enough for the next day's experimenting, Tim he decided it was time to hook them up with an IV.

"Well fellas, I figured you would appreciate a good shower and an update on your predicament. The shower you've already had, so here is for your good news: The Pitoni are now history, which is win-win for everybody. So continue to cooperate and you just might make it out of here alive. I will be back bright and early tomorrow as I have some tests I'm going to need you around for. And pending those...well, let's just wait and see what happens." Tim was talking as he inserted the IV needles into them.

"I'm sure the two of you are also very hungry, so I'm going to inject you with something special. Any requests? Double bacon cheeseburger? Filet mignon, perhaps?" Tim laughed mean-spiritedly as he finished hooking them up. "Seriously though, fellas, I am interested to see how you react to my virus."

The men's eyes seemed to bulge out of their heads at hearing this, and attempted to shake their heads in denial with what little energy they had left. "Oh, don't worry, I'm not talking about the typical sort of virus you are thinking of, like Ebola or HIV. Think of this as more like a computer virus...like the Trojan Horse; it is a piece of code that is capable of replicating itself."

Looking none too comforted by Tim's explanation, Nero and Nikki glanced at each other and then back to Tim. Before leaving them alone once again in their dank prison, he finally injected both Nero and Nikki's IV with his "virus" to carry out what the armor would have done on its own.

Drained from the day's events, he headed up to the second floor of his house to clean up and get ready for bed. Taking off his damp and soiled clothes he hopped into the shower and stood in the stream for what seemed like an hour. Once he finally felt clean, he turned off the spray and stepped out. Drying off and wiping the steam off the mirror, he was confronted by his reflection again.

As he gazed at himself, he still saw no signs of a monster. Out of anger he clenched his fist and punched the mirror. After one strike he saw his new reflection fractured. Pleased with the result, he cleaned up the blood from his hand and went to bed, exciting thoughts of the next day's experiments racing through his mind.

CHAPTER TWELVE
Hard Time

"One, two, *tree*, open says me!" Turning the safe handle with a slight 'thunk' noise, he then said in enthusiasm, "Look at what we have here, my little apple dumpling. It's all for us!"

The woman stared into the safe with a hungry gleam in her eyes and cried out "Ohh baby, we're rich!"

"Yes sugar plum; now grab that bag right there and hold it out to me while I fill 'er up."

"Okay my darling, but are you sure it's safe now? Can we really take it all this time?"

"Diligence is the mother of good fortune, no? The Strigoi doctor - or that crazy clone as you like to call him - captured Nero and Nikki and burnt down the building full of the Pitoni. I knew as soon as I met him that the vengeful Strigoi was the answer to all our problems. Using him to take care of our obstacles for being together once and for all was like taking candy from a baby. So don't be scared...our problems are finally over, my sweet, sweet Lily."

The two embraced and kissed passionately, and once Lily finally caught her breath she whispered "Oh Vinnie binnie, I love you."

Sergeant Tibbs was at his desk reviewing some final paperwork for a recently closed case when the Lieutenant walked up.

"Tibbs, you and a couple officers need to take a drive over to Nero Lombardi's place. We need to try to get to the bottom of all the retaliation activities that have been happening lately. All paths seem to lead back to the Pitoni."

"Of course, Lieutenant, but why Nero Lombardi? As much suspicion and as many leads that we have had on the creep we've never been able to connect him with the Pitoni. Inevitably all the leads turn cold and we do nothing but hit dead ends."

Forbidden Origins-apostasia

"Well, we may have finally gotten a break in that regard. When we questioned those girls that were from the abandoned bus one of them that spoke English said she remembered hearing the name Nero."

At hearing this Tibbs sat up straighter in his chair in peaked interest. "You don't say? Huh. I suppose all the girls have looked at mugshots by now...?"

"Yes, but none of them can recall seeing much of anything. Blood tests showed that they were drugged heavily and they were likely blindfolded for much of their captivity. So that is why I want you and Charlie to go and have a chat with Nero, to see what you can dig up. Obviously don't say anything to tip him off about the girls, the last thing we want is to worry about the Pitoni trying to locate them. Even though they are in protective custody there is no saying what the gang would be willing to do to get their hands on them again."

As they neared Nero's house, Tibbs said to his partner "Now remember Charlie, we are just here to question him, we don't actually have anything concrete to be able to bring him in with yet. But he is a pretty tough character and is unpredictable, so be sure to keep on your toes."

167

"Got it, Sarge." As eager as they both were to get this notorious criminal off their streets, the last thing Tibbs needed was for Lombardi to bring in another high priced lawyer to claim that they were abusing their authority and get out of more potential charges on a technicality.

As they walked up to Nero's house, right away Charlie spotted something wrong. Before knocking on the door the young officer whispered, "Sarge, look," while pointing to what he could see through the window.
Some blood splatter on the wall and what looked like a hand peeking out from the bottom of a closed door.

Tibbs whispered back, "Okay, I'm going to radio it in and request back-up. You go around to the back entrance and then wait 60 seconds; I will go in through the front."

A loud crash echoed through the house followed by the sound of footsteps coming towards them.

"Vinnie you told me it would be safe!" Lily yelled.

"Shhh!! It would be in our best interest to keep quiet and escape, sugar puss," Vinnex said, grabbing at her hand to try and pull her towards him while attempting to calm her all at once. But her hysteria knew no bounds as she continued while slapping his hands away from her.

"I just knew that you would lead us into more trouble and screw this up, just like you screw everything else up! Now Nero is going to kill us both for taking his money! I HATE YOU, I HATE YOU, I HATE YOU!!"

As the officers in the house would have to be deaf to not hear the arguing, they followed the sounds to the office that the couple were hiding in. Officer Charlie was the first one to the get to the door and hollered out.

"ON THE FLOOR NOW!" The pair froze and were quiet for half a second, and then Lily blurted out

"It's all his fault officer! I had no part in this."

Vinnex stared in disbelief at his love who had just betrayed him at the drop of a hat, and then just shook his head as he raised his arms up and placed them behind his head and lowered himself to the floor.

"Well, it was awfully nice of you gentlemen to have dropped by. This crazy woman doesn't know what she is talking about; we are just here to housesit for a friend that is out of town."

By this time Sergeant Tibbs had entered the room and was looking into the bag full of money that was at Vinnex's feet. "Housesitting you say? Well, I suppose you were just going to 'watch' this money for him too, then? And I suppose that the dead body I found in the closet is just there for decoration, huh?"

At that Vinnex kept his mouth shut, and Lily started crying. After cuffing and reading them their rights, the officers took the two suspects outside. Just as they were walking up to their cruiser, a few more squad cars pulled up.

D.K. Ratcliffe

Meanwhile, Lily continued to cry and proclaim her complete innocence, while dramatizing everything and making a scene in general.

Charlie looked at Tibbs and said, "Does the female have to ride with us?"

Tibbs shook his head and stated, "Nah, I think we should keep them separated. Have Wilkins and Jones take her." Charlie exhaled in clear relief and then walked her over to the other officers' vehicle as Tibbs put Vinnex in the back of their car.

"I don't suppose you want to save us a lot of time and just tell us what you were doing here exactly, and where Nero is? He's the bigger fish to fry anyways, so if you can give us information on that then I'm sure the DA will come up with a great deal for you and your little girlfriend."

Vinnex mumbled something that sounded like 'You will have to talk to the Stree-goy for that.'

Tibbs narrowed his eyes and said, "What was that?"

Vinnex just looked back at him for almost a full minute, and then said, "What I said was, I want to speak to a lawyer."

During their trip back to the police station, Tibbs continued to try and get Vinnex to say more about what he was doing at Nero's house, and about the dead body. Refusing to speak in English anymore, the only responses he got from him were in Romanian. He also kept saying the 'Stree-goy' word, but of course neither Tibbs nor Charlie knew what it meant.

170

Forbidden Origins-apostasia

Once the caravan returned to the police station, Tibbs went straight to the Lieutenant to explain what went down at the Lombardi place.

"There was no sign of Nero, but instead we picked up a prostitute and a Romanian. It could be that they really have no connection to Nero and were just there to rob the place, but they seemed to know how to get into the safe and did not have anything else in their loot bag but the money. Plus, we have the dead body, and it looks like he was killed without much of a struggle, which could indicate that he knows them. I'm inclined to believe that he's associated with the Pitoni, and just hasn't had any arrests until now. While cuffing him we did find a snake tattoo on his forearm."

The Lieutenant took all of this in and sat deep in thought without speaking for a few moments. "Well, if that is true Sergeant, then this could be the break we have been looking for. Perhaps we can finally have something concrete on this blasted gang to be able to take them down once and for all."

Tibbs looked hopeful, and replied with, "That would be ideal, sure, but he isn't talking, at least not in English. I have started the search for a lawyer that speaks Romanian, but that could take some time. In the meantime, we do have the woman that we can question."

"The prostitute? What makes you think she knows anything?"

Tibbs answered, "She pretty much hasn't stopped talking since we arrested them, but so far she hasn't said anything helpful yet. Except that it seems clear that she and the Romanian are pretty close and have known each other for a while."

"Good. Get her in one of the interrogation rooms as soon as possible, and try to get something we can use."

Tibbs agreed to this and then said, "In the meantime, Lieutenant, I think it would be prudent of us to call Dr. Phillips and have him come in."

"The famous clone scientist?" he asked. "What for?"

"When he was in the hospital Charlie and I had him look at some mug shots of prominent Pitoni members, including Nero and Nikki."

"Yes, yes, I remember. But nothing came out of it, he didn't recognize any of them."

"Right, but suppose if this Romanian character is part of the Pitoni, then it is possible that he was involved in the kidnapping, right?"

"Good thinking, Tibbs! Make the call and have him get in here ASAP."

Forbidden Origins-apostasia

For several days Tim had been examining Nero and Nikki for any sign of changes. When nothing seemed to be happening he even went so far as to try torture, mostly mental. But to his surprise and confusion there was still no change. Not even a new dark blotch. The exception being that they appeared to heal very quickly and their skin seemed tougher. This was mildly impressive to Tim as they didn't have the full body armor to start out with. But he was still surprised these were the only deviations within them that he could find.

Puzzled by the lack of results, he leaned back in his chair with his hands behind his head. This should be a good sign, that this armor may not be what was causing all of his own changes.

'But then what is making me change?' he pondered. In frustration he looked around his basement laboratory as if somewhere written on the walls was the answer. Only one thing popped into his mind. It was him.... *he* was the monster. He began this project thinking he was doing the noble thing to help mankind escape from a potential disaster, and stopping Federal Duplications from moving forward with selling the body armor. But instead it seemed that it was turning into a journey of self-discovery. Could it be that the trauma of losing his beloved and unborn child had unleashed a monster within him that had been there all along?

He decided it was time to do some more tests, but in this go around he was planning to use all his DNA instead of separating his from the armor cells. In effect he would be creating a new 'Trojan virus' with more of his DNA, which hopefully will have more of a detrimental effect on the captives and corrupt their entire systems. The end result will determine once and for all if the beast was a side effect of the armor...or that he was the beast all along.

Walking out of his lab, he began to talk to his captives from above the pit in an almost frantic manner.

"Well apparently my first test failed. Which is technikcalie good for the human race, but might be bad for you. Because I have a problem, and I need it answered." With an ungraceful lumbering crash, Tim unexpectedly fell on his rear into the pit. But he looked no worse for wear as he staggered to his feet and stood in front of the two men.

"Neruh, I believe you once called me a muhnster? I think it was only meant to be a prejudiced remark from a biguht, but as it turns out, you might be right. But if I'm a muhnster then that means potentially all clowns could be. I don't know if you can tell, but I started drinking a little while ago when I was in the other room. And I don't drink...ever. I had bought the bottle for my wife in celuhbration of an important leguslaytion getting passed for my kind, but little did I know that she was pregnant at the time. So there it sat in our kitchen, gathering dust. And now that she's dead, and soon enough we all will be, I

figured, what the hail? But honestshlee, I wasn't all that worried about it going to waste. Do you want to know the real reason I was drinking? Cat got your tongue? Haha," (BURP).

Since at the end of this monologue Tim was speaking just inches from Nero's face, he flinched and strained against his bonds. He looked like he was trying to say something, just not the answer Tim was asking for. Either way he couldn't because of his gag.

"Let me tell you. Do you know what my wife's last warrds were? It was her cereal number! Yeah, all clowns have 'em. So if you think that all clowns are muhnsters, then are you trying to tell me my wife is a muhnster too?!" Tim slapped Nero's face.

"You should learn some manners!" Tim raged. Taking a couple of deep breaths to steady himself, he injected Nero with the new virus, then proceeded to Nikki.

"Well, so long boys! Let's hope we get some real answers this time around." Tim's mood seemed to change directions like the winds; going from manic then depressed, to furious and then back to manic. He left them as quickly as he came, and then covered the pit back up.

Walking up the stairs and to his couch, Tim couldn't hold back the tears any longer and cried himself to sleep.

(RING) (RING) (RING) Rubbing his eyes, Tim blearily looked around as he tried to identify where the offensive sound was coming from.

(RING) (RING) (RING) Seeing a little light glowing on the coffee table, he finally realized it was his phone going off. He grudgingly picked it up and answered, "Hello?"

"Is this Dr. Timothy Philips?"

"Yes."

"I'm sorry to disturb you Dr., but this is the Sheriff's department. If at all possible we would like for you to come in as soon as you can. We currently have in our custody someone we believe is a member of the Pitoni. In the event you are wondering, we did get permission from Federal Duplications to call you. We were told that your help in this matter would be at our disposal. I'm required to tell you this by law because of the Clone Safety Act (CSA)."

'Oh great, this is the last kind of hassle I need right now while I'm hungover and so close to finishing my research,' Tim thought to himself.

But to the officer he just replied with, "Okay, I'll be there shortly." After hanging up, he looked at his watch and realized that he had passed out for a couple hours. With no small amount of dread Tim tucked in his shirt and fixed his hair as he starting heading out the door and to the police station.

176

CHAPTER THIRTEEN
The Demon Within

"Sorry for the wait Dr. Lately it seems as though this town is falling apart, which is actually why we called you to come in. We have someone in custody that we believe is a member of the Pitoni. Once we suspected his affiliation with the gang, we wanted to see if you could identify him out of a group of mugshots in the event he might have been one of the kidnappers involved in you and your wife's abduction."

After hearing what Officer Tibbs had to say, Tim thought to himself, 'It has to be Vinnex, he is the only member I left alive besides Nero and Nikki. Both of whom are safely locked away in my cellar.'

But out loud he said, "Wow, you really think so, Officer? Well of course I would be more than happy to do my part. There is nothing that would help me sleep better at night than to have one of the culprits finally brought to justice."

"I figured you would feel that way Dr., so again, thank you for your time. Before I get the pictures out, I want to let you know that once we were finally able to get this suspect's cooperation, your name came up. A lot of what he is saying is mumbo jumbo mind you, but there are two things that are definitely coherent. One is your name, and he also keeps referring to you as Strigoi. Would you know anything about that?" he asked.

Tim squirmed at hearing that Vinnex had been blabbing about him. But considering how loquacious the guy was he also was not entirely surprised. Somehow he managed to keep his cool in front of the officer. Giving some thought about the best way to answer, he figured he might as well tell the officer some version of the truth.

"Yes, that's what they called me when I was kidnapped. It's a Romanian word for a troubled soul from the grave, a being that transforms into an animal, sort of a cross between a vampire and a demon. It wasn't until later that I found out what it meant. I'm assuming it is because I'm a clone; they were all quite opinionated about how clones are inferior and unnatural if I recall." Tim attempted to sound hurt and indignant.

Forbidden Origins-apostasia

"I'm so sorry for what you endured Dr., but your testimony is going to be critical in helping us to build a case. Hopefully not just against the suspect we have in custody, but also against whatever Pitoni members were involved with your abduction and your wife's murder.

So here are some mug shots, and I would like to know if you can identify any of these men." The officer opened a large manila envelope and pulled out a dozen pictures of mug shots and laid them in front of Tim.

"Please let me know as soon as you think you remember a face."

Tim started viewing the shuffled pictures, again thinking that Vinnex was the only person that had ever called him Strigoi. But for appearances sake he took his time studying each photo, as if trying to remember. Even then, it did not take long before he came across that proud Romanian face with the prominent bone structure.

"This one! This guy is definitely the kidnapper that got away. I think I can remember now what they called him...Victor? Wait, that's not quite right...Vinnie?"

"Very close sir, but it is Vinnex. This is the man that we have in our custody. Another officer and I were going to Nero Lombardi's house, because of all the racket that's been going on." The officer threw more pictures on the table.

"Obviously these are of the crime scene from your kidnapping...the guys you killed in self-defense, tattoos associated with the Pitoni. Then a few weeks later, a barn burns down with bodies inside. As it turns out, they were all identified to be Pitoni members. Around that time, a bus arrives in a small town not far from here. It was full of young girls that we believe were to be sold off, and guess what? One of them mentions they heard the word Nero.

And finally, shortly after that an old bank that happens to be associated with Nero catches on fire, and lo and behold, dead Pitoni inside. Naturally we felt it prudent at this point to ask Nero some questions. So today my partner and I rode over to his place, and guess what we found?" Tibbs didn't pause long enough for Tim to respond, but he still shrugged his shoulders as if to say he had no idea what they found.

"We found *another* dead Pitoni member in Nero's house, and with no sign of a struggle. Then after searching the house we find Vinnex, who you have just identified. You know what is weird, though? He's been saying that all of these happenings are actually you, and not a rival gang that is responsible. As unlikely as it is that one person could be responsible for that much murder and mayhem, even you have to admit that you have strong motive for revenge."

Tim was feeling more and more uncomfortable. He knew this was just simple questioning, but the accusations were making him feel sickly. He couldn't afford to lose control anymore. Staying calm, he replied with "I wish I could have gotten revenge. There's not a day that goes by without missing

Forbidden Origins-apostasia

my wife. Of course I want them all to pay! But wanting that and actually performing the atrocious acts that you are talking about are two very different things, Officer. Like you said, how in the world could one person accomplish all those things on their own? If I were you, I wouldn't take a lousy criminal's word for it. He was more or less responsible for the death of my wife and unborn child, and because of that my life has been completely turned upside down. And now he wants to blame the death of his gang on me!

All I know is that the day I was kidnapped, he was talking to another member about a new beginning; a takeover of some kind. Not any specifics of who or what, nor did I care at the time. I just wanted to escape with my wife! You said it yourself, you went to this Nero's home, someone was found dead, and Vinnex was there. I'll bet he's the one to blame for all this mess."

"I know Dr., and of course we feel that is the most likely scenario, but it is our job to ask questions and follow every lead possible. Please understand that I don't believe you did it, and hate to have to put you through this kind of stress after everything that has happened to you." Tibbs said this with sincerity, but then leaned forward in his chair and stated, "However, I think at this time it would be best if you do not leave town without checking with us first. We may need to call you back in for additional questioning, and I would be prepared with some alibis for the dates of the burning barn and bank murders."

181

The next morning, Tim went down to the basement and gave Nero and Nikki their morning "shower", then raised them out of the pit to thoroughly examine them. It didn't take long to notice the dark blotches on their skin near the injection area. He took fresh blood samples as he wanted to compare them with other samples he had taken before. After so much waiting and nothing happening until now, what he found was shocking; the cells were mutating.

The DNA strands from Tim and his armor were finally cohabiting with Nero and Nikki's DNA. Tim's DNA was making deletions from Nero and Nikki's DNA. And not only manufacturing replacements from his own and the armor, but also creating duplications of them. The proteins from Tim seem to be designed to take over, yet leaving important chromosomes for them to still function and live. This new breakthrough could be a clue on how he was becoming different himself.

At the rapid pace they went from just healing quickly to having major DNA changes, Tim guessed that the progression of the virus would be exceedingly aggressive. And once it overtook their DNA completely, they would become something different. He was confident they would still have the ability to function like a human, but essentially that person would be dead. There would be little to nothing of the original human being left in the

Forbidden Origins-apostasia

body. But instead someone or something new would take over, sort of like a new birth. The closest thing that Tim's mind could compare it to would be like a swift acting cancer. It would kill them while at the same time a new form of physicality would inhabit their bodies. He was not sure how it would affect the consciousness or mental state, but it seemed that stress or adrenaline sped up the process. Or at least contributed in some way, which was consistent with what Tim had been experiencing.

The DNA from the armor was made to react in severe conditions, which could explain why the changes sped up under certain conditions; Nero and Nikki were definitely under a lot of stress. Tim had been looking forward to the real torture of the two men, but had been trying to wait for a day like today. He had to be certain that there were enough DNA changes for conditions to be prime for collecting more data. So as he stepped away from his microscope he could barely contain himself as he hurried back to the pit to finally get to the really fun part of his scientific research.

Tim finished his last torture technique he had in mind to try and realized there was no hope for his captives to turn into some kind of monster like he had. He would have thought that as fast as his virus was taking them over, the added stress of torture would have pushed them over the edge. But it seemed it was too early to tell. His examination of the DNA and the results suggest that something would happen eventually, but he did not have the time or the patience right now...he had bigger fish to fry.

Feeling drained all of a sudden, Tim placed Nikki and Nero's gags back on. Figuring that they weren't in any shape to try and escape, he decided not to place them back down into the pit for the time being. All he wanted to do was go back upstairs and take a nap.

As he started to walk away and go towards the stairs the lights in the basement started to flicker. Almost instantaneously a sharp stabbing pain materialized in his head, causing him to stumble. He was able to keep his balance enough to not fall down by using one hand to grab onto the handrail for the steps, while placing his other on his forehead trying to fight the pain. Just as it seemed like it would become unbearable, it stopped. The pain and the light flickering had both stopped at the same time. A slight movement behind him caught his attention, but before he could turn his head to see what it was, he heard his name being rasped out in a strange, deep gargling voice.

He spun around and saw that his two captives were just as he left them, except that Nero's gag was off and on the floor. In shock Tim slowly edged closer to Nero, thinking to himself, 'Was this it? Did he turn Nero into the beast after all?' But nothing on Nero had changed besides the blotches on his skin, which had become a little more prominent. All of a sudden he spoke again, and the voice said his name again.

"*Tiiiiiimmm.... Don't be afraid, just let go. Let him take control.*"

When he spoke Nero's lips moved, but the voice definitely did not seem to be Nero's, and his eyes looked completely soulless and black.

Tim, at a loss for words, could only ask, "Who are you?"

A slight chuckle came from Nero. "*I am knowing. I know what you've done to the Pitoni, you destroyed them all without any mercy. Then you treated these men as your own personal lab-rats, and tore them up so ruthlessly. Just let him in and never feel weak. You can be all powerful.*"

Tim had so much nervous sweat pouring down his body it felt as if there was a heat lamp on him. Tim did not ask the creature who he was referring to because he already knew.

"What do you want from me?"

"*Freedom...*" the voice said while fading out.

Meanwhile the lights flickered again, and this time Tim did fall to the floor from the pain in his head that followed. After a moment the pain and the flickering stopped once again. Everything seemed to be back to normal, as even Nero's gag was back on his mouth. In fact, it was as if time had stood still while the conversation took place.

CHAPTER FOURTEEN
Final Preparations

Over the next couple days Tim went over his plans with the utmost care, giving less and less time to Nero and Nikki. Ever since the strange incident in the basement, Tim felt apprehensive about spending much time down there. Instead he focused almost all his efforts on how to take out Paul and Federal Duplications. He and Paul worked at the Federal Duplications headquarters, which was a building of super advanced technology. While cloning is the generalized focus of the company, they are also heavily involved in different types of technologies to advance and evolve the cloning process.

Forbidden Origins-apostasia

Once upon a time the company was known as Genetic Duplications, when it was part of just the private sector. But since then it became controlled and run primarily by the federal government, at which point funding became a non-issue. Tax payer dollars are a huge part of the budget, but besides that there are many sizable donations made from sympathetic citizens. Anyone with deep enough pockets that want to further the cause. Having the social platform of helping childless parents obtain clone babies and with soldiers returning from war to get limb replacements looks very good for any organization or philanthropist.

And since that important piece of legislation that Tim had a hand in getting passed was approved, hospitals and health insurance companies had been paying hand over fist. They all wanted to have cloning stations made available in every major region in the world, so that clones and regular humans alike could benefit from their uses.

And then of course there was the military, which was paying exorbitant costs to fund the armor research. So needless to say, Federal Duplication's funding, influence, and power knew no bounds. Tim had to be very thorough in his attempt to find a weakness to exploit.

Luckily Tim's high level security clearance allowed him to access documents for finances, future plans, and even some simple blue prints to the building. He was careful about his snooping, wanting to make sure that his poking around did not raise any red flags. Tim was more than competent with computers, so that shouldn't be a problem. His programming ensured that he had all the necessary skills to be a top notch researcher as a geneticist, so this type of work was right up his alley.

It did not take long for him to realize that there was not enough information available to him at his clearance level, though. He wanted to know every little detail possible to take out Federal Duplications, but he kept coming up against firewalls. Then Tim remembered that Paul had some of the highest clearance in the building. It wasn't until the day that Paul had taken him to see the armor that Tim had realized just how high his security clearance was. But now he was glad to know this information as Paul would often keep important work documents on his home computer, and he was fairly certain he should be able to hack into it. Well, much easier than he could get into Federal Duplications files.

And if he was then able to decipher cryptic codes on the buildings security measures and other such valuable information, it would go a long way to helping Tim to carry out his vengeful plot. If he could find any weak points, it would help him decide the best way to take out Federal Duplications. Whether that be through bombing, gassing, or perhaps even hiring a terrorist group, Tim was open to almost any possibility. He recognized with no small amount of regret that all these plans would involve the loss of innocent lives. But ultimately the

Forbidden Origins-apostasia

big picture was of more importance to him; yes, the greater good will cause some collateral damage, but this sacrifice of hundreds of civilians was so that many more could live.

After remoting in to Paul's computer and digging around and decoding secret files, Tim discovered something he was not expecting. Tucked away in the list of files he saw something labeled MUD PIT. The file was password protected, so immediately Tim knew he was on to something. Trying a couple of password guesses to start with, Tim started to worry that he may not be able to get in. Generally, only 3 attempts were allowed and then after that a security feature on the computer will lock the user out.

After some intense thought, finally Tim decided to try "PrincessDi11"; Princess was the sarcastic nickname of Paul's beloved cat, Diana, and 11 was Paul's lucky number. She was such a spoiled thing that Tim and Aavah had often joked that Paul treated her like she was royalty, so the inside joke between the three of them was that she was his little 'princess Di'. Tim had already tried Diana11 as one of his attempts, but he should have known that Paul would not be so naïve as to use such a simple password to guess, as many amateurs use their pet's names. But only Aavah and Tim knew the nickname, so it would make sense that Paul would feel safe using this as a password.

Sure enough, Tim's guess was right; he was in! There was only one document in the file, which needed decoding.

189

After hours more of deciphering the code, what Tim found was quite surprising. It appeared to be about missile technology. This seemed strange, seeing how Paul was more involved with cloning rather than military grade missiles. The only connection he could make was the neural-computer. Paul was the lead scientist that designed the clones programming. And from what Tim understood about advanced missile technology – which was limited – was that the programming used by neural-computers could be similar technology that could potentially program smart missiles. Weapons that could think or have a type of consciousness seemed revolting enough for Paul to experiment with.

Suddenly a light bulb went off in Tim's brain and he had flashbacks from when Paul was giving him information on the armor he is now wearing.
While riding in Paul's car on their way to the company building, Paul had asked Tim about the new job they had for him at work.

"Your assignment for this project is going to require you to start working in the lab more. Not on the road promoting clones and all the nonsense that went along with that. That stuff isn't everything you were made for."

After arriving to the compound, Paul led Tim into the basement research and laboratory.

"Do you know what section we are in right now?"

"This is the section that requires the highest security clearance, so I have never been here before. I knew that you

were working on something big, but I didn't realize that it was this big. Even if you have the authority to come in this section, how is it that I am allowed in here?"

"I've been working on a couple new projects, and one of them is for some of our elite military special forces. Right now it is still considered a top secret project, but I've convinced the company to allow you some access. Let me show you why...Tim, imagine a military that didn't have to die. Whether the soldiers are clones or standard individuals, death doesn't have to be an expected result of war; at least not for the U.S."

Tim remembered being brought over to a glass chamber, where he looked at the armor that he is now wearing.

"Why are you showing me this now? I would have seen it when it's issued to the military."

"Eventually the armor will be able to save the lives of millions of civilians. But in order to do that, it has to be concealed. The technology cannot get into the hands of the enemy."

And then before they left the room, Paul warned strenuously that he couldn't even share the details with Aavah.

"Remember Tim, everything in this room is top secret."

This was all starting to make sense for Tim, with the exception of maybe a few details. The more he was able to decipher the notes in the file, though, the more it became clear that the file was all about the technology for smart missiles. In his reading he quickly discovered how the technology all came together through the use of the mind. The missile's launcher contained a neural-computer much like the one used for programming clones. A soldier would be implanted with a neural-chip which then would read the soldier's brain activity. The neural-chip sends the thoughts of the soldier to the launcher's neural-computer where it reads and translates the information into the missile's guidance system. In other words, the soldier could use mind control to launch a missile to its destination. Just by visualizing the target the launcher's neural-computer picks up the soldier's position, then calculates the coordinates of the visual and delivers the airstrike. It would seem that with the neural-chip and the bio-armor any person could be the ultimate killing machine.

Tim realized Paul was involved in much deeper things then he could ever imagine. Even though at this point he no longer considered him a friend- but an enemy- Tim felt even more betrayed. All this time he thought their jobs were supposed to be giving and protecting life, not taking it away. Tim knew that the military took special interest in their projects, but he always thought that it was for noble purposes, like healing wounded soldiers. And in the case of the armor, protecting soldiers from wounds and loss of limb. But with what he discovered he was finding that the current technology the military desired is to not just kill people, but to totally annihilate.

Forbidden Origins-apostasia

Everything Tim knew suddenly felt as if it was all a lie. Tim had originally set out to get revenge on both Paul and Federal Duplications, and now more than ever he wanted to hinder (if he couldn't completely stop) what they were planning. And what better way than to use their own missiles against them.

It took him a great deal more time and research to figure out how to use Paul's clearances to hack the launcher that controls the missiles, but this would have been even more difficult if Tim didn't already have insider knowledge. There were enough similarities to his own programming design that he already had a deep understanding of how it all worked.

It wasn't much longer after discovering the use of Paul's mind control system that Tim was able to locate the actual missiles. There were six missiles ready and waiting to be deployed, likely for testing. Tim was confident he could hack them through an upgrade; the missiles and its launcher were mobile, and were made to receive upgrades while overseas or on the battlefield.

This was meant to be a smart failsafe system, but these online upgrades would leave the software vulnerable for hacking. That is the beauty of technology; the more advanced it becomes, the more susceptible it becomes for hacking. Tim was going to create his own update to download onto the software, with a date, time, destination and an irreversible launch sequence.

Between everything he found in Paul's MUD PIT file on his computer and information on hacking missiles from the

Internet (isn't it amazing what one can find on Internet?), to Tim it seemed like taking candy from a baby. While it involved some time and learning, it was easier than some of the work he had to do in the past.

He knew it wouldn't solve all the problems he came up with, like another facility opening up with the research continuing and the armor eventually being given to the military. But hopefully with the destruction of the Federal Duplications headquarters building and important members in it, it would at least cripple the process. The hidden military base where Tim will be launching the missiles from would be exposed and revealed to the public. And if it was portrayed in the media to be a government conspiracy, that certainly may shut down certain operations.

The more he thought about it, the more Tim became convinced that it was the right thing to do, and the best way to go out with a BANG. Chuckling to himself at his own morbid thoughts, Tim decided it was time. He was ready to set off his silent ticking time bombs, and he couldn't wait to see the grand finale. But first, Tim had to make a call.

"Hey Tim! How are you doing, it's been about a week since I've heard from ya."

For the first time in a while, hearing Paul's voice was like music to his ears. The difference being that now he knew pretty soon he would never have to hear the traitor speak again.

Forbidden Origins-apostasia

"Hey Paul; I've needed some time, but I'm ready now. I would like to come back to work this next Monday."

Sounding a little taken aback, Paul responded with, "Well, you know you're welcome back at any time. Are you sure you're ready though?"

"I'm positive," Tim replied.

"Well I'm glad to hear it! We've all been missing you around here and can't wait to see your ugly mug!"

After a few more minutes of small talk, Tim got off the phone and proceeded to set the missiles to launch for his return date.

CHAPTER FIFTEEN
Blowing up the Past

Today was the day. All the careful planning, diligent work, and waiting was all about to come to a close. Sitting on the edge of his bed and staring at his clock, Tim wasn't able to get a wink of sleep all night. Thoughts of his mission were racing through his head. And as much as he tried to stop them, thoughts of Aavah kept popping into his head as well. Not that he didn't want to remember her, but he wanted to be at the top of his game in the here and now. Not living in the past while reminiscing bittersweet memories. Just as he started to get a little drowsy from all his intense thoughts and staring...

Forbidden Origins-apostasia

(BEEP) (BEEP) (BEEP) the alarm went off. Quickly regaining his awareness, Tim turned his alarm off and began to get ready for the day. With everything that had been going on lately he had let himself get pretty scruffy, so he needed to clean up, and look as normal as possible.

Paul had called Tim the day before, making sure he was still okay with coming in. Tim was more than ready to come in to work; in fact, he was so eager he asked Paul if he wanted to ride in together, like they used to do. Paul sounded especially pleased to have Tim suggest this, but declined as he mentioned that he had to go in quite a bit earlier for a special project he was in the middle of. Despite the fact that he was the one that made the offer, Tim was relieved to hear this. He didn't really want to be in such close proximity with Paul before the BIG moment. He just wanted to make sure everything seemed as normal as possible as to not tip Paul off that anything was amiss.

Tim went through his final plans one last time. He double checked that the missiles were still ready to be launched with his update, and everything looked good to go. Next he headed down to the basement and opened up the hatch for the pit. Nero and Nikki looked so different from when they'd first arrived. Thinner, gaunt, badly beaten, blotches on their skin as well as the toll from being in constant agony. They almost could pass for being in their 70's or 80's even though they were closer to 40 and 20. Tim lowered some smoke bombs in the cell with a long fuse.

"Well boys, this is where we part ways. I'm sure you will be relieved to see the last of me, but believe it or not I am actually going to miss our special times together. Thankfully I don't have to think about it for too much longer though, as none of us are going to make it past today."

With a humorless laugh Tim lit the fuse then quickly closed the hatch. Next he grabbed his bottle of silicone so he could line the hatch with it, ensuring that it would be air tight. The smoke inhalation should be enough to finish them off, but if not then it shouldn't be too much longer that they would succumb to starvation and dehydration.

Not wanting to think on the fact that this was the last time he was ever going to see the house that he and Aavah had lived in together as man and wife, he hastily went upstairs and grabbed his keys and briefcase, then dashed to his car. As depressing as it was to pull out of the driveway and see the house disappearing behind him in his side mirror, the thought of what was awaiting him at work boosted his spirits and put an authentic smile on his face. All he could think to himself was 'At last....'

Pulling in to the security post once he reached the compound, he got a nice warm welcome from Ernie. Short and round, bald on top, and slightly inappropriate, Ernie never failed to greet with warm smiles and good laughs to start off the day.

"Tim! How are you doing buddy!?"
"I'm fine, good to see you Ernie." Under normal circumstances Tim would be happy to see Ernie, but today he

Forbidden Origins-apostasia

was mostly sad to see him. While making his plans he knew that many innocent lives would be lost, but he forgot that some of those lives were people that he knew and had grown fond of. Although his guard post was on the outer rim of the compound, chances were even Ernie's life would not be spared from his missile attack. During Tim's inner battle to come to terms with what was going to happen, Ernie took his silence to be for another reason.

"Listen Tim, Paul told me what had happened. I'm so very sorry, she was a wonderful woman. The Lord seems to take all the good ones early, doesn't He? But who are we to question his plan for us, no matter how painful.

Well, I just want you to know that if there is anything you need at all, let me know. I may be old and broken, but I know a thing or two about heart ache...and heart burn... and even heart attacks! If you can believe it."

His little joke snapped Tim back to the present and he laughed at this. "Haha Ernie, nice one. I'll keep that in mind."

"All jokes aside Tim, see that you do. Hey, I know, maybe we can have lunch today? If I let my boss know in advance that I am going to take my lunch break today away from the guard's post, I don't think that should be a problem."

Perking up at the suggestion, Tim responded with, "Yeah Ernie, I would like that!" He was relieved to hear the suggestion, as this gave him an idea on how he could save at least Ernie from the disaster.

"I was actually too nervous about returning to work to be able to eat anything this morning ('at least that was true enough', Tim thought to himself). So I wouldn't mind going early for brunch, say in about an hour and a half? Let's meet at the Higgins Cafe that is just down the road, my treat."

Ernie scratched his chin as he mulled this over. "Well I just ate breakfast...but what the heck. A man like me can always eat, right?" Gesturing to his wide belly and chuckling to himself. "I'll get on the horn right now and arrange for someone to take my post. Want to say about 10?"

Tim quickly thought about the timeline of events and figured that time should work out to have Ernie far enough away to be out of immediate danger.

"Sounds perfect."

And with that, Tim pulled away from the post and parked in his usual parking spot.

As Tim looked up at the six story building all the positive feelings he had from his short interlude with Ernie faded and was slowly replaced with rage. The company that he gave his entire life to, his utmost loyalty, betrayed him with lies and deceit. But worst of all was that they did nothing to save his dying wife when they could have done everything. Opening his briefcase, he pulled out some muscle relaxers and tried controlling his breathing. He definitely couldn't afford to lose his control now and risk throwing his meticulous plans down the drain.

Eventually regaining control of himself, he exited his car and began making his way to the sixth floor. He was actually in a hurry, but along the way people kept trying to greet him and talk with him. But after a while he had no more time or patience for small talk. So after about the fourth attempt someone tried stopping him, he just gave a quick, simple smile and a wave and continued with a brisk pace; leaving anyone trying to talk with him in his wake.

Unfortunately it wasn't enough, and he arrived just in time to hear the *DING* of the elevator door, and it shut right in his face. Growing more frustrated and sickly with anxiety, he was just about to take the stairs and walk it off until a work friend grabbed him from behind.

"There's the man of the hour! How are you doing, buddy?" Tim wasn't in the mood for friendly socializing at the moment, but still kept his cool.

"Yeah, I guess that's me. I'm hanging in there." With beads of sweat running down his face Tim turned around to face his old friend Mike Walters.

"Gee, Tim.... Are you feeling ok?"

Tim just wanted some air and an ice cold glass of water, but knew he had to press on.

"Yeah, I was just at the gym," Tim replied with a lack of interest.

"Well it's good to see for myself that you're up and around!" Mike said, while slapping Tim on the back.

(DING) During this little interlude the next elevator had arrived.

"Just in time!" his colleague said with enthusiasm, guiding Tim towards the elevator.

Stepping in, Tim pressed the 6th floor button, and as he saw more people approaching he quickly pressed the "close door" button as well. To his dismay it did not shut immediately, and as people were still getting in, more were coming their way. He frantically tried pushing the button again and again until finally the door shut, and he breathed a sigh of relief. Mike looked at him strangely but just continued to blather on about menial things that held zero interest for Tim.

Finally he made it to his floor, and his colleague walked out with him, still talking about useless sports stats and women. He was starting to think Mike was never going to leave him in peace. Until he walked through the door leading to his department, and suddenly it made sense why he had followed Tim.

As the door opened he heard, "Welcome back Tim!" And a round of enthusiastic applause followed. This seemed to be the last straw for Tim attempting to hold back his anxiety, and he fell to his knees, not able to catch his breath.

The 'surprise' staff rushed to his aid trying to help him back up. While he had one hand on his chest over his heart, he used his other to wave them off. After a scary and tense 30 seconds he was able to pick himself up off the floor and right himself.

He looked at his co-workers and said with derision, "Well that's one way to welcome someone back to work, scare them half to death!" Although he wasn't really joking the group took it that he was and laughed. Since they were able to see that Tim was okay, they gave him one last round of applause.

As he started making his way around the room, he was surrounded with a mixture of condolences for his loss and well wishes for being back to work. Tim hardly heard any of it and responded with one word answers or grunts. The entire time he was looking around the room at all the faces, trying to find one person in particular. Finally one nameless woman said something that caught his attention.

"What did you say?" Tim asked her.

Smiling she repeated herself. "Wasn't it so nice of Dr. Sullivan to plan your welcome back party? He's even invited some important political figures here; I think they're towards the back."

"Where is Paul? Err, Dr. Sullivan, that is?" Tim asked with concern.

The woman shook her head with regret and said, "You know, he's been so sick with the flu this past week, he had to call in again today, the poor man."

Tim's heart stopped and time stood still as what she told him registered in his brain. Paul was not here...but that's

203

impossible, he told him just the day before that he would be here, and even said he would be coming in early...and then as the realization hit him, he almost lost his fragile hold on control as the rage tore into him.

'That SOB lied to me!' Tim thought to himself. Dashing towards his private office and brushing off both the small and the important people in the room. Closing his door and locking it shut, he took a couple deeper breaths, trying to get it together. Changing into the beast right now was not going to do him any favors, and it definitely wouldn't get him Paul. Pulling out his phone he stabbed the familiar numbers with enough force that his screen cracked. But that was the least of his worries...

(RING) (RING) (RING)... "This is Paul; I can't take your call right now..."

It was just a voicemail, so then Tim tried his work number.

(RING) (RING) (RING)... "This is Dr. Sullivan, sorry, but I'm not in today."

Not only could Tim not get a hold of Paul, but he was also finding out that he had changed his voicemail messages. Tim knew he couldn't have been sick. Looking at his countdown timer he had on his phone, he had only a little over 5 minutes' left until the missiles launched. Tim was not about to leave this world without taking Paul with him, which gave Tim only one option...he had to get out of the building and find him.

Forbidden Origins-apostasia

Tim ran out of his office and directly into a sea of people. Some of them attempted to grab and tug on him to get his attention, but he just kept moving forward, completely throwing aside any manners he had left. Not wanting to get stuck in the elevator again, he ran down all six flights of stairs to get back to the main floor. By the time he made it across the parking lot and to his car he was completely covered in sweat, to the point of having his clothes sticking to him like a second skin (well, third skin if you count the armor). Jumping into his car, he threw it into drive and tried to call Paul again.

Just as he was exiting the parking area he remembered Ernie. Frustrated he hung up the phone and glanced at the timer. There was just 90 seconds left before the launch. Tim dropped the phone into his cup-holder and drove as fast as he could to the entrance post. As soon as he saw that Ernie was still there he slammed on his brakes and yelled out at him.

"Ernie, get in!"

"Oh, there you are Tim! I just tried calling your office. After I got to thinking about it I thought it would make more sense if we rode together rather than meet at the cafe..."

Before Ernie was allowed to finish his reply Tim yelled louder and with more intensity. "Get in now!"

"Tim I can't, my replacement hasn't shown up yet. You know that I can't leave my post unattended. I could be fired!"

While Ernie was going on and on about how unusual this was and he couldn't understand what has gotten into Tim, Tim

had decided enough was enough. He was out of time and
patience, so he got out of the car and grabbed Ernie by the arm.
Dragging him over to the car and shoving him into the passenger
seat, Tim then got back in and drove away with haste.

"What is the matter with you?! Did something go wrong
in the building? Another one of those hazardous chemical
spills??" Ernie was trying to make sense of Tim's strange and
rude behavior, which he had never seen before.

But Tim wasn't interested in having a heart to heart at the
moment, he was still trying to reach Paul via phone. After
hearing the voicemail response yet again, Tim cursed and then
threw the phone down.

Once he figured they were far enough away from the
compound, he pulled the car over to the side of the road. "Out!"

Ernie looked at Tim like he had grown horns and a tail.
"Right here? But this isn't even the restaurant!"
Then he closed his eyes for a second, took a deep breath, and
then spoke in a calmer and gentle voice.
"You look like you're under a lot of stress, buddy. Maybe this is
too soon for you to be back to work. I think that you should let
me drive you home, and then I will take a taxi back to work."

"Ernie, I'm fine, I just really need you to get out of the car.
You'll be safe this far away. Just whatever you do, do not go back
to work. Trust me when I say it is a matter of life or death," Tim
stated earnestly.

Forbidden Origins-apostasia

"Oookay, Tim, if that's what you want, I'll get out," Ernie replied and finally stepped out of the vehicle.

Tim sped off immediately, barely leaving enough time for Ernie to close the door. As he stood there staring at the back of Tim's disappearing taillights with his mouth hanging open, six passing flames split the sky and the clouds followed by cracks and shouts from sonic booms rattling in the ear. Immediately following was the sounds of crashes and explosions.

At hearing the sounds Tim looked behind him and could see smoke rising in the background. His plan was executed perfectly, but in his mind it was far from successful. He still couldn't believe that Paul wasn't there; they were both supposed to die in that explosion. Just as Paul had ruined his life when he allowed Aavah to die, he ruined his death as well.

Arriving back to his little suburb community, he drove right past his own house and pulled into Paul's driveway. By the time he parked the car Tim was so nerved up he couldn't get his fingers to work right and struggled with getting his seat-belt off. Getting out of the car and walking was becoming a chore, as every step felt like stumbling.

"Paul! PAUL!" Tim was yelling at the top of his lungs while making his way to the front door.

"I KNOW YOU'RE IN THERE!"

All of a sudden he heard a muffled shot ring out from somewhere behind him. Feeling some pain and then numbness in his back, Tim tried to turn around to look, but everything seemed a blur. Falling to his knees he saw a shadowy figure approaching him. He tried to ask the person what they wanted, but before he could confront them, everything went dark.

CHAPTER SIXTEEN
The Unfolding

Tim was drifting in and out of consciousness. Somewhere amidst the surrounding blackness would come beams of light and fragments of sound. But when he'd try to focus on these moments, the darkness would engulf him again. Suddenly red eyes came towards him from a distance, coming closer and closer. The red glow from the eyes was so bright that it lit up part of the creature's face. Tim did not recognize it, but he knew somehow that it was the beast from within.

The hand of the monster seemed to pierce right through his body; trembling, he felt the very life source of his body leaving him. Was this it, death at last? Was the beast about to take him to the underworld? All he wanted was rest and to be reunited with Aavah.

At just the simple thought of her name, Tim was ripped out of the darkness and transported to a place of intense light. After his eyes finally adjusted to the abrupt change, he realized that he was standing on a beach. The sand was white and hot on his feet and he could even feel a cool yet gentle breeze caress his cheeks. He glanced out to the sea and saw foam bubbling and floating in off the waves about a hundred feet in front of him. The color was a startling blue-green, which reminded him of Aavah's eyes. When he looked down at himself, his body was intact and functional with no blotches on his skin and the armor was gone.

All of a sudden the breeze turned into a strong wind, and in its wake he heard his name, like a soft whisper blowing by. It was the sweetest, most beautiful sound he had heard in a while. There was no doubt in his mind that it was Aavah's voice. Frantically scanning up and down the beach, he finally saw her standing on the shore line in the distance.

Speaking aloud he asked himself, "Am I in heaven?" But the answer did not matter to him now that he knew where she was. It seemed as if all his problems and worries drifted away in that moment. Starting out at first with a slow and shaky walk, eventually his strength returned to him and he broke into a jog.

"Aavah! Aavah!" he yelled in excitement.

She turned her head and looked right at him with a soft smile. Now that he knew for sure that it was her, Tim started sprinting as fast as he could.

Forbidden Origins-apostasia

"Aavah!" he cried out again. Little by little he could make out more details as he gained ground and became closer to her. She was wearing a white flowing sundress with her hair down and both were being carelessly blown around by the wind. His arms ached to hold her again, and feel the beat of her heart against his chest. His calves burned from the exertion in the sand and his heart was pounding furiously. But he was so close! He pushed himself even harder until she was only an arm's length away.

Reaching out to grab her hand, the once beautiful scene blew away like the dust in the wind. The sun became too strong for words, and the heat felt like it was radiating through his skull. No longer able to withstand the penetrating rays he threw his arm in front of his eyes.

"Aavah!" He tried calling her one last time as everything disappeared into blinding pure white light.

Tim jerked up right, sweating and breathing heavily. He looked around in panic for Aavah, but in front of him now was not the beach, but an unfamiliar bedroom. And he wasn't standing or running in sand, but sitting up in a bed.

Feeling disoriented and bereft, he slowly laid back down. Staring up at the ceiling he closed his eyes. He did not wonder where he was or why, but all he could do was try to hold on to the images of the dream that had just left him. Conjuring up the precious image of his beautiful Aavah on the beach, he let the grief overtake him and his tears flowed freely down his face and onto the pillow.

After allowing himself a time of grieving that was long overdue, the sound of birds singing through an open window grabbed his attention. Taking a look at his surroundings, he realized that this was somewhere he had never been. Extending his senses, unusual sounds were heard somewhere in the distance; but then he realized they were the sounds of pots and pans clattering in a kitchen. As he pondered on the noises, the smell of a good breakfast reached his nose. The smell wound its way through his body till it reached his stomach, which suddenly felt ravenous. Curious, Tim rose from the bed. After glancing around he noticed a little note on the bed stand.

Tim,
Don't worry, you are in a safe place. I know you are angry and have questions; I will try to answer them as best I can.

Tim didn't recognize the hand writing, but wherever he was, one thing was certain: he wasn't in any immediate danger. Whoever had him would have already killed him if that had been their intent, and he wasn't chained down or in any type of restraints. Hungry and anxious to explore his new setting, Tim ventured out from the room he woke up in.

Forbidden Origins-apostasia

He wandered down a small hallway until he reached a staircase. The sounds from what he had assumed were coming from the kitchen were louder here, obviously coming from downstairs. Descending down the steps to the landing, he looked around. To his right he heard more noises coming from an open doorway. Tim advanced with caution, trying to catch a glimpse of whomever was in the kitchen. He saw a man walking around with his back to the door. Silently Tim made his way into the room and leaned against a counter nearest to the doorway. The man still had his back to him but he looked more familiar now that Tim was closer to him. Turning around, the man gave a slight start when he realized someone else was in the room.

"Heaven almighty, Dr.! Make some noise when you enter a room! Or give a man some signal that he's no longer alone."

With an unobstructed view of the man's face, it only took Tim a moment to place the face he was looking at with a name. The man wiped his hands that were covered in some kind of white powder off on his shirt and extended one of them in greeting.

"I'm sorry, where are my manners? I'm..."

Tim held up his hand and cut him off. "I know who you are."

He strode past the gentleman and took an apple off of the table from a bowl that was in the center, brought it to his mouth and took a bite, never once taking his eyes off the other man. There was a few beats of awkward silence as Tim took several mouthfuls of his apple and the two just stared back at one another. Finally, the man decided to finish setting out the food and sat down at the table.

"Please Dr., have a seat and have some breakfast with me. I don't usually have the time to cook, but I assure you that when I do it is quite good."

Wanting to argue but having his stomach telling him to just be quiet and listen to the man, Tim decided that he could eat first and then ask questions later. As it turned out, the man really was a good cook, and after a few minutes of eating Tim was finally able to organize his thoughts.

"Your reputation precedes you, Dr. St. Clair. Although we have never met, I am well aware of your work. But what I do not understand is where I am and why am I here? What exactly are you planning on doing with me?"

"Well first of all, please, call me Luke. And second, I could say the same of you, Tim. I have followed your career for years, and I must say it is quite impressive. I have been very excited to work with you, although I'm sure you have no idea what I'm talking about. Which brings us to all your questions, but I'm afraid that I am not the right person to answer everything for you. I am however a little surprised that you're not reacting badly to my presence here. As you have already mentioned it, you know my reputation."

Forbidden Origins-apostasia

"All I really know is what the media has said about you, and of course what you yourself have said in all your interviews. You have become quite the leader of groups that have taken a stance against cloning. Or at least certain aspects of it. I also know that you're well known for breakthroughs in the medical field and for discovering vaccines for rare diseases. They say that you have come the closest to a cure from cancer as any scientist or researcher has ever been, outside of cloning, of course. Very impressive resume, but I am not concerned about any of that right now. What I do want to know is what you meant by saying that you aren't you the right person to tell me why I am here?" As Tim poured more syrup onto his pile of food, he heard footsteps from up above. A few seconds later the steps came bounding down the stairs with a voice.

"Luke, while I appreciate your hospitality, your guest rooms need some major repairs." Tim could not believe what he was seeing. It was Paul, and he even had the audacity to nod in greeting to Tim as he crossed the kitchen to pour himself a cup of coffee.

Before Paul even had a chance to move away from the counter, Tim sprang up and had Paul's head pinned against the overhead cabinets with his forearm.

"Oh, hey bud... you're finally awake," Paul said.

"You have a lot of explaining to do, starting with Aavah!" Tim said with a low growl. Tim could feel his control starting to slip away and felt that he could transform into the beast as quickly as a blink of the eye.

"She was a clone and you never told me. And you just let her die." With that he then smashed him into the refrigerator.

"Ugh! Enough of the melodramatics Tim," Paul grunted out. All that did was to incite Tim's anger even more, and so he put more pressure on Paul's neck.

Luke interjected with as calm of a voice as he could manage. "Tim, I realize you're angry and want answers. You'll get them. And if you don't feel they are satisfactory then you can always kill him later, right? In whatever horrible way you see fit. But if you damage his larynx too badly or kill him now, you will never find out all that you want to know. We brought you out here for a reason...please just give him a chance to explain."

Taking some deep breaths and regaining control of himself, Tim let go of Paul with clear reluctance and returned to his seat.

"Look what you made me do, my coffee is all over the place!" Paul said with frustration as he refilled his mug.

Before Tim could react again, Luke responded mockingly, "Let's not cry over 'spilled milk', Paul. Better that than a crushed neck."

At hearing this Paul – who was cleaning up the liquid mess – glanced over at Tim and saw the serious look of animosity on his old friend's face.

Forbidden Origins-apostasia

"Touché." Paul joined them at the table and sat down looking pretty nonplussed.

"Kill me in any horrible way he sees fit, eh Luke?"

Luke shrugged. "He let you go, didn't he?" And after giving Paul a pointed look, went back to giving his food his full attention.

As Paul helped himself to what was on the table, Tim decided to start asking the questions. "So why am I here Paul? And why is living-up-to-his-name "Dr. Saint" here as well?"

"Ha ha! You hear that Luke? You're a true Saint!" Paul said with hearty sarcasm.

It was obvious that Luke was uncomfortable with becoming the subject of conversation, so he ignored the jab and continued to eat; therefore silently excusing himself from the discussion.

Tim was not in the least bit entertained by Paul's joking manner. It may have been a quality he admired of the man in the past, but no longer did he find it in the least amusing. With a stern voice that told Paul it was time for business he redirected his attention. "Let's start with Aavah."

Reading Tim's expression and realizing it was time for some explanations, Paul dropped the façade.

"Tim, I am truly and deeply sorry for what happened to Aavah. What happened at the hospital was awful and I know it looked bad, but I never wanted her to die. I am also sorry for having to keep the truth from you. I know you are desperate for

217

answers, so please bear with me as I explain everything."
Dropping his fork and knife and pushing his plate away, Paul
continued.

"As you've probably suspected by now, I've been involved
with a lot of top secret operations with Federal Duplications,
some of which you've had a basic understanding of. However,
what you didn't know is that everything we have been involved in
has been mostly a lie. Every piece of work and information was
and is for one goal and one goal only: Project Eden." Paul took a
deep breath while playing with his silverware on the table.

"Project Eden on the surface appears to be all about
advancing the human race, which seems logical and good.
But the more I worked on certain projects and the more time
that passed I realized Eden was all about putting the human race
into a forceful extinction; eradications of anyone unwilling to
evolve. Everything is supposed to come to a new order, but the
problem is the people that make up and run that order. Cloning
was never really about harvesting organs, filling in niches or
helping out third world countries. Indeed, we did do those
things, and advertised them thoroughly, but it was all stepping
stones for a much bigger purpose. It was to ease the public into
the Eden mindset, which was to create the perfect race...a
Utopian society, so to speak. The name of the game is survival of
the fittest, with letting the government enable your fitness...but
once you sign up with this gym membership, it owns you." Paul

Forbidden Origins-apostasia

paused for a moment to look back and forth between Tim and Luke and asked them,

"Have either of you heard the phrase used by politicians 'Never let a crisis go to waste'?"

When both of them nodded, Paul continued. "Well, this was more or less our main business model. It took some pretty major crises for the general public to accept these types of changes, right? So we would find a problem, exploit it, and then give the world our solutions. In some cases, we've contrived problems just so we could act like the heroes when we came up with the best answer. It's an effective tactic to promote an agenda like cloning or to help a leader gain trust from the people, but it's all done dishonestly. As far as the government is concerned, the means justified the end. People will generally believe anything they see in the media, and it'll leave them blind to what is happening right in front of them. It's not too far from brainwashing and it's very efficient. This is just one of the dark underlying ways we've introduced cloning (Eden) to the public."

Paul gave a sarcastic grin and attempted his best cheesy TV sales pitch voice. "Lose a limb while in the service? Or perhaps gangs are running rampant in your town and you or your friend have been shanked? Well call now and fix an injury! We have all the cloned parts you need." Paul snickered at his own idea of such a ridiculous sales pitch would go. But after seeing the unamused face of Tim, the grin disappeared and his mood and tone became more serious as he moved on to the extremely difficult topic of Aavah.

Paul's eyes watered and turned cloudy with sorrow. "Aavah.... sweet, sweet Aavah. Yes Tim, she was a clone, but not just any clone. I know I don't talk about my first marriage very much, but I know I have mentioned it to you before...?"

Even though Paul was making a statement he trailed off at the end with it coming out more like a question. When he didn't continue Tim gave a curt nod to indicate he knew what Paul was referring to, but he didn't understand the quick change in topics.

"You may remember me telling you about when I had prostate cancer, which has been my motivation for finding cures, particularly in the cloning development. But what you don't know is that there was another factor for my passion in that field that I never talk about.

My first wife and I wanted a child in the worst way. However, we met each other after I was recovering from the cancer. I loved her to the point of wanting to move heaven and earth to make it happen for her. With the work I was doing at the time it seemed logical to just clone a baby for us. I was so emotionally invested in the idea and professionally driven that when I approached the company with the idea, I did not care what contract I would have to sign or what motives they might have. All that mattered to me was that they were a means to end of helping me get what I wanted...what I *needed.* So after

Forbidden Origins-apostasia

creating a perfect test tube specimen, the clone was artificially inseminated in my wife.

Unfortunately, after several months there were some complications. As you know, cloning back then had more risks and failures. So I told her that we would have to abort it and try again. But my wife had already grown attached and refused to let me do that. I begged and I pleaded with her trying everything I could think of to make her understand that it was not just the baby, but her own life at risk. Nothing worked. She said she would leave me if I forced her to get rid of it, and I could not bear to even think of that. In the end the baby survived, but my wife did not. As I'm sure you have figured out by now, that baby was Aavah.

But Tim, I want you to know that Aavah never had any programming or animal genetic modifications like most other clones. She may have been a designer clone, but she was still fully human. I regret to say that I was so distraught over my wife's foolish decision to give her life up for a clone, that at the time I couldn't even stand the sight of the baby. I knew that I would not be the best person to raise her, so I immediately put her up for adoption with the company's approval. The only way I could get them to agree with it was if no one else would know she was a clone and I had to continue to monitor her and her progress. As far as they were concerned she was still a piece of their property and they wanted to keep track of her development

221

for the sake of the cloning research. So the adoption was open and I had mandatory visits so I could monitor her.

As she became older I eventually was introduced as the 'family friend,' with her never knowing I was her father. I can't say I regret giving her up for adoption. I feel that her adopted parents raised her better than I ever could have. But as she grew up I struggled to hold on to any bitterness I may have had when she was first born. Aavah was the sweetest child with so much love to give to everyone around her. My visits went from tortuous memories of my late wife to where I looked so forward to them they were the highlight of my entire month. That is until she was old enough to start dating...then they became more torturous than ever before." This last part Paul chuckled at the irony before continuing on.

"Seriously, though, that was a hard time for me. I knew she was so much better than the boys that she was dating, and destined for so much more. Then it finally dawned on me how I could start becoming a good father and influence her life in a real positive way...with you, Tim. Believe it or not, I programmed you with my daughter in mind. An intelligent, worthy man that I could be sure would take care of her. Of course you can't program love, and what you two had was very real, but in the beginning I was able to influence the both of you to come together. After she completed her schooling and certifications I was able to get her into the company working as our laboratory nurse. And as you know, the rest is history."

Forbidden Origins-apostasia

After hearing all this information Tim was quiet for a few minutes, with tears running down his face in silence.

"Her father, Paul? This whole time, and you never told me...or her! She at the very least had a right to know. But what I really don't understand is that if she was your daughter, how could you let her die? We both know you could have saved her! What kind of inhuman monster – ?!"

"I did want to save her Tim! Get that through your head! There's more to explain, much more!" Paul shouted in frustration. Suddenly feeling exhausted, and every bit of his 60+ years of age, he tried to take a moment to calm down. He wondered how to explain the next part, which he knew was the information that Tim was impatiently waiting for. After debating on how to soften the blow, he finally decided to just give it to him straight.

"Aavah's death may have been prevented, I guess we'll never know for sure. I tried pulling rank, I tried cashing in every single favor I had, I even told them about her pregnancy to see if that would entice them. Yet none of it was enough, and I was given direct orders to stand down on the issue.

I was given one bio-armor. And to be frank with you Tim, you're an extremely valuable asset for Federal Duplications. Any potential risk of death or prolonged recovery for a valuable asset such as yourself is unacceptable to the company, even if it means that someone else would have to die. It did not matter to them that Aavah's condition was much worse, their priority was you,

223

and you alone. Not to mention that the government will always capitalize on any potential sob story to activate the next step for their agenda. After a suitable mourning period, their plans were to have you go back on the road and promote another step towards Eden.

Obviously they didn't realize that it would back fire and you would go rogue and try to destroy the very company that created you, but then they would not have thought that it would be possible for you to stray so far from your programming."

Tim was not at all happy with that statement. "Did you kidnap me just so you could explain that Aavah and I are only pawns to some covert government project, so you could feel better about yourself?! Because so far it's not working, in fact, despite my 'programming' I've never felt so inclined to tear you apart as I do right now!"

At this vehement outburst from Tim, Paul suddenly backed his chair away from the table and stood up so fast that the chair toppled over.

"For your information, no, I don't feel any better about myself!" Paul yelled as he started pacing back and forth in the kitchen. "In fact I feel as low and slimy as anyone is capable of feeling. Do you think that I don't realize that I deserve to be judged in the deepest pits of hell?! The government had their eyes on me since college. When I joined a secret fraternity I had absolutely no idea what I was getting myself into.

Forbidden Origins-apostasia

It was so easy for them... they used all my dreams and ambition against me for their own gain, but that was just the beginning. And believe me, they're not the sort of people you can say no to once you're in. It's truly a type of mafia.

So no Tim, I did not bring you here to tell you all this just so I could get it off my chest and feel better about myself. To the contrary, I brought you here so you can take your revenge out on everyone responsible, including me! I have a plan that you might be interested in, but there is still much more that I need to share with you."

A bit taken aback by the crazed look in Paul's eyes and not used to seeing him so serious on any topic, Tim couldn't help but be curious. "Okay Paul, I'm listening. Regardless of what you have to say, though, I can't promise I won't kill you in your sleep."

Paul flinched at this response, but then shrugged it off. "Fair enough." With that he stopped pacing and picked the chair up off the ground and sat back down at the table.

"The research facility you blew up was just a stage for the people. The real research is happening underground for project Eden. What most people don't realize is that the company was always run by the government, even before it was called Federal Duplications. But initially, because of the general distrust of the government, we thought it would be easier to accept if it was thought to be privately owned and run. I'm not saying that all the research you did or that was going on in the Federal

Duplications headquarters was useless. Every project served a purpose towards improving Eden. But the civilians needed legitimate reasons for cloning research to overcome their squeamishness on the topic, so we provided contrived reasons.

Take Aavah for example. We were already proving that a fully functioning human could be created through cloning. But we still had to ease the public into the thought process slowly, until they were practically begging us to further the cloning research. Organ transplants and limb replacements for trauma victims - particularly for veterans - gave us huge support. Before we knew it, it had become hugely profitable. But the research we were doing was well beyond simple replications for organs and limbs.

What you need to understand is that THE biggest goal - the real goal from the beginning- of Project Eden for the past several years was to create an elite class of super soldiers. Every single project that we had was another way for us to test out different attributes and to see how different technologies and DNA additions would affect their strength, intelligence, immunity, skills, etc. Anything that would give these guys the tools they'd need to be undefeatable in any type of combat situation."

Paul leaned back in his chair, arms folded behind his head, giggling to himself as he remembered. "It was amazing! We used DNA strands from sharks, alligators, monkeys, leopards...anything that we could think of to improve upon their

Forbidden Origins-apostasia

muscle capacity, natural body armor, and immunity. We also discovered ways of making genetic metallic materials for extra protection. These guys could take bullets to the chest and keep moving! It was simply incredible. Much like your bio-armor, Tim. But you should have seen some of the first super soldiers. Faces that only a blind mother walrus could love."

While Paul was explaining these things, Luke started choking on some of his breakfast.

"Hey, are you okay?" Paul asked while slapping him on the back.

Finally able to safely swallow his food, Luke responded with, "Yeah, I guess I just never get used to how you phrase things, Paul."

Paul laughed and carried on with his explanation. "So anyways, these initial soldiers ended up becoming more like super Frankensteins, but were still effective for what the government needed before disposing of them. The next step was the programming, but we would need a super computer to help us understand the complexity of the brain. This is the real reason for developing the neural-computer. To control an elite group of soldiers that could carry out certain agendas with no limitations. And then eventually control the masses for Eden with their new bodies. But we needed to start on a smaller scale, so we tested the programming by making clones with specific skills. You were also part of that test."

Paul took another deep breath to get ready to tell Tim more upsetting news that he was certain would not go over well. "Tim, because of the CSA (Clone Safety Act), it's my job to monitor you. You have a neural-chip that allows me to do that."

"I have what?! So you've been spying on me!? All this time??" Tim was clearly outraged.

"No! Well, at least not until later... let me explain. I never used your chip to spy on you and Aavah. I wanted as normal of a life as possible for you guys. The chip you were implanted with when you first came into being was a monitoring chip meant to give us your vital readings and also acted as a location device...essentially a GPS. But you already know all that as you have inserted them in other clones yourself. So with that chip I could never 'spy on' or control you. I did get high stress alerts the day you and Aavah were kidnapped. I honestly thought it had to do with the baby on the way and the new job opportunity. I knew you were on a date with her that night, and I thought maybe things weren't going so well, or else maybe they were going very well and you were just feeling overexcitement. So I ignored them... that is until you were shot and I was getting vital readings that were at dangerous levels. So I tried getting ahold of you and when I couldn't I sent an ambulance to your GPS coordinates.

It wasn't until you were in the hospital and under surgery, that the neural-chip was implanted. I told you about the bio-armor at that time -not that you could miss it- but I was given

Forbidden Origins-apostasia

strict instructions not to inform you of the neural chip. It was mandatory for you to have it with the armor so to keep track of your recovery. And, if necessary, implant suggestions to speed up your mental recovery and get you compliant for going back to work on the road. I promised myself I wouldn't spy on you and I was giving phony results to the company, but I kept getting more and more distress signals. So I had to keep monitoring you...however I never once controlled you."

Tim was trying his absolute best not to reach across the table and strangle Paul. "So you know everything?"

Paul replied, "Mostly. Because of the new neural-chip, I was even able to see when you changed into the...umm...creature. The first time was at the barn, and again at a Pitoni hangout. Despite my concern about your loss of control, I didn't want to interfere with your revenge. I wanted that scum responsible for Aavah's death off the streets every bit as much as you did."

"Ok Paul, whatever you say. But what I still don't understand is how Aavah was able to recite a clone serial number with her last dying breath, and yet you claim she never knew she was a clone...?"

"Ohh Tim, I was so excited to hear the news of you guys expecting a child, but I was also terrified. As I told you about my own experience, going through a clone pregnancy was very hard on my late wife and ultimately ended her life. I know that our technology is a lot more advanced now, but I was still worried about Aavah's health. So that day that you and I went to the lab together, after I dropped you off I went back to the building and found Aavah. I congratulated her and told her that I wanted to make sure that everything went smoothly for her pregnancy. I gave her that clone ID to memorize in case anything went wrong. I led her to believe that would be the number for the baby, but while carrying the child the number was good for her to use for herself in the meantime. So I told her that I would start prepping emergency organs for her. But it was that same night that she was killed, so there was no time. You have to believe me Tim, there was nothing more I could do."

Tim ignored Paul's plea and just moved on to the next issue at hand. "So tell me Paul, why now? Why the sudden change of heart towards this 'Eden'? And if you knew all about my thoughts and plans, why didn't you try to stop me from blowing up the Federal Duplications building, knowing that it was not going to take care of the real underground research?"

Paul exhaled with a heavy sigh, knowing that this emotional roller coaster was far from over. "Eden was my pipe dream for so long, the perfect place and perfect bodies with no violence or death. That would sound good to anyone, right? But I learned quickly that achieving that dream requires you getting your hands dirty. It got to where I knew I had to leave the morals I once had at the door, and accept the fact that the cost was going to be innocent lives. In order to create perfect, new ones -"

Pausing he clenched his jaw trying to keep himself together, but to no avail. The tears started running down his face while his voice quivered as he continued. "I've killed to attempt to make things better. My daughter was considered just collateral damage that would help promote another agenda...in the process, I lost not only her, but my best friend! Do you think that is how I wanted my life to turn out Tim?! The two of you were my only family. Even if Eden becomes a reality in my lifetime, what then? Who will I share my success and happiness with? Will it help me sleep at night and forget the crimes I had to commit to make it all possible? I've learned that the majority of those who enter into Eden will become no better than puppets. That's the true Eden dream for those that are in power. The master puppeteers will decide everything for all and control them with the programming in their new bodies.

So I thought that I could deal with the consequences of whatever it took to achieve Eden, but I found the cost was too high! That's my sudden change Tim...I have nothing left for me on this godforsaken earth.

As for the Federal Duplications building, after figuring out your plans, I basically led you to hack my computer. Like I said before, I wanted you to seek revenge, and not just with the Pitoni. Surely everything I just told you about the company helps you to understand why I feel no loyalty to them. They have to be stopped! But I want to do this with you, not against you, Tim. I thought that if I didn't let you at least get in a little bit of vengeance before bringing you in, you would have killed me before I would even have had a chance to explain everything, and what I want us to do.

And because I know your thoughts, I also know that next to your revenge the only desire you have left is to no longer live with the pain and misery that is your existence. But I have more for you to do, so I needed to stop you before it was too late. I know that in all your plotting you did worry for humanity, so you can't tell me you don't care what the government is planning. So what I am offering you is an extension of your retaliation. The opportunity to save the world and the satisfaction of knowing that at the end of all this we will both rid our awful selves of this world. In other words, I am letting you settle your score with me as well, provided that we finish this."

Sitting in his seat, Tim looked deflated and sick. "I spent so long hating you and wishing for your demise that I can't even wrap my brain around the fact that you are pretty much serving yourself up to me on a silver platter...and to top it all off, finding out that you are Aavah's father! But you sure know how to make an offer I can't refuse. Okay Paul, I'm still listening."

Sitting in his seat, Tim looked deflated and sick. "I spent so long hating you and wishing for your demise that I can't even wrap my brain around the fact that you are pretty much serving yourself up to me on a silver platter...and to top it all off, finding out that you are Aavah's father! But you sure know how to make an offer I can't refuse. Okay Paul, I'm still listening."

Forbidden Origins-apostasia

Feeling somewhat renewed and energized at the fact that Tim seemed now slightly less inclined to kill him in his sleep, Paul continued with enthusiasm.

"Part of Project Eden is to make a formal first appearance to the high ranking military personnel of our elite forces. Fifty super soldiers will be put to the test, using weapons and technology that up until now has been virtually unknown. If you thought that the mind control missiles were bad, this technology contains a whole new level of mind control destruction. This is going to take place in a base that's unmarked and unnamed; not even the President of the United States knows where it is. Those of us that actually know of its existence and have been there refer to it as the MUD PIT, which stands for Military Underground Defense and Phantom Intelligent Technologies. What I want from you is to help us program the soldiers to work for us, use them to destroy the base, then have them go out and assassinate the other leading scientists involved.

I know that all this sounds impossible, but we have a lot of the ground work already covered. Luke, you haven't said anything in a while...why don't you fill Tim in on the rest?"

A little startled to finally be brought in on the conversation, Luke stumbled a little bit over how to begin. "Uh...yeah...sure, Paul. Um…. Tim, you're at my cabin, and I'm here to help you through to the end. Paul has informed me on what was going on with you and your...unusual transformations. I'm here to help keep your stress levels down and maintain your

233

current state of being, so to speak, so you can continue your work. While you've been passed out for the past couple of days I've analyzed some of your blood samples in my lab..."

Tim cut Luke off. "Don't bother giving me the results, I've done my own testing. I know it's irreversible and time is short. I also know that this could be contagious through blood or fluid swapping. But since I'm not planning on living any longer than I have to, and I won't be kissing anyone, I don't think there is anything to worry about."

Paul spoke up once Tim finished. "Tim, after I tranquilized you, I went into your house to grab your clothes and toiletries. I also went in your basement and found a trap door opened with an empty pit and a window broken. I was rather surprised that your attempt to finish them was unsuccessful."

"They escaped?!" Tim was utterly shocked and taken aback by Paul's remarks.

"Don't worry, I'm sure your prisoners will be caught by the police, and once they are, Luke is going to get in touch with them right away. Without us able to perform more testing on them we have no way of knowing what strain of the virus they have or whether they can infect other humans, so obviously we want to make sure to give the authorities specific instructions for their containment. Either way, you don't have to worry about them or the police coming to look for you, as it has been all over the news that you were killed in that explosion.

Forbidden Origins-apostasia

By the way, I was rather pleased that you saved Ernie from all that, as he was always my favorite security guard there. Unfortunately, that did leave open a loose end, so I ended up having to offer him a lot of money to go on an extended vacation in the tropics, with the agreement that he won't do any talking to the media or investigators. I guess since I'm not planning on being on this planet all that much longer my life savings is better off spent on Ernie having an early retirement then ending up being seized by the government...but I digress.

So, I've shown Luke all the data I've had on you since you left the hospital, secretly of course. So he is completely up to speed on everything, and he has been willing to help without exposing you. It made sense to me to go to one of the leading scientists that have been vocal against cloning and Federal Duplications, as I suspected one of them would be more than willing to help take them down. As it turns out, Luke was perfect for the job. Other than the fact his cabin could have been in a little bit nicer of condition for guests," Paul mentioned wryly, which was quickly followed by Luke tossing a biscuit at Paul's head.

Ducking just in the nick of time, Paul finished with, "Now please Tim, don't continue to be your difficult self and allow our host to study you so he can get valuable information to help others in the event your virus spreads."

Tim looked like he was about to argue, but then stopped himself and gave a grudging nod. "Just one question, though. If

235

this has been all planned out for some time, why did you grab me after I was at the building, instead of before? Weren't you worried I would get blown up when I had every intention of staying there? Why did you wait for me at your house?"

"The simple answer is I thought it was too risky to go to your house and take you. From your neural-chip I could tell you were awake all night, and I didn't know how paranoid you would be. I also knew you wouldn't blow yourself up without me, so I waited. Look Tim, we can go back and forth with Q&A all year long, or we can get down to business and finish what you started. So, what's it going to be, buddy?"

Tim rolled his eyes at Paul's impatience, but in a way it was comforting that some things never change. "Okay, I'm in."

CHAPTER SEVENTEEN
Crash Course

"I was optimistic that you would let me get this far in my explanation about why you are here, so I set everything up in the living room," Paul remarked as he got up and gestured towards the other two men to follow him into the next room.

"Well come on, don't be shy," he said while trying to get Tim and Luke to hurry it up.

After taking one last quick swig of what was left of his coffee, Tim followed Luke and Paul to the living room. He wasn't sure what to expect, but it wasn't the chaotic mess that he found. It looked as though a tornado had flown through and tossed papers, pictures, and documents everywhere. He turned to look at Luke.

"I think you've been vandalized," Tim said wryly, trying to cover up how overwhelmed he felt by the mess.

Luke looked around the room with a guilty expression on his face. "No, that was me. I was looking at everything earlier and it kind of dazed me."

Clapping Luke on the shoulder, Paul chimed in, "It's probably more organized since you moved it around from the way I originally had it," he chuckled.

"Ok, enough about this disaster. Please get back to the point already," Tim stated trying to get back on topic.

Paul rolled his eyes and sighed "Okay, take a seat." He sifted through one of the piles and then pulled out a red folder. As he rifled through the pages in front of him, he started to tick off the steps already completed on his fingers.

"Allow and provide ways for Tim to seek revenge: check. Heavily sedate and then kidnap him: check. Explain everything: check. And finally, show him The Plan." And with that, he went back to shuffling through the papers looking for whatever it was he needed.

Tim was not amused with Paul's sarcastic and joking manner, but he still couldn't help but be curious about what 'The Plan' was.

"Aha!" Paul exclaimed. Handing out some of the papers to Luke and Tim, Paul continued. "As I said earlier, a number of super soldiers are going to be fully operational and ready to be released for the military very soon. These clones will have the same genetic problem as you, Tim. The difference being - and please don't take this the wrong way - these guys are all from a much superior design. We need to give the public a taste of what these soldiers can do; they have to see the horrific possibilities of these creatures. My plan is to destroy the secret base (The MUD PIT) using the same soldiers made on the base to do the dirty work. But that phase of the plan is just the beginning. It would be far too easy for the government to cover up the details on the base and the research that occurred there.

Phase two will be to send the soldiers to take out the leading scientists (yours truly being the exception of course, as I need to be around long enough to coordinate the final phase) and also the generals behind all this.

And finally, phase three will be to destroy the National Human Resource for Genetics building. The destruction of this building is imperative to our plan, as this is the hub for all the initial research for cloning. To take it out of the equation will set the government back for years.

I also can't stress enough how important it is that the public has the opportunity to see what these guys are capable of. Between losing their main labs and cloning facilities and having backlash from the public, they will have a difficult time starting everything back up again. Unfortunately, the truth is that cloning and genetic modification can never be stopped for good; the best we can hope for is to delay it. I take personal responsibility for this generation of clones, and that is why I am doing everything that I can to stop it for a time, and hopefully for a long time. I've already talked with Luke at length about most of this already, and he agrees that the death and destruction that we are planning is nothing compared to what will happen if we don't do something to stop it."

Tim sat very still and was silent through all of Paul's talking. By the time he finished, he also felt personally responsible for how far cloning advancement had become in the short time he was involved. He may not care about much else besides joining Aavah in an early grave, but he did feel that he was being called to action to carry out Paul and Luke's plans.

"Okay, what do we need to do?"

"Well, the first thing we need to do is to alter the super soldiers' programming. As you can see on the papers I handed you, our first task is going to be the hardest. Luckily the task I was assigned for the MUD PIT base was to design and create their neural-chips. From the beginning I have been planting and hiding code within the code so that none of the plans are actually visible yet. The difficult part is going to be unlocking those codes without any of the scientists or other staff being aware of it. So basically I need apples turned into oranges while still looking like apples; that's how convincing it needs to be. I'll be able to continue working at the military base because as far as they are concerned I was just the poor schmuck whose best friend hacked his computer to blow up the Federal Duplications

Building." With that he looked pointedly at Tim who unabashedly stared right back at Paul.

"So Tim, I need you to help unlock and then re-hide these codes. Seeing as how you've already done some of this type of work with the missiles, you shouldn't have too much trouble. While at the base I will be overseeing the clones and ensuring that the work you are doing doesn't raise any red flags. I will also have access to any information that you may need, and will send to you through an encryption so it can't be traced. Once you're finished with the codes and new software that we need, I will take the information back and download it. During all this Luke is going to study your condition and monitor you, making sure you don't have any more episodes.

Now that technology is much farther advanced from when you were created Tim, stop and go cells have been manipulated enough to where we can create a fully functional adult clone in just under a year. They had started making these specially created clones a little over 6 months ago, so in just a few more months they will be ready. I know that this gives us a tight deadline to get all our tasks finished, but between the three of us working together I know it can be done.

There is going to be a group of fifty of these soldiers, and they have it timed perfectly that ten a day for five days will be 'waking up'. Each individual will need their own programming because each one will have their own separate mission, in addition to contingency plans. Phase one will take place on the fifth day, when the last ten of the fifty clones awaken. The software that you help create that is downloaded to their neural-chips will make it so that they immediately know what they need to do.

Because of the momentous occasion of the last clones coming into consciousness, it is mandatory that all staff be at the base that night. So I will be there as well to make sure everything goes as planned. I will give you the blueprints for the building as well as positions of every guard, security camera, and weapons storage. That way you can be sure to add this information into their programming. The soldiers will steal guns, ammo, and all the explosives we need from the armory. The base itself then needs to be wiped out. Since this base technically doesn't exist, if we successfully destroy everything, no help will come. There are some black armored buses on the base that we can use to transport the soldiers and bring them here. Luke has about seventy acres of wooded property that surrounds this cabin that should help keep everything hidden well. That would be the start of phase two, for which we will need to make up fake I.D.'s for the twelve soldiers that will be commissioned to assassinate key scientists and government officials. And during that time the rest of the soldiers will begin preparations for the big event.

Once the soldiers come back from their assassinations we will be ready for the third and final phase. The soldiers, Tim, and I will go to the National Human Resource for Genetics building to guarantee that everything goes as planned. And of course to eliminate all the soldiers...and ourselves." At the end of this Paul noticed that Tim was looking a little shell shocked from hearing all the information.

After taking a deep breath and let it out dramatically, he quipped, "Believe it or not that's the shortened version; the more detailed version is in all these papers and documents that you see here." Paul gestured towards all the paperwork strewn about. "Seriously though, do you have any questions so far?"

Tim looked thoughtful for a few moments and then finally asked, "Is this why you've been calling in to work sick?"

Looking pleased with Tim's assessment Paul exclaimed, "You've got it, buddy! I've been 'sick' so that I could have time to get everything ready. Plus, that way there was a plausible explanation about why I wasn't in the building the day you blew it up into smithereens. Now that I have you here, I am going to have a miraculous recovery and start going back in, but this time only to the MUD PIT. Obviously there isn't much to go back to at the other lab," he joked while laughing at his own irony.

Tim – as always seemed to be the case lately – was no-nonsense. "Well, what are we all waiting for? Let's begin."

Over the next couple of weeks, the men delved into their individual tasks. Tim figured out the code within the first couple of days. So from there he was spending the bulk of his time deciphering all the pages Paul had collected, trying to figure out the patterns. If he could find the patterns, then it should be no problem to incorporate the patterns into the code, so that they would be virtually undetectable.

Luke was hard at work studying Tim's data, taking daily samples from him to perform more tests. And of course Paul spent all his time at the MUD PIT, collecting more information to be sent to and analyzed by Tim.

Over the next couple of months Luke was completely managing his own laboratory from his cabin. He couldn't afford to leave Tim alone in his worsening condition. Despite being heavily medicated it was getting harder and harder for him to not change.

One day after Luke was wrapping up an important phone conversation for work, he heard Tim yelling and cussing from downstairs. Walking into the little spare room that they had set up for Tim's office, Luke found Tim sitting at the desk with his head cradled between his hands. As Luke walked into the room, he saw that there were busted glass shards and some type of

Forbidden Origins-apostasia

liquid all over the floor. Carefully he maneuvered around all of it and sat down on an old wooden chair next to Tim.

"I can't do this Luke," Tim said brokenly when he realized he had come into the room. "I can't control myself enough to function properly."

Tim lifted up his hands to show Luke how bad the shaking was. Even more of a surprise to Luke however, was Tim's tear-stained face. With the exception of his unconscious state that he was in when he first came to the cabin, Luke had never seen a moment of weakness in Tim. Seeing the usually stoic and closed off man in such an emotional and raw state was unsettling for Luke. Not knowing what to do or say to comfort Tim, he decided to try a change of topic.

"You know Tim; you've never really told me anything about Aavah. But just from the little bit I've heard here and there from Paul she sounds like she must have been an amazing person."

Tim lifted his head and wiped the tears from his face, then after a couple attempts to clear his throat he finally responded. "Yes, there is no question about that. She was the best. Want to know something funny? I don't think she had ever seen me cry. I've seen her cry on many occasions, of course." Tim gave a little smile at that thought.

"She was my entire world, Luke. I've known her ever since I became conscious. You can learn a lot in a fourteen-year incubation stage where you are being raised to maturity, but

245

flirting was something I had to figure out on my own. The first few attempts were pretty pitiful, let me tell you. At the time she was seeing someone else, so she made sure that I knew that she was only doing her job and that I was just her project to take care of. So every time I would try asking her out, she would tell me that she already had to deal with me at work and didn't need a 'project boyfriend' in her outside life. She was not mean-spirited, it was a joke of course, but used it to make a point. Finally, one day after she said that I told her 'Well maybe I wouldn't be a project if you were better at your job'. That stopped her dead in her tracks until she realized that I was teasing her and then she playfully slugged me in the arm as she laughed and laughed. After that it was like she looked at me in a whole new light, but even then it still took time and patience. She wanted to make sure it was not a Florence Nightingale syndrome situation...but eventually she accepted the fact that she had fallen head over heels for me." This last statement caused Tim to start to break down in tears again.

"I never thought I would be a father, Luke. I was blindsided when she told me, but soon after I felt a joy that I can't even explain. She died the same night she told me we were going to have a child..."

Luke was surprised to feel wetness on his own cheeks after hearing Tim's story. He tried to brush the tears away as nonchalantly as he could, but it seemed as though Tim still noticed. Deciding that maybe he had chosen the wrong topic to

Forbidden Origins-apostasia

distract Tim with, he thought that maybe he should try again, only with something less emotional this time.

"You know Tim; you have been working yourself to death. I don't think I've seen you sleep more than two hours at a time since you've come here, and you barely remember to eat anything. It's no wonder you are struggling with control and don't feel like yourself. You have to start taking better care of your body if you don't want it to rebel against you."

The change of topic did seem to distract Tim, but he didn't look as though he agreed with Luke's advice. "No, no, I'll be fine. I have to finish this code writing I started. I think I figured out..."

As he turned back to the desk to study the papers he had laid out, Luke pulled a syringe out of his lab coat pocket. He had made it a habit to carry a couple of tranquilizers around just in case Tim had an episode. Tim was already so distracted by his work that he hardly seemed to notice when Luke moved closer to him. But as he rolled up his sleeve and started to inject him, Tim stopped what he was doing and looked questioningly at Luke.

Luke told him, "Don't fight it Tim, just let yourself relax." Feeling drowsy, Tim tried to speak but all that came out was, "Whaaah..." then slumped down in his chair. Not long after that he was breathing heavily, but in a deep sleep.

Luke soon realized that he should have laid Tim down first, but in the moment it seemed like a good idea. Picking Tim up by the armpits he started to drag him towards the living room

247

D.K. Ratcliffe

so he could put him on the couch. Just as he was leaving the office he heard a raised voice.

"What did you do!?"

Startled, Luke dropped poor Tim on the ground with a loud THUNK. Looking up he saw Paul standing there laughing at him. "Very funny, ha-ha...instead of cracking jokes why don't you help me move him to the living room." Still chucking, Paul complied and lifted Tim's legs and together they moved him to the couch and laid him down.

"So really, what's with sleeping beauty here?" Paul asked Luke.

"Well, he hasn't been sleeping and his condition is getting worse, so he needs some rest. I'm glad that all this is almost over, I don't think he can hold out too much longer...hey, what are you doing here by the way?"

Paul smiled, realizing just how much he startled Luke and replied. "Things have been going smoother than anticipated, and so I thought I would bring over the final work that Tim's going to need my help with. So I came to share the good news with you both, but instead I come back to find you dragging an unconscious Tim all through the cabin." Always the smart-aleck Paul couldn't help but to put one more jab in.

"At least now I know what you guys have been doing with your spare time while I've been away."

Luke could only roll his eyes as he continued to try and catch his breath. Tim was not a small man, so it took a lot of

248

effort to get him as far as he did on his own. But as usual, no retort was necessary for Paul to carry on.

"Anyway, it's almost time. The programming as far as I can tell is successful and hasn't raised any type of suspicion. All I need are those security hacks for the base and the fake IDs."

Luke smiled in relief that this was finally coming to a close. "I can hardly wait."

•

CHAPTER EIGHTEEN
The MUD PIT

(beep) $-^-$ (beep) $-^-$ (beep) $-^-$ (beep)

The rhythmic sounds of a heart monitor was flowing through the ears of clone #43 as he was coming into consciousness. Listening to the beeps, he found that he could expand his hearing outward and hear other sounds outside of the repetitive beeps. He recognized the different sounds as people's voices, without understanding how he knew this. Even the words registered in his brain, although he'd never heard human speech before. Somehow he was able to comprehend not only what the words meant, but the tones that went along with them. He was able to determine there were two people speaking with one another, the first being soft spoken and questioning, and in contrast the second voice was much deeper and had an edge of superiority to it.

Opening his eyes proved to be difficult, as there was something bright that caused him pain and discomfort. Somehow he knew that placing his hands over his face and turning to his side would help dim the brightness. Having never used his eyes before, he quickly became frustrated by the fact that everything he saw was blurry. Knowing that things should be clearer and in better focus, he tried rubbing his eyes, which only seemed to make it worse. So he tried opening his mouth to complain to the two voices, but the only sound that escaped was a croak. Beyond aggravated at this point, he angrily slammed his hand on the surface he was laying on, and the voices suddenly stopped. The next thing he knew, a firm but gentle hand touched his arm and pushed his upper torso back to a laying position.

"I know this must be disorienting, but can you please stay on your back for me?"

He nodded yes, and the soft voice answered, "Thank you. It's good to see you awake forty-three. I'm going to open each of your eyes one at a time and you're going to feel some liquid drop into them. It's going to help your vision clear and focus. If you can understand what I'm telling you raise your right hand, please." Just as he had raised his hand the person applied the drops to his eyes, then instructed him to blink several times rapidly.

Once he had, the voice thanked him again and said, "Now hold your eyes very still while I count to ten. Once I've reached ten you can open your eyes."

The voice started counting and when he heard ten, he opened his eyes to the world, seeing it clearly for the first time. The person standing in front of him was slight of frame, but looked firm. He recognized that it was a female, and a good looking one at that. She had almond shaped brown eyes, full red lips and long black hair that flowed down her back in a ponytail. She smiled at him expectantly, and he realized she was waiting for him to say something. He tried to clear the scratchiness from his throat, but all he got was a rough feeling tearing at the back of his throat.

"I'll grab you some water," she said, then proceeded to the sink and returned with a cup.

"Drink this, it'll help your throat." Just as he was taking a drink, a ruckus started happening on the far side of his room, where there appeared to be another man lying on a table.

She noticed where his attention went and informed him, "They've been keeping an eye on forty-eight, but it's not looking good." Just as she finished her statement several doctors flooded into the room. Their appearance was followed by desperate words such as "we are losing him" and "multiple failures of the organs."

He couldn't see the other clone from where he was laying, but some blood had squirted across the room. The nurse that was taking care of him quickly stood up and pulled a separating curtain to reduce the distraction and gruesomeness.

"Sorry about that, sometimes things don't go as planned."

Although his throat still felt scratchy, #43 was finally able to get out the words, "Who are you?"

"I'm Nurse Stefanie, your personal care taker and therapist until we get you out of here," she said with a proud tone in her voice.

This was disappointing news for #43 to hear; he realized in that moment that before he made his escape, she would have to die.

After a day of vigorous testing and exercises, #43 was escorted to his small holding cell for the night. Making his way to a military style bed placed to the other side of the room, he laid down on it and patiently waited for the perfect time to strike.

Out of the fifty soldiers created, forty-nine survived. And each one of those soldiers were intricately connected through the neural-chip. Just as computers can send and receive messages to one another, the soldiers were able to do this telepathically. This was meant to be part of their original design as it would enable them to be more efficient soldiers and work together as a formidable team. That aspect of their programming was not meant to be 'turned on' until their military demonstration, but Paul made sure that it was effective immediately upon their awakening. He needed them to be able to communicate in this way for their takeover of the underground base. In addition to this he included in their software the ability to manipulate all the computer systems in the cloning facility.

Just after the midnight hour, the soldiers started using their mind control to do exactly that. They made one hour loops on video surveillance recordings, shut down emergency alarms, and opened all the electronic locks on the doors, including the ones on their holding cells. From there the forty-nine soldiers moved on to their individual tasks of taking over the cloning department of the MUD PIT. Mostly using their bare hands, they killed anyone who stood in their way. This did not take much, as most were lab techs and scientists, so were unarmed. And as for the guards, the weapons that they had did not help to save them...the soldiers were just too fast and powerful. They collected all the firearms they came across, but for stealth reasons knew not fire them until it became necessary.

Just as one of the guards was about to come out of the bathroom, he thought he heard some commotion coming from the hallway. Opening the door just a little bit, he looked out to see what was happening and saw one of the clones dropping a fellow guard to the ground after having his hands around his neck. Just then some radio static was coming in through his radio earpiece. Startled, he quickly closed the door while trying not to make any noise. Since he knew better than to try and take one of those things on by himself, he rushed to a stall and stood on the toilet to hide his feet.

Pressing the talk button on his device he whispered nervously, "Attention Phoenix, this is Dragon... Attention Phoenix, this is Dragon..." (~static~)

"Dragon, this is Phoenix" (~static~)

"Ice Burg, Ice Burg, Ice Burg. Sector Delta 1-0-9. At least one casualty, maybe more, I repeat at least one casualty, do you copy." (~static~)

"Roger Dragon, copy that on the Ice Burg in Sector 1-0-9 with casualties." (~static~) "Sending reinfor..." (~static~)

The guard was alarmed that the communication got cut off, but at this point there was nothing else he could do. Taking a minute to catch his breath, he untucked his uniform and used it to wipe the sweat off his face. Only two minutes or so had passed since he saw the clone kill the guard, but to him it felt like it had been an hour.

All of a sudden he heard a couple gun shots and screams. The next thing he knew the bathroom door was flung open followed by the sounds of someone in total agony. Then a loud smack echoed through the bathroom as if someone had fallen. The moans drew nearer as he could hear the individual dragging himself towards the stalls. Before the injured man could reach one of them, the bathroom door opened again, but this time sounding like it was going to fly off the hinges.   Next there was a loud cry of "NO!!!" followed by three gunshots, each one more deafening then the last. There was a brief moment of quiet until he heard a loud snapping sound.

Covering his mouth to keep from making any noise the guard tried to be as still as possible to not be detected. Solid footsteps approached closer to his hiding place, and his breath caught in his throat. The steps were going at a normal pace, but to him it felt like slow motion. The side profile of a boot coated in blood appeared just on the other side of the stall. Blood dripped down from higher up, quickly followed by three crushed bullet fragments. What seemed liked hours later, the boot finally turned towards the opposite direction and a faucet was running. When the figure finally made its way back out the door, the terrified guard slowly slid down against the wall and got his feet back to the floor. He let out a shaky breath and sent out a quick prayer of thanks to the fates that had allowed him to remain undetected.

The clones fought their way to an armory that was designated for their field training. At this point in the attack there was no hiding it anymore, so they were gathering up all weapons to assist in their takeover of the MUD PIT base. The objective was to directly kill anyone with major importance and obtain all

Forbidden Origins-apostasia

advanced weapons and ammunition. Any survivors would be taken care of with the blast that would demolish the entire base. #43's specific mission was to locate the armored buses, and bring them closer to the supplies so that other clones could help load them up with the stolen goods.

The echoes of screams and gun fire became dimmer as they faded in the distance. The guard in the rest room decided it was finally time to leave the safety of the stall. His side arm raised and aimed at the ready, he cracked opened the door and slipped out when he saw the bathroom was indeed empty. As he saw a fellow colleague lying on the ground mangled and with his neck twisted at an unnatural angle, he spun around back into the stall, losing his lunch in the toilet he had just been standing on. After regaining his composure, he once again left the stall and this time avoided looking down on the ground. Opening the door to the bathroom and peeking down the hallway, seeing that it was clear he cautiously made his way down the corridor.

As he passed one of the rooms he heard some whispering coming from inside. Making sure that it was clear, he moved in and quietly asked, "Is someone in here?"

Another voiced loudly whispered back. "Yes! Over here, behind the desk."

Walking behind the desk he saw two ladies crouched down, one of whom was Nurse Stefanie. Kneeling down he asked Stefanie, "Aren't you one of the techs working with these clones?"

Taking offense, she replied with some bitterness in her voice. "Yes, but I didn't foresee them doing this, nor do I know how to make them stop."

Taking a deep breath, the guard then sat down beside them. "Relax, I wasn't accusing you of anything, I know that you aren't to blame. I always had a bad feeling that these unnatural soldiers were ticking time bombs that could go off at any moment. I was just wondering if you had any idea that this could happen. But obviously someone has to be responsible. Truth be told, my money is on Dr. Sullivan."

Taken aback by his comment she said, "Well I don't know who you think you are, but I know Dr. Sullivan personally and he would never allow this to happen."

Giving a smirk he responded to that with, "Yeah, well its happening. So directly his fault or not, clearly something went haywire. But don't you find it suspicious that just a few months ago some missiles go off and hit the Federal Duplications building, supposedly the blame being 'faulty wiring'? And Dr. Sullivan not only had a hand in the programming of the missiles, but also was one of the few people assigned to the building that day that conveniently avoided the disaster? And now this?"

Forbidden Origins-apostasia

The other lady finally chimed in. "Look you two, we can keep arguing or we can try to get out of here. Do you have a plan, officer?"

Giving a sigh he responded. "I wish I did. I'm sure Stefanie here can attest to the fact that the three of us are no match for these guys. But you're right, we can't stay here...I have a feeling this place won't be standing too much longer. And before you ask, yes, I base that opinion on what we all know happened to the Federal Duplications building."

Putting their differences behind them, all three decided it was time to escape.

Moving down the blood soaked halls, the unlikely trio passed dead bodies of familiar co-workers as they pressed on. Finally nearing an exit, they took cover in a nearby room to assess the situation outside before jumping out in the open. As they cautiously approached the window, to their surprise they found Paul sitting in a chair with his head down in his hands.

"Dr. Sullivan?" Stefanie asked, checking to see if it was really him and if he was injured.

Looking up Paul replied "Yes."

"What are you doing, and what's going on?!" Stefanie questioned.

Paul felt dazed and didn't know how to reply, so he didn't.

"We have to get out of here," the security guard said with urgency, while pulling the blinds at the window open just enough so that he could see out.

Paul still had no response. As soon as the guard saw that all was quiet outside and the exit they were near did not appear to be watched, he demanded to the whole group, "Come on, now is our chance! Let's go, before it's too late!"

Seeing that Paul still was not making an effort to understand or reply to the dire situation at hand, Stefanie said "You guys go, I'll stay with the Dr. Maybe if I can get him to talk we can fix this. Don't wait for us, just get out of here and alert the authorities on what is going on."

Frustrated with Stefanie and her refusal to leave without the non-responsive Dr., but seeing that it would be pointless to try and stay to change her mind, the guard shrugged and grabbed the other lady's hand and started to lead her out of the room and towards the exit. He had a feeling that they were running out of time, and there was no sense in all of them being suicidal.

"Dr., do you have any idea about what is going on? If anyone can figure this out and stop this, I know it is you! Please, work with me here! Say *something*! Don't let any more people die. You've done so much to save countless lives, so let's *do* this!" Stefanie tried begging, pleading, and anything else she could think of to try and get Paul to come to grips with the situation. She was determined that they fix the problem. Or at the very least to get out of there and escape.

But Paul just continued to have a blank stare and occasionally shook his head back and forth, as if to say 'it's no use'. Giving up on her other tactics that did not seem to have any

Forbidden Origins-apostasia

effect, she tried placing her hands on his and attempted to cajole and comfort him to come back to reality.

"Dr., if there is nothing we can do, then we need to get out of here. Don't you understand what will happen if they find us? The world can't afford to lose a mind like yours, so we need to leave now!" Strangely enough, Stefanie heard almost her own exact words repeated coming from behind her, but in a much deeper voice.

"It's time to leave now, Dr."

After a split second she realized that she knew that voice, and with that recognition her hands started shaking and her breath caught painfully in her chest.

"Dr.?" she cried out in question, hoping against hope that Dr. Sullivan was not part of all this like the security guard suggested.

"I'm sorry," Paul whispered, finally appearing to come back to reality.

Stefanie then turned around to see the figure standing behind her, and it was exactly who she was expecting, Forty-three. "Why?" she looked back at Paul with tears running down her face. Paul met her eyes finally but never even had a chance to answer.

Stefanie felt a cold and sharp object being placed on her neck, and suddenly she looked down in horror to see her life's blood pouring right out of her. She grabbed at her throat as if to

261

try and stop the flow, but it was too late. She fell face first to the ground, unmoving.

Paul looked down at her in heart break, but he knew that there was nothing to be done.

#43 knelt down on the ground and gently turned beautiful nurse Stefanie over so he could check for a pulse. Feeling none, he started to stand back up. At the last second he impulsively decided to close her eyes; he couldn't stand the look of fear and accusation that he saw in them. So far, this was the only kill that he felt regretful to complete. Standing back up from kneeling over her body, he signaled Paul to come with him.

Outside, the security guard and the other woman ran as fast as they could. It had been quiet enough when they had first made it outside, but shortly after it seemed like a bona fide war zone out there. They stayed low and tried to find cover as often as they could. But trying to avoid the cross fire from heavy machine guns, grenades and sniper fire was no simple task. Buildings constantly sounded like they were exploding, while fire lit up paths that led to more destruction.

Avoiding these paths during one of their mad dashes to the next point of safety, all of a sudden the guard felt a stinging pain come from behind on his left side. He let out a cry of agony and ended up tumbling face first into the dirt.

Realizing he'd been shot, the lady turned back around and grabbed him under the arms and with all her might starting dragging him. She hadn't made it too far when another shot was fired and she fell straight back.

The guard had a feeling that this was sniper fire, so he laid lifeless for a couple minutes. Hoping it was safe, he finally inched forward on his elbows to see if the woman was still alive. Unfortunately his suspicion was right, a sniper had put a bullet right into her head. Looking up ahead he saw that he was pretty close to the outer woods, so he had to keep moving. Crawling on his belly he finally made it to a tree and used it to prop himself up to view the base. Just at that moment he saw four black buses pulling away from the compound and within seconds the entire base blew up and lit the night sky.

The man couldn't believe that all this had happened when just over an hour ago his life had seemed so normal. Gingerly he felt his exit wound and he knew that it was bad; the pain was becoming unbearable, and breathing was quite the chore. He knew that he had lost a lot of blood in his struggle to reach the woods, so he came to the realization that he likely was not going to be found until it was too late.

Painfully reaching into his pocket, he pulled out his wallet. Opening it up he dug out a picture and threw the wallet to the side; it was a picture of his wife. "I'm sorry baby, I won't be around for much longer. I'm sorry for all the things I said to hurt you, and wish that I could have another chance to be a better husband." He started sobbing. "I would give anything to hold you one last time -" His last couple words had become such a struggle, he broke out into a sweat and starting panting. The picture he had been holding fluttered to the ground as he let the weakness overcome him and he took his last, painful breath.

CHAPTER NINTEEN
A Task for Laski

After a full night of driving through back roads, four black armored buses with Paul and forty-nine soldiers transporting advanced explosives, weapons and ammunition, arrived at Luke's cabin.

When Tim and Luke saw the buses pull in, they both felt relief and amazement that the plan had worked this far. They hurried outside to meet the soldiers and greet Paul, who had jumped out of the bus he was in the second that it had parked.

D.K. Ratcliffe

"Well, how did it go?" Luke asked.

"Fine," Paul stated flatly.

"Are you okay?" Luke said.

"Yes, I just need to take a shower and get some sleep. Make sure you have the soldiers start cleaning and preparing the equipment. Hide the buses with the ghillie tents and pass out the ID's and rental cars to the clones on the assassination missions." Paul said all this in an abrupt manner as he pushed past them to walk in the cabin. Tim and Luke looked at each other and shrugged their shoulders, then proceeded to do as Paul instructed.

As Luke dispersed orders to all the other soldiers, Tim gathered the five clones that were assigned to kill key government officials and other important figures in the cloning world. Because they already had the plan downloaded in their software, there was no need to go over any details. So instead he showed them the rental cars they would be using and presented them with prepaid credit cards for gas and miscellaneous items. He also ensured that they had all the weapons they may need, including firearms with silencers. Then he showed them the assorted tools and items that were in the trunks of the rentals that were for any contingencies, including the possibility that a kidnapping would need to happen. Finally, he passed out the five fake ID's that Paul had created for each of the five assassins.

Forbidden Origins-apostasia

Calling out their clone numbers one at a time he had them take the ID with their new name. "Okay #43, you are now Marc Laski."

#43 walked forward and took his ID card. After him #49 was called, so the newly named Marc Laski took this time to glance briefly at the picture and information on the card. How strange it seemed to not know if the picture resembled him, as he had not had an opportunity yet to see his own reflection. During his musings the rest of the clones had turned and walked away towards their assigned vehicle. Dr. Phillips was gazing at him curiously, probably wondering why he hadn't left yet. Without saying a word, he tucked the ID into his back pocket and turned around and went to the rental he was to use, ready to begin his next mission.

'Marc Laski' traveled day and night, only stopping for food and gas. When he arrived at his destination it was late in the next day. He decided it would be best to park across the street and wait for the family to go to bed. He was to assassinate the leading geneticist – Matthew Lenten – from a specialized department in the cloning community. Then he needed to gather all the man's research, but he had instructions to not to hurt the family.

As the hours passed and it seemed as though the family would never go to bed, suddenly there was quite the commotion coming from inside the house. Yelling and screaming, with sounds like breaking glass. Not long after the commotion had started a man appeared, storming out of the house. After slamming the door hard, he went up to the SUV parked out front and got in. Laski had to act quickly before he lost the guy, so he turned the engine on and threw it into gear. He drove up the man's driveway and pulled in behind the SUV before he had the chance to back out.

The man opened his door and started yelling furiously, but by this time Laski had already jumped out of his rental and was halfway up the drive. Sooner than the angry man could step out of his vehicle and finish his rant, Laski was upon him and thrusted his knife into the man's throat. The man flailed his arms in surprise, but he was already dead by the time Laski pushed him down to the floor of the SUV. Upon closer inspection Laski was able to verify that it was the geneticist he was here to kill. He then closed the vehicle door, leaving the body inside. It was now time to look for everything the geneticist had in terms of research lying around that needed to be taken and destroyed.

Walking up to the door that the geneticist had just stormed out of, Laski tried the handle and found that it wasn't

Forbidden Origins-apostasia

locked. Grabbing his side arm, he stepped inside the house with his gun raised. It was a big house, so he made sure to check all the rooms that he passed, but was pretty certain that the family members were towards the center of the house. He could hear their voices getting closer as he circled around through the long, winding hallway. Eventually he reached what appeared to be the living area where two young boys, no more than six and seven years old were playing.

The older of the two boys noticed Laski first and cried out in a panic, "Mommy!"

Quickly following her child's call an angry feminine voice hollered from a different room. "That better not be you Matt, I told you to leave!" The voice became louder as she neared the living room. Expecting it to be her husband - or maybe soon to be ex-husband, by the sound of things - she furiously entered the room with a phone tucked close to her chest. She stopped short immediately, being caught off guard as she realized that it definitely was not her husband. She stared at the strange man and the gun in his hand for a few heartbeats, unable to move or speak.

Laski leveled the gun at her and mouthed the words "Hang up the phone."

Trying to stay calm and not make any rash decisions that could wind up getting her kids or herself hurt, she lifted the phone to her face and with a firm voice said, "Mom, I think I'm going to have to let you go. I love you."

Without waiting for any response she hung up, then directed all her attention to the gunman. "Listen, I don't know what you want, but I'll give you anything. Just please, let my boys go." Other than the crack in her voice, she did not let her terror show. She knew she had to keep it together so she could do everything in her power to protect her sons.

His gun still aimed, Laski reached into his jacket and pulled out some duct tape, which he threw in front of the mother. "Restrain them."

Looking down at the item she realized he was ordering her to pick up the tape and do his dirty work. She looked back up at him with water filled eyes, and she felt like a dam about to burst. "I can't," she said.

Laski looked at her more intently. "Your arms are in working order. You are capable."

Feeling overwhelmed, she could not hold back the flood of tears any longer. "I know I'm *capable*. Just please, give me your word that you won't hurt them. If you've been hired by my husband, just take me and leave them out of this."

Laski realized then that when she said she couldn't do it, she wasn't referring to not being physically able. Rather she was too concerned about the welfare about her boys to be able to handle it emotionally. In order to have her compliance, it seemed he needed to provide reassurance that he was not going to harm them.

Forbidden Origins-apostasia

"You have no need to worry about their safety, I have orders to let them live... if you comply. You have my word."

Wishing that she could have more encouragement that they would be ok, but realizing that was the best guarantee she was going to get out of him, she reluctantly picked up the tape and went over to her boys. While restraining them, she tried her best to comfort and keep them calm. "Ok now boys, we are just going to play a little game. You know how much you like to play 'cops and robbers'?"

The boys looked at her with wide eyes and solemnly nodded their heads.

"Well, this man is going to pretend to be the robber, and if we are very good then the cops will come and rescue us. Now, won't that be fun?"

Because the boys could sense her fear they looked as though they were not so sure this was fun. "But Mommy-" one of the boys started to whine.

"The mouths too." Laski said to her, just as she was finishing up. She glared at him with undisguised hatred, but did what he told her to. As one last attempt to shield them from anything that was about to happen, she gave them their tablets with the headphones connected so that they could watch a movie, which should prevent them from hearing anything more that was going on.

Laski was curious about what she was doing but decided to let her continue if it helped to keep the children from being frightened. He did not enjoy playing the 'robber' as he knew this made him the bad guy, but carrying out his mission superseded his feelings on the matter.

After Mrs. Lenten finished with the boys, Laski walked over to her and took the tape from her hands and proceeded to tape her hands and legs. Pushing her gently onto the couch, he then took the boys and placed them onto the couch next to her. Coming back to the mother, he squatted next to the couch to be eye level with her.

"You have done well so far Mrs. Lenten, so I just want to remind you that I won't hurt any of you if you continue to do what I ask. If you scream or try to do anything else stupid, I can't make any promises."

She nodded her head to indicate she understood and then asked, "So what do you want? You never answered my question from earlier. Did my husband hire you?"

Laski grinned and replied. "No, he did not hire me. I was actually hired to kill him..." Just as he said that she started to build breath to let out a scream. Quickly he covered her mouth; she tried biting his hand, but it was no use.

"Listen, I keep trying to tell you that I did not come here to hurt you, so please don't make me." The woman struggled with calming herself down, but finally shook her head and he was able to lift his hand away from her face.

Forbidden Origins-apostasia

"I need you to help me locate all your husband's work. Any computers, papers, letters, and books that he has, plus anything that he's ever even looked at. Understand?"

Confused, but not wanting to argue, she again nodded her head in agreement.

So that she could lead the way, Laski took the tape off her legs but left her hands confined behind her back. After taking him down a different hallway than the one he had used, she led him to a large room that was filled with books and filing cabinets.

"This is his office, he kept everything in here."

He sat her in a corner of the room away from the door, so that he could work and keep an eye on her at the same time. Immediately after he got down to business, pulling out some heavy duty trash bags from his pocket. He began to throw everything he could find that had information on it into them.

After watching him do this for several minutes Mrs. Lenten finally asked, "Do you have a problem with my husband?" Laski was focused on his task and did not bother to answer. Seeing that she wasn't getting a response, the lady gave a little mirthless laugh and continued. "Who am I kidding, everyone has a problem with him. If she had ever met him, I'm sure even Mother Teresa would have had a problem with him. Matt was one arrogant, selfish, pig-headed SOB, that's for sure. I don't even know if I should feel sad or relieved that he's dead now."

After all that and the man still did not appear interested in talking, so she tried one more tactic to get his attention. "Well if you won't tell me anything, could you at least do something for me really quick?"

To his credit, Laski stopped for a moment and looked at her in question.

"In the top drawer to the left is a carton of cigarettes. They're my husbands, but I sure could use one at the moment...and it's not like he's going to need them anymore." At that she gave another one of her terrible little laughs. She did not expect him to agree to her request, but when she saw that he was headed that way she quickly added, "And don't forget the lighter next to it."

Laski grabbed the cigarettes and lighter like she asked, if for nothing else than to shut her up. Bringing them to her, he took one out and placed it in her mouth.

Just as he was focusing on trying to light it for her, she brought up her foot and kicked him between the legs as hard as she could.

Laski was neither amused nor fazed, and rolled his eyes.

Mrs. Lenten was a bit shell-shocked that her well-placed kick seemed to have no effect whatsoever. But then she was even more amazed when he lit the cigarette that was still hanging from her mouth, and then continued working. Sighing in defeat she accidentally took a drag and then ended up coughing

violently from the smoke. She then proceeded to spit the
cigarette out and frantically started stomping it out.

"Ugh! Those things are even worse than I remembered! I
haven't tried smoking a cigarette since high school."

Her antics gave Laski a slight grin, finding her somewhat
humorous. "You don't say? I would have never guessed."

After a night of throwing any little bit of information in
plastic garbage bags and piling them up in his rental car, it was
now time to leave and meet back at Luke's cabin. Before leaving
he threw the mother and the kids in a hallway closet. After
restraining her legs again and taping her mouth, he told her, "I'm
going to barricade you three in here, but I will send help after
just a little while."

Then he closed the door and put a heavy piece of furniture
in front of it. He wanted to make sure that the woman was not
able to get out until the help arrived and he was long gone. It
would not do to get caught at this point as he still had one more
mission to carry out. Once he was well on his way and out of the
area he made a 911 call on his prepaid phone and gave the house
address, then tossed the phone out the window.

Arriving back at Luke's he immediately started to unload his car full of trash bags and throw them into a fire that was going. Paul had started the fire earlier, in preparation of the five assassins bringing back all the research and any other information that they could find from their targets.

After everything was unloaded and starting to burn, Laski noticed a picture that had fallen out of one of the bags, just on the edge of the fire. It was in a beautiful wooden frame, and somehow had escaped the flames completely and was not damaged. After walking over closer to inspect it, he saw that it was a picture of Mrs. Lenten. Through the process of grabbing documents and such, her picture somehow had ended up in one of the trash bags. Grabbing the picture before it was consumed by the flames, he walked back and sat on an old log bench near the fire.

As Paul came around the back of the cabin he noticed that while the other soldiers were busy preparing for the next big event, one clone was sitting in solitude by the fire, intently focused on something he was holding. Walking over to Laski, Paul politely asked if it was alright to sit by him.

"So everything went well?" Paul asked.

"The mission was very successful, sir," Laski replied.

Forbidden Origins-apostasia

At this formal response Paul chuckled a little under his breath, then said, "I'm glad to hear it. You're #43, right?"

Laski looked at Paul, then nodded his head. "Yes," he said, then looked back down at the picture. "Do I stand out from the others, Dr.?"

Paul looked at Laski, then stared for a moment at the fire; years of collaborated research burning to ashes. Paul knew his work very well, so it was clear to him that 43's behavior was a little off. But what was most strange was the fact that the clone soldier recognized that he stood out. "What makes you think that you're different from the others?"

"We are all telepathically interconnected, so I know the thoughts of all the other clones. They follow their programming, but beyond that there is nothing. They may look human but are really just empty shells with neural-software. They don't feel emotions, have any curiosity or desire to do anything more than what they know they need to do."

"And you do?" Paul asked curiously.

Instead of answering his question, Laski surprised him with, "I know how #48 died."

Paul was startled at the diversion as well as the revelation. "Oh yeah? And how is that?"

"#48 was different, like me. I don't know why, but when he awakened it seemed as though his body rejected his mind. I know this because he was communicating with me just before he died. He fought so hard to stay, but the battle was too much for him."

Paul was a little speechless about what this clone was saying. Finally, after a moment he said, "It's never been my job to 'soul search', but when I was just a boy I was forced to attend church. It was here that I first learned about souls and a higher being...it's probably all just nonsense, but after these last few days I feel like anything is possible. I know that Luke has his own theories about the natural order of things and never agreed with the process of cloning, but I always felt that if it is scientifically possible to do, why not?

I can only tell you what I do know, which is that the human body is more complex than I care to even think about. You, the other soldiers, my dear friend Tim, all have a severe genetic disorder. Maybe because I'm not near as good at my job as I once thought, I don't really know for sure. Some type of 'virus', if you will, is taking over your genetics; it's what I'm calling an interdimensional mutation. I have no idea why it's happened or what's going on exactly. All I know is that the DNA mutations are somehow allowing for another entity to come in and host your body.

Unfortunately, although this mutation seems to be coming originally from clones, it does appear that it can act as a contagion and infect naturally born humans. Whatever this entity is, could put the human race into extinction. Or perhaps end up leading into a different phase of evolution, I don't know.

I realize now that it's silly to think we are here in this universe by ourselves without someone or something else waiting to take over.

Either way, if there is such thing as a soul, then maybe that is what makes you different, forty-three. My advice to you would be to not allow yours to slip away. If you have to keep fighting for it, then fight for it. Help us with this final mission to preserve the souls of others. Because if we do not succeed then the mutation will take over and by then the matter of 'souls' will be moot, as there will be none left."

After the doctor walked away, Laski started to throw the picture back into the fire, but couldn't seem to bring himself to do it. He stared at it for a few moments longer and then finally decided to take the picture out of the frame and stick it in his pocket. As he started to fold it, he realized there was something written on the back. Smoothing it back out Laski flipped the picture over and saw the inscription: 'XOXO, Maggie'.

Heading back into the cabin, Paul saw Tim and Luke playing cards. They looked up at him as he walked in and invited him to join the game. "Nah, thanks, but I'll pass for right now. Do you guys want to know something interesting? I just talked with one of the soldiers out there, and apparently he's turned me into a philosopher. I blame you Tim," Paul said jokingly, while shaking his head. Without waiting for a response he proceeded to the kitchen, mumbling to himself about how even creations think they are experts on life now. Tim and Luke looked at each other and laughed, then continued playing their game.

Paul could hear Tim and Luke laughing in the other room as he was pulling a cold beer out of the fridge. It felt good to hear Tim laugh again and enjoying a little happiness. Unfortunately, that happiness would have to be short-lived, as all they had left was the next couple of days.

CHAPTER TWENTY
Out with a Bang

"So this is goodbye huh?" Luke asked while Paul and Tim were about to enter the bus.

"Yeah, I suppose so," Paul replied.

Luke took a deep breath and finally spoke his mind. "I know we have had this argument numerous times, but I can't help but ask you one more time if you're sure you want to do this. I know we haven't quite found the cure yet, but if I just had a little bit more time..."

"No!" Tim said abruptly. "It's just too dangerous. It was all I could do to make it this long without transforming again, and I can't stand the thought of becoming the beast even once more."

Luke hung his head in disappointment at Tim's answer, knowing that there was nothing he could do or say at this point to talk his friends out of their part of the final mission.

"Alright, well then...I'm really glad I had the opportunity to get to know you. Say hi to Aavah for me when you get to the other side."

Reaching out to shake Luke's hand, Tim realized just how much he had started to like the man. "I'll do that. Thank you for everything Luke." Not wanting to be overcome with emotion, Tim quickly grasped Luke's hand and gave him a hearty clap of the back, and turned around and got onto the bus.

After that it was Paul's turn to give his final goodbye. "You know Luke, I used to think guys like you were fools to fight against our research and say it was 'immoral'. I thought that Eden was the end all and be all for the human race, so I felt like your efforts were not only ridiculous, but insulting. The ironic thing is now that I see who the real fool was. Whatever you end up doing for the rest of your life, never stop fighting for what you know is right."

Luke wasn't sure what to say to all that, but before he could even form a response, Paul was already talking again.

"Well, no sense in wasting any more daylight, it's time to get this show on the road." With that, Paul gave a brisk shake of Luke's hand and followed after Tim onto the bus.

Luke wasn't sure why, but Paul's words affected him in a place he couldn't quite put his finger on. He remained standing there in pensive silence and watched Tim and Paul ride off into the distance along with four buses, forty-nine soldiers, and an obscene amount of weapons and explosives. After having been part of something so big that was now drawing to a close, he wondered how in the world he was going to go back to the routine of his normal life.

Some hours later, the four buses neared their destination. Intense anxiety ate away at both Tim and Paul, to the point where both of them took turns to vomiting in the bus. Paul's anxiousness stemmed from his memories of what it was like at the MUD PIT during their hostile takeover. He was not looking forward to reliving that nightmare...the screams, the blood, the death. It did make him second guess if it was true that the means justified the end. That was always the motto for the company he worked for, so it hardly seemed as though anything they lived by could ever be the right thing to do. But he also knew that mankind would not continue without the elimination of cloning and the power hungry people in charge of it. He just couldn't stomach the idea of the carnage that was about to happen in their plans to destroy it all.

Tim had it even worse, but his was due to the monster inside wanting to be unleashed. All the stress and the progression of his virus made him very close to his breaking point. Paul was careful to inject Tim with relaxers continually. It was important to him to have his old friend by his side and to complete the mission with him. And if the beast came out, it would no longer be Tim, that's for sure. Who knows how much worse the carnage would be if that were to happen.

As for the forty-nine soldiers split between the four buses, they couldn't have been calmer; for them, this was their moment. The carrying out of this final mission was the culmination of everything that they were programmed for. Even Laski was feeling completely composed, with perhaps even a touch of eagerness.

As they turned a corner the federal building was now in sight on the horizon. Paul's heart felt like it dropped to his knees. 'And here I thought I couldn't get any more nervous', Paul mused to himself, losing his lunch one last time. But at this point he felt that it was too late to look back now, so they had to keep pressing forward.

Looming closer and closer, the buses neared their target. Paul guided Tim down on the bus floor so that the two of them would have cover. They heard as the first bus sped up and crashed through a security post's arm gate. Shortly after, theirs sped up, heading towards the front entrance. The soldier driving

Forbidden Origins-apostasia

the bus swung it around, then shifted quickly into reverse and floored it to ram the fancy glass entrance.

(CRASH) the sound of glass breaking into a million pieces was all around them. The people inside were stunned and disoriented, with no idea on what just hit them. Glass, debris and bodies scattered all over the place from the impact, including some of the security guards. The back doors of the bus flew open, releasing the soldiers within. Jumping out, they started taking control immediately and making demands.

"To the corner! Move it! Move it!" the soldiers yelled, organizing the captives. The people that tried running away were gunned down.

Panic and screaming arose from the crowd, "What do you want from us?" some of them cried out.

The soldiers did not answer or acknowledge the distress of the people but continued their single-minded tasks. From a distance, the hostages could see what seemed to be an endless array of weapons, ammo, and barrels being rolled out of the buses. They soon realized this building was going to become a war zone.

Once everything was unloaded, the soldiers began to structure themselves into the separate groups they were assigned for. Nine soldiers dispersed about the ground floor, keeping some hostages near the front entrance. Five soldiers were tasked with setting up the explosives they had brought with them around the building. The rest of the soldiers were divided into three more groups (one of which included Laski) to take over and guard the rest of the building and to gather more hostages. There was just one more clone that was not assigned to any of the other groups, as he was to escort Paul and Tim to the upper floor. Tim's weakness was getting so bad he needed Paul to help get him out of the bus and to walk.

Their escort clone came up to them and said, "It's time." With Tim's arm wrapped around Paul's shoulder they began their trek. They passed small groups of soldiers striding briskly through the halls, scouting out all the rooms and offices. They were to execute anyone they found on the spot. There would be no chances taken that anyone could escape.

Meanwhile, amidst all the chaos, federal agents that worked in the building started suiting up because of all the ruckus and alarms that had been going off. Before long, yells of, "On the ground!" were shouted by both the soldiers and agents, followed by storms of bullets raining down through halls and from room to room.

On the second floor Laski and two other soldiers were searching through the cafeteria, collecting and gathering more people for execution. The workers in the kitchen heard the commotion, and

Forbidden Origins-apostasia

after they peeked through the swinging doors they saw the terrifying soldiers pointing weapons and shouting orders at those within the cafeteria. Before they even had a chance to back away from the door, one of the soldiers looked up and started storming towards them.

Two of the chefs were even more horrified than the rest at the events that were happening, because they had the bad luck of having their seven-year-old daughter with them at work that day. It was not uncommon for them to have her there with them lately, as the daycare they used to send her to had permanently closed at the start of summer, and they had yet to find an alternative for her. She was such a sweet and well behaved child that none of the other employees seemed to mind, and in fact treated her like the kitchen mascot. She was their little unofficial taste tester that got to try all of the desserts and treats before they were sent out to the cafeteria. They had considered it such a blessing to be able to spend this special time with their daughter, but on this particular day it seemed like a nightmare.

Frantically the father cleared out a large shelf in the food pantry while the mother whispered, "We need you to be a good girl and hide in here sweetie. Just remember to be quiet as a church mouse and that mommy and daddy love you." They hugged her fiercely and placed her into the pantry. Just as they had closed the door Laski entered into the kitchen ordering everyone out and into the cafeteria.

The escort soldier leading Paul and Tim made sure every stairwell, hall, and office were clear before entering. The longer that Paul had the burden of Tim's weight, the more he struggled with keeping up with their bodyguard. As the clone was checking one of the last hallways before they reached their destination, he entered the doorway and spooked an agent that was just on the other side.

Tim and Paul could see the agent and clone shoot each other multiple times in the chest with assault rifles. The clone soldier spat some blood out of his mouth, then disappeared from their sight. Tim and Paul could not hear much of what was going on, so they moved slowly to the door, nervous to see what would be on the other side. Suddenly as quickly as he had disappeared, their escort reappeared scaring the wits out of the two men. The soldier was completely covered in blood, almost looking like he just walked off the set of a zombie apocalypse movie. Paul and Tim could only stare at him in shock.

"All clear. Let's move," the soldier said, completely cool and collected as if nothing at all had just happened.

Coming out of their state of shock, they continued to follow the escort into a high level office, containing a floor to ceiling window with a panoramic view of the city. Paul could finally sit Tim down and take a breather.

Forbidden Origins-apostasia

"Paul, are we the bad guys?" Tim asked in a raspy voice.

Paul took a good look at his friend and saw how much closer to death Tim appeared. Paul leaned his back against the wall and sighed.

"I thought that by destroying everything that I had helped to build, I was doing the right thing. But now Tim, I just don't know. If I could go back in time, I would have rather stuck with my first job at a grocery store than where I am today." At this Paul paused and ruminated for a moment about the direction his life had taken. "Maybe no matter which path we chose, we were destined to be the bad guys. Or maybe there is a God out there and he is punishing us for everything we have done. Who really knows?"

Shocked that Paul would make such a statement, Tim looked over and said, "Wow, I guess it is true that there are no atheists in a foxhole."

Within twenty minutes all the explosives were set. During this time the police and FBI had arrived outside and were getting situated. With the recent assassinations that had been reported combined with the Federal Duplications building being blown up just a few months prior, they weren't wasting any time to make a breach. There would be no peace talks, no negotiations of any kind. The orders were simply to recapture the building. Hundreds of brave officers from just about every branch of service had been called in to participate in the rescue. The Special Forces task team was ordered to save as many hostages as possible, but to shoot any terrorist they came across.

After scouting the area, they found the best potential points of the building for entry. They shattered windows and broke down doors to get in, ready for action. Mini battles started breaking out through the building again, with casualties increasing by the minute. The Special Forces team had years of experience of intense training and fighting, but nothing had prepared them for the powerful opponents they had before them. With the amount of bullets it took to take this enemy down, naturally it made the task force guys wonder who (or what) they were up against. But due to the sheer numbers of the task teams, the soldiers were finally starting to drop.

As the war waged on, Laski and his team prepared to stand their ground in the cafeteria. Laski was near the kitchen when he heard something moving somewhere on the other side of the door. Curious, he moved slowly into the kitchen to find where the noise was coming from. Honing in on the noise, he came to a pantry. Opening it up he discovered a small girl cradling herself and crying. Laski just stood there in a daze, suddenly flooded with memories of Maggie Lenten and her children.

As shots began to fire from the cafeteria, he snapped back to reality. From the sounds of it, the battle had finally made its way to their guarded area. Kneeling down, he reached out a hand to her.

"Don't be afraid. I am going to help you."

The little girl hesitated at first, but then stood up and took his hand.

From their position in the high rise office, Tim and Paul had the perfect vantage point to see the officers storm in and enter the building. Little did these brave men know that instead of saving the building and the captives within, they were only adding to the death count for when the whole thing exploded. Paul looked over at Tim and said, "This is wrong! We have to stop this." He started to walk towards the soldier but Tim grabbed the back of his shirt, trying to stop him.

"Paul, no! It's too late -!"

Paul broke free from Tim's grasp and rushed towards their bodyguard, who at this point had started firing out the hallway at the advancing task force.

"Stand down! STAND DOWN!" Paul yelled at their escort. The soldier did not listen to Paul and continued firing.

"I told you to stand down soldier! That's an order!" But even then the escort would not stop, and he starting to aim out the door again. Paul tried grabbing the clone's rifle, but was pushed back and he stumbled to the ground. As Paul got back up to confront him again, a stray bullet coming from outside came in and hit him in the neck. Paul rolled for cover, grabbing at the wound and putting pressure on it.

Tim saw what happened and started crawling over to Paul. Arriving to his friend, Tim saw how bad the wound was. Taking off his bullet proof vest he started ripping his shirt to make a field dressing.

"Tim?"

"Yes Paul, I'm right here."

"I guess I'm more afraid of death than I thought I would be."

Tim let out a breath that came out sounding like a sob. "I know...me too pal."

"If there is a God, do you think there is a chance he could save me?" Tim wanted so much to comfort the friend that he thought he had wanted to kill himself not that long ago. But instead, he answered him honestly.

"I wish I knew."

While Laski had his back turned from the entrance of the kitchen, another one of the soldiers came in.

"What are you doing #43? You are dangerously close to being considered AWOL right now. I sensed that you found another captive, so execute it and get back to your post."

With his back still to his fellow clone he responded, "I was just about to, #45. I will return to my post once I've completed my objective." Laski pulled out his sidearm, aimed it at the little girl, then pulled the trigger.

At that precise moment, #45 felt a huge pressure hit him right in his midsection. Looking down at himself, he realized he had been shot. He glanced back up just in time to see Laski turning, and the little girl standing there completely unharmed. He then realized that the other soldier had tricked him, by planting a false image into his head of what was occurring.

The next thing he knew, Laski was rushing towards him, aiming and firing more devastating blows to his body. Before he took on too much damage, he dove behind one of the kitchen islands to take cover and have time to pull out his own weapon.

Both men were now using their side arms for the short range, fast paced shootout. And at this point they both were using their telepathic communication to play mind games with one another, trying to throw each other off.

It was a very even match that could have lasted hours, but luckily a squad of officers entered, taking the other clone's attention off of Laski. Laski was hidden behind the sink area where the men who just entered could not see him, but the other clone was open to their view. A whole new battle began. The clone picked them all off one by one, but not without taking on severe injuries to himself.

By the time the coast was clear and Laski decided it was safe for him to come out, he saw the other clone in a sitting position, barely able to function. He walked towards the soldier and kicked the gun from the clone's hand, and knelt down beside him to get a closer look. With the small amount of strength he had left, the clone slowly lifted his hand and tried choking Laski.

"Nothing but an empty shell," Laski said with disgust to the clone and finished him off. As he stood up he noticed one of the dead task force officers appeared close to his size. Switching from his camo uniform and military gear he had since the MUD PIT base, he put on the officer's uniform hoping to blend in. Opening the pantry once more, he lifted up the girl and carried her out in his arms.

Forbidden Origins-apostasia

Tim closed his eyes tight, then opened them again. But the horrific scene was still before him. This was no nightmare that he could wake up from. In front of him was the escort soldier's body lying lifeless but still receiving bullets from the squad. Tim looked down at Paul to ask him what they should do now, but he was no more. The overwhelming sadness led Tim to cry for his deceased friend, even though he knew that soon enough his own end was imminent and there would be no more time for tears.

Just as the thundering and cracking of gun fire and bullets stopped, Tim could faintly hear a different type of noise. After straining hard to hear it, he realized it was a light ticking sound that was coming from Paul's pocket. Reaching in, Tim grabbed a device and pulled it out. It was the detonator, and the countdown had somehow started.

"But how?" Tim asked aloud to the empty room. It was only supposed to start with the key turned and a code entered, and Paul died before they had done that. In fact, before he died Tim was certain that Paul had decided against blowing up the building. There had been too much death already. Tim looked back at the escort lying in front of the door and noticed something. The clone's eyes were still opened and were slowly closing, and there was the slightest movement coming from his chest. Tim knew now that the soldier must have started the countdown for the detonation. All the technology and explosives they had brought with them had originally come from the MUD PIT, and each of the clones had complete telepathic access to the software.

Tim had no idea how he was able to hang on for this long without changing, but now he was truly on the cusp. Hearing the footsteps of the Special Forces inching closer, Tim felt compelled to reach in his jacket and use all the tranquilizers he had left. Tim did not want himself changing and potentially setting himself loose into the public. Just as Tim injected himself with the last needle, he saw the men closing in on him; as they approached they became blurrier. He could hear them shouting something, but the voices were muffled. He thought he heard them saying something about him being a hostage and that he needed medical attention. While he may have not been the type of hostage they meant, he did consider himself a hostage of sorts. He was a hostage of grief, revenge, and death. All the things that had seemed so important these past months since losing Aavah now seemed so pointless, and he knew she would have been disappointed in him. This caused him more sadness than he had ever felt in his life. Ironically, the men he thought needed to die for a greater good were now trying to help revive him. It felt comforting as well as heartbreaking. As his life slowly slipped away, he hoped his silent prayer for forgiveness was heard, and that he would be able to see Aavah again.

Forbidden Origins-apostasia

Running down the halls and finding his way outside with the little girl in his arms, Laski saw some paramedics in the distance. Just as he reached the medical staff, explosions started going off behind him. The building was totally engulfed in flames, and glass and debris started flying everywhere. Suddenly everyone was in a frenzy as the building began to come down. Laski had no choice but to keep running and get the girl to safety. He ran, and kept running, without having any idea of where he was running to. When he made it just outside of the city he finally stopped.

Looking back towards the building that once stood, he saw smoke and dust, as well as more emergency crews passing by. He had meant to save the girl, but it was part of his mission to be in that building when it came down. He had no purpose left. He was alive and didn't know what to do. Setting the girl down, he grabbed his wallet from his back pocket, and pulled out his prepaid credit card. He placed it in the bewildered little girl's hand and told her, "Here, there's some funds left on this card. Take it. Find a good family to live with."

Then he turned around and proceeded to walk away to figure out what to do next. It was his destiny to be part of that explosion. And now that he failed in that mission he had to decide on how to make up for it; even though there was nothing in his programming for a contingency for this happening.

Laski didn't make it more than five steps before the little girl rushed to him and started tugging on his hand.

"Mister, please. My mommy and daddy said police are supposed to help me if I get lost. Well, I'm lost and you are the police." She said this in tears but with strong conviction.

Laski was confused for a moment, but as he looked down at her he noticed a badge stitched on the shirt he was wearing that he had taken from the Special Forces officer. He was just about to correct her when he realized that *she* was going to be his new mission.

CHAPTER TWENTY-ONE
A New Mission

Laski was determined to find this girl a family, and he already had one in mind. Maggie Lenten and her boys should do the trick. Laski knew that walking on foot was not going to be practical for too much longer. The little girl was exhausted, and even by car the Lenten family was many hours away.

After passing a 'For Sale' sign for a vintage truck made in 1995, he decided to withdraw whatever he had left on the pre-paid credit card and inquire about the vehicle. With it being an older model from a private seller, there was a good chance it wouldn't be too pricey. It wasn't too long after trekking into town that they came across a bank. There was an ATM outside, so he checked the balance on his card and found that all that was available was $1200. After withdrawing the full amount from the machine he continued to follow signs for the vehicle for about another mile and a half.

These led the ragtag pair to a nice suburb just outside of town, which is where they finally found the truck. Since the signs advertised it was made in the 1990's, in his mind that meant a cheap old automobile, which would be serviceable enough for the short time he would be needing it.

But upon arrival he saw that the truck was not beaten up at all, and although old it was in beautiful condition. The price of the truck was written on the windshield, which said it was going for $5,800. The disappointment was overwhelming. He contemplated stealing it for the greater good, and just use it long enough to help the girl get a family, then he could return it. Despite the temptation, something was telling him it was wrong and he didn't know why. Maybe it was the fact that he could get caught and would end up jeopardizing the whole mission. Either way, he decided against stealing it, and started to walk away.

Forbidden Origins-apostasia

Just then the owner of the house noticed Laski and the girl and rushed outside. "I can help you if you're interested in my truck!" the man yelled out, hoping to grab them before leaving and to make a sale.

As Laski turned around he could see an elderly man approaching them, moving rather quickly for someone his age.

As the owner came to an arm's length distance, he saw that Laski and the girl were rather dirty and rough around the edges. And upon closer inspection, he also noticed the police uniform Laski was wearing. The man stood in silence not knowing what to say.

Breaking the silence, Laski responded with, "I'm sorry, but I can't afford your vehicle. I only have $1200 cash." At that he turned around once again to walk away.

"Wait! Hold up," the elderly man cried out.

Laski turned back around to see what was the matter.

The man approached him again. "I was just watching the news, so I'm wondering if you both were near that building when it collapsed?"

Laski was a little startled at the question, however the man didn't appear to be making accusations of any kind. So he answered honestly, but with caution.

"Yes, we both were in that building, but I managed to pull her out before the building collapsed. Unfortunately, most of the emergency vehicles were tied up with trying to help the injured

301

or were damaged from the explosion, so I had to get her out of there by foot."

Chuck must have been a very soft-hearted man, as his eyes teared up after hearing of their narrow escape from death. "I see. Where are her parents?" he asked.

Without hesitation, Laski replied, "Her parents were both killed in the attack..." Before Laski could finish his answer, the little girl began to cry at his brutally honest wording.

"Careful now, you mustn't be so descriptive around young children," the man said to Laski while bending down to get to the little girl's level. "You know, I'm a grandpa, and my wife is a grandma, so do you know what that means? She's always ready to bake some yummy cookies. Does that sound good?" The man asked kindly, and she nodded yes. He stood up at looked Laski in the eyes and said, "Well, that settles it! Why don't you both come inside and clean up? We'll provide dinner and dessert, it's the least we can do for our two brave heroes."

Before walking into the house the man stopped short, suddenly realizing that he forgot to introduce himself. "I'm sorry, where are my manners? I'm Chuck, Chuck Meyer. What's your name?"

Laski was about to say #43, but then just in time remembered he was given a name. Before today no one had asked him his name. "Marc Laski," he replied, after a short pause.

Forbidden Origins-apostasia

Chuck heartily shook his hand. "I'm glad to meet you, Officer Laski." Then he looked down at the little girl and asked her, "And what's your name, darlin'?"

Looking up at the man she replied, "Hannah."

He gently took her hand in his and shook hers as well. "Well it is most certainly nice to meet you, Miss Hannah."

She blushed and looked down at her shoes, but he could see the small smile on her face after he let go of her hand.

As they walked in the house Chuck introduced them to his wife Nancy, who was waiting just inside the door for them. She was a small, plump woman that always smelled like she was baking something fresh (which she usually was). Chuck explained to Nancy how Officer Laski was in the building that collapsed and how he had saved the little one. He also whispered in her ear that Hannah's parents tragically perished in the building and asked if she could whip up a fresh batch of chocolate chip cookies.

The Meyers offered the guest bathroom on the main floor with a tub for Hannah to wash up in, and then directed Laski upstairs to use their master bathroom shower.

303

"I'll have Nancy help Hannah wash up, and after that she can take care of your clothes. In the meantime, I have some clothes laid out on the bed for you." Chuck was talking through the door while Laski was in the bathroom trying to figure out how to work their shower. "My wife has kept some of my son's clothes from his younger years; she hates getting rid of things. He was pretty tall, and a linebacker when he played football in college, so I think this will fit you fine."

Chuck began laying the clothes on his bed for Laski. "Nancy is getting some clothes ready for Hannah, as we have some extra outfits of my granddaughter's here as well. It is such a blessing having you both here...she sure loves children!"

At that moment Laski finally figured out the shower and had it running.

Chuck waited a few seconds longer, but still did not get a response. "Well then, I guess I'll just see you back downstairs when you're finished. No rush!" Chuck exited the room, realizing he was probably getting annoying with all his chatter.

Stepping into the hot, steamy shower was a feeling Laski had never experienced. At first he wasn't sure what to think with three different shower heads spraying hot water all over him, but soon enough he got used to it and began really enjoying it. The therapy of washing off all the sweat and blood he had been carrying for the short, but violent time he was alive, felt soothing. Finishing up his shower, he dried himself off and walked into the master bedroom and saw the clothes that had been laid out for him. A pair of faded blue jeans, a white button up collared shirt, a white, black and blue striped sweater, and finally a soft looking white t-shirt.

Feeling overwhelmed at what to do with all these pieces of clothing, Laski decided to start with the part he was sure about. So he picked up the jeans and put them on. In deep thought and concentration, he figured the shirts couldn't be too difficult to piece together, he just had to think of it like a puzzle. He ended up trying multiple combinations before he was satisfied he had them all in the right order: t-shirt, dress-shirt, then sweater.

As he was about to walk out the door, he noticed his reflection in a full length mirror which was standing next to the dresser. This was the first time he had ever seen himself. Dark hair, dark eyes, a strong jaw line. It was lucky that these clothes fit him as his muscles were hard to conceal. As he looked at himself from head to toe, a ghost of a smile appeared on his face. He had to admit, he looked pretty darn good.

Heading down to the dining area he saw Chuck, Nancy and Hannah sitting at the table waiting for him. When he came into view Chuck gave a low whistle.

"Wow...now that is one sharp looking young man! What do you ladies think?"

When both Mrs. Meyer and Hannah agreed, Laski couldn't help but to smile for real this time; perhaps the first genuine smile he had. Sitting down at the table he saw that Hannah had cleaned up real nice, too. Her silky blonde hair was pulled back with two pink hair clips, one on each side of her head parting her hair, which almost reached her shoulders. She was wearing a modest pink and white dress that matched her hair clips. Chuck and Nancy also dressed up a little nicer than when he had seen them last.

The food that they served was great; Laski had never experienced such a variety of flavors. But the biggest surprise was that he enjoyed the conversation almost as much as the food. Laski was quiet for the most part, but loved seeing the interaction between everyone else. After some delicious dessert - that they were all almost too full for - they continued the pleasant conversation for a while longer.

As that died down, Nancy asked Hannah if she would mind helping her to clean up.

"Ok," the little girl answered shyly.

The two grabbed up the leftover food dishes from the table and disappeared in the kitchen.

Both men satisfied from the great meal, just sat in companionable silence for several minutes. But when Chuck looked at the time, he suddenly remembered what situation his two guests had just come from.

"You know Marc, I can't believe it has slipped my mind this long, but I imagine that you need to call the station and let them know where you are and that you are ok."

Chuck pulled out his phone and handed it to Laski, who looked at him blankly for a moment before it dawned on

306

Forbidden Origins-apostasia

him what he meant by that. This whole time Chuck assumed that
Laski was an officer of the law, so of course he would believe he
needed to check in with his superiors.

"I cannot call the police, sir." As he began to answer the
old man, Laski stealthily slid the cutting knife that was left on the
table up his sleeve. "To be honest with you, I'm sort of a
considered AWOL right now."

Chuck started in surprise at hearing this answer. "What
do you mean by that, Marc?"

"When I found Hannah alone and scared, I left my post
and went against my orders. My new personal mission was to get
Hannah out of that building safely, so that was what I did. Once
that building came down, I didn't know what to do. But I
realized that if I took personal responsibility for Hannah, I could
get her to her new family. They do not live close by, which is why
I was looking for a vehicle to make the trip."

Chuck did not interrupt while hearing Laski's truthful
explanation, and did not speak right away once he was done.

"Do you wish to call the authorities now, after what I just
told you?" Laski asked him, while handing him back his phone.

When Chuck looked down at it, Laski took the opportunity
to ready the knife in his hand. Little did Chuck know that his
answer would decide his fate.

"Well now, if we are both being honest here, Marc...I
never was one to be a stickler for the rules." After saying this, he
tucked his phone back in his pocket.

Laski was relieved, as he really had not wanted to kill the kind man.

"The way I see it, you may have defied your original orders, but it is your job to serve and protect. And that's what you did. You saw someone that was in need of your help, so you did what needed to be done. As far as I'm concerned, you did the right thing."

Laski did not respond to this, so Chuck just continued.

"Ok then. It's getting late. So, in light of the fact that you may be considered a fugitive, I think that it would be best if you both just stayed here for the night."

"I appreciate that, sir," Laski said.

After Chuck let Nancy know that their dinner guests would be sleeping over, she made up the couch for Hannah and began tucking her in while Chuck showed Laski into the guest room.

Some hours later while deep in sleep, Laski suddenly jolted awake after hearing the sound of footsteps creeping into his room. He started reaching for his pistol he had hidden under his pillow, but just as he was about to pull it out the footsteps stopped before reaching his bed, and then all was silent. He stared at the empty doorway in puzzlement and then finally looked down towards the floor. There on the ground right next to his bed was Hannah, all wrapped up in blankets.

"Hannah?" he asked.

"Yeah?" was her muffled response.

Forbidden Origins-apostasia

"What are you doing in here?"

She stood up so she could be near eye level with him. "I keep having nightmares."

"Nightmares?" Laski asked.

"Yeah, very bad dreams. Every time I close my eyes I see my mommy and daddy get chased by monsters covered in blood that are trying to eat them," she said in a quavering voice.

"So why did you come in here?" Laski was still confused what bad thoughts or dreams had to do with her invading his room.

"Because I was scared, and I knew that you would protect me from the monsters."

In that simple way that children have of putting things, Laski realized just how much she was relying on him to take care of her. His heart was touched and so he decided to let her stay there on the floor next to him for the rest of the night.

The next morning Laski was awake before anyone else, sitting at the dining room table by himself. He was all dressed up again in the nice clothes Chuck had given him the day before.

When Chuck came down later in the morning, he realized that he had forgotten to place the officer's freshly washed uniform in the guestroom before bed. "I hope you slept well, Marc. I'm sorry that I hid your uniform on you last night. I didn't mean for you to have to wear the same outfit again today."

"That's ok, I wanted to look nice this morning," Laski replied.

309

Chuck couldn't help but smile. "You know what, you look really good in that outfit. You should keep it. In fact, there's something else that goes with it." While saying that, Chuck went over to the hallway closet and came back with a blue moto jacket with little zippers all around on it. Chuck signaled Laski to stand up and try it on.

After putting it on, Chuck told him to check the pockets. When he reached inside he pulled out some keys. Laski looked up in question, confused at what this meant.

"I talked with Nancy last night and we both agreed you should take the truck." The old man picked up a piece of paper he had set on the table when he first came downstairs and handed it to Laski. "Here's the title; I've already filled out my information. Come outside and let me show you the features and what all I've done to it."

Heading outside Chuck began to explain, "Many years ago I had bought this for my son and I to work on together. I thought it would be a good way for us to spend some father-son bonding time. Once it was finished I gave it to him as a high school graduation gift. It's a 1995 Toyota Helix. You don't find too many of these bad boys in the States, I can tell you that. These things will take a licking and keep on kicking!" Chuck said with a laugh. "Anyways, we added a lift kit and oversized tires. The engine is original, but completely rebuilt, so it's almost like new. We repainted it this black color (the original was white) and we re-did the entire interior as well. And as you can see, it has an

Forbidden Origins-apostasia

extended cab with a Hardtop canopy for the bed." Chuck placed his hand on the truck. "It's funny really; my son and I never liked the style of vehicles from the 90's. But when I found this one at an auction I just knew there was something special about it. My son and I both have a lot of fond memories with this truck." He said this last part with sadness.

Laski was happy to receive such a gift, but after Chuck was done talking it seemed as though something was wrong. "Do you mind if I ask why you put it up for sale? Wouldn't your son be upset about you just giving it away?" Laski had to ask.

Chuck looked down at the ground to hide the tears that started welling up. "That's just it, Officer Laski. He loved this truck, but nearly a week ago he died. He worked on a military base, but something went wrong and he was one of the many casualties. See, I was trying to sell the truck because I can't handle having it in my driveway...it is a constant reminder of what I've lost. But Nancy and I have decided that instead of selling it, we would rather give it to you. We don't need the money and I feel better about giving it to someone who is a hero, like my son."

Laski had an awful feeling from what Chuck was saying that his son was one of many that had died at the MUD PIT. Laski wanted to say something, but couldn't find anything appropriate to say. "I'm so sorry for your loss." Laski finally said.

311

Chuck wiped his eyes with a hankie he pulled from his pocket, and then after composing himself he took a deep breath and then said, "Marc, please don't take this the wrong way, but I've felt compelled to ask you if you know where you're going when you die? I'm not saying you'll end up like my son, but especially after what you have been through you know as well as anyone that we are never promised tomorrow."

Laski was a bit taken aback by the question, but realized it made sense with how the conversation was going. "No, I don't, but I've wondered..."

Chuck smiled. "It's okay, many do. If you are interested, I do have the answer." Laski looked at him with a puzzled expression, so Chuck went on to say, "The body is just a dwelling place for the soul. When the body dies the soul can either be tormented or live in paradise..."

Just then Hannah came running out of the door of the house. "Look! Look! I have a new purse!" She lifted up her pretty blue purse that Nancy had given her and showed the two men. Shortly after, Nancy came outside carrying a plate of homemade, warm coffee bread wrapped in plastic.

"Mr. Meyer and I are just so pleased to have had the honor of having the two of you stay with us! It truly did us good to have some people to take care of and spoil, even if it was just for a little bit."

Laski accepted the plate from the generous woman and replied, "Thank you for everything ma'am, but we should get

Forbidden Origins-apostasia

going. We have a long way to go." Laski was curious about what all Chuck had to say, but he felt that he had a mission that needed to be completed first.

"Okay, but at least let me give you one more thing before you leave." Chuck said.

Chuck and Nancy went inside and came back out with their hands full. Nancy gave Laski and Hannah their clean clothes and some extra snacks for the drive. Then Chuck gave his last gift.

"I want you to read this; this explains what I was trying to tell you earlier. It will help you on your journey."

Taking the book Laski saw that it was very thick. He had never read anything before, but he did know how to read. "Okay, I'll look into it."

After shaking Chuck's hand goodbye, he helped Hannah into the car then got into the driver's seat, turned the engine over and pulled out of the driveway. Hannah waved at the elderly couple that had taken such good care of them until they were completely out of sight.

Not even ten minutes after being on the highway the questions started rolling off Hannah's tongue. "I keep hearing you say that you are finding me a new family. Who's going to be my new mommy and daddy?"

Laski pulled out the folded picture of Maggie Lenten. "This is your new mother."

Grabbing the picture from Laski she said, "I like her hair; it's like mine that's short, but not so short. Is she nice?"

Laski considered the question. Finally he answered, "Not to me, but she seems to love children."

"Well, if she loves children, that means she's nice. What about the dad, he's not in the picture...is he nice?"

Laski responded to that with, "The dad died." Poor Hannah looked crestfallen after hearing that. "That's so sad. What happened to him?"

"I kille—" before Laski answered honestly, he remembered from Chuck how not to be so blunt with children. "He choked," he corrected.

At this Hannah nodded her head as if to say she knew it. "Well, that's why you don't run with food in your mouth. Will she get married again so I can have a new daddy?"

Laski thought about this and finally said, "I might try to get a father ready for you later."

"Okay, but he has to be nice too. Will you stay with me?"

"I don't think so. You will have two brothers that will stay with you."

Hannah seemed displeased when she heard the first part, but perked up immediately with the news about having brothers. "I've always wanted brothers. Are they older or younger?"

Instead of answering this time, Laski replied with a question of his own. "Why do you ask so many questions?"

Forbidden Origins-apostasia

Without skipping a beat Hannah said, "Well, I think it's because I like to know things, and my questions are important. Where are your mommy and daddy?"

Laski sighed, resigned that this was going to be a very long drive. "I do not have parents. I am a genetically altered soldier created for a mission I couldn't complete."

"Oh...Are you an American soldier?"

"Well, I was made in America, if that is what you mean."

Hannah was more comfortable with that answer then the previous. "Okay; I was made in my mommy's tummy."

Laski looked at her then back at the road. 'What did I get myself into?' he asked himself.

CHAPTER TWENTY-TWO
Hungry

(CRASH)

Startled out of reading one of the *Forbidden Origins* comics that Shem had given him, Cody realized that the loud crash he heard was coming from the room next to his. As he quickly laid the comic down on the bed and got up to listen closer at the door, he heard the faint sounds of moaning coming from the next room. Frantically throwing some clothes on, he followed the moans and heavy breathing to Shem's room.

Opening the door, he found the reverend on his hands and knees on the floor, struggling to stand up. Cody rushed to him and cried out, "Are you ok?!" He attempted to help the older man to his feet, but he was almost like dead weight.

Forbidden Origins-apostasia

"I feel like an elephant is sitting on my chest," Shem rasped out.

Finally Cody was able to get him on his bed, but he knew that the situation was serious.

"Cody, I was there when my father had his heart attack, so I know that is what is happening to me. The good Lord is going to take me the same way that he took him..."

"No! Don't talk like that, you are going to be fine. Tell me where the phone is so I can call an ambulance." Cody was trying his best not to panic, but he had just found the kind reverend and already considered him a friend; he was not ready to lose him just yet. Shem pointed with a weak hand across the room to where his phone was sitting on the dresser. But when Cody picked it up, Shem shook his head.

"What's the matter, is it not charged or something? Is there another one I can use??"

But again Shem shook his head and motioned for Cody to come closer. "The guitar...bring me the guitar."
Cody stared at him for a moment in disbelief. The man was having a heart attack and all he could worry about was his stupid guitar?

This time Cody was the one to shake his head and he turned the phone on and said, "We will worry about the guitar later, Shem. Right now we need to get you some help." As he started dialing, the reverend grabbed his hand and with a sudden surge of strength he pulled him down closer.

317

"Silas, if anything happens to me, I need you to remember everything that I've taught you. It's important, it will help you when all else seems lost..."

Towards the end of what Shem was trying to say it was clearly difficult for him to speak and it was getting harder to make out his words. "...need you to understand...the guitar..."

Cody never got a chance to ask him what in the world he was talking about, because just then the 911 operator answered the call.

"911, please state your emergency."

In the time that it took to explain to the operator what was happening, it appeared that Shem had stopped breathing. Cody frantically relayed this to the lady on the other end, and she asked him to perform CPR on the man to try and revive him. He worked non-stop for as long as he had the strength, but it was to no avail; Shem was gone.

"Sir, the EMTs should be there any time, but please remain on the line with me until –"

Cody hung up the phone and dropped it to the floor. He wanted to just curl up in the corner and ball his eyes out. Not just for the loss of his newfound friend, but for his entire, miserable life that continued to seem to go from bad to worse. He wondered why in the world he seemed to be such a curse to anyone that he had contact with. A few months ago when he tried to get back in touch with Dr. Phillips, he saw on the news that he was blown up in the Federal Duplications building. He

Forbidden Origins-apostasia

knew that the man was set on revenge, but he had no idea he was suicidal. He wished that he could have found him before the tragedy, but with his luck, the guy probably would have just ended up offing himself sooner.

Cody walked over to the guitar that Shem thought was more important than his own health. He picked it up and looked it over, but the answer did not seem to be written on it. Hearing sirens coming from far away, he realized he had to get out of there before they arrived. He had managed to stay under the radar since the barn incident and dropping off those girls, so the last thing he needed was to be detained and questioned by a bunch of cops. He took the guitar with him to his room and quickly threw a few of the things that Shem had given him into a duffel bag. Even though the comics would take up too much room and not allow for him to bring more essentials like clothes and such, he couldn't bear to leave them behind. Shem wrote them, and besides that he had been hooked on them since he had moved in with the reverend. He figured he could always get more clothes, but chances were slim that he would be able to find these comics anywhere else. So grabbing up his bag and the guitar, Cody slipped out the back entrance of the building just as he heard footsteps approaching from the front.

Hearing the sound of a door opening, he woke up and found himself in a dark room. Even though it felt like there were a mountain of blankets on him, he felt freezing with a chill that seemed bone deep. His throat was also unbelievably dry, and he couldn't remember a time he felt as hungry as he did just then.

"Still not feeling any better, humph? I don't know what I'm going to do with you. You're eating my life away. I don't have time to play nursemaid all day long, weeks on end. I need to get back to work. You know Nero, when I allowed you to step foot back into my house it was only for the sake of our son. So you should be grateful that I did not just leave you outside to fend for pathetic self. I told you that being part of that stupid Pitoni gang was going to end up getting you and our son killed, but no, of course you never listened to me! And then you tell me that some deranged clone doctor performed experiments and tortured you both, and do you let me call the police? No! Of course not, because you are such a low life scum of a criminal that you can't even do anything about it when someone is TRYING TO KILL YOU!" Nero's ex-wife Claudia screamed this last bit at him while she stood there with her hands on her hips and her foot tapping on the floor.

After taking a second to squeeze in a breath before continuing her massive nagging session, she instead let out a

Forbidden Origins-apostasia

startled "Oh!" when Nero started sweating profusely and convulsing. She rushed over to his side to feel his head and it burned her hand to touch him. "Nero, this has got to stop. I'm sorry, I know I promised you that I wouldn't take you and Nikki to the hospital or get the police involved, but I have got to call an ambulance!"

As Claudia started to pull her hand away from Nero's forehead, his hand grasped hers and he started to bring it towards his cheek. "I'm sorry Nero, but it's too late for that. No amount of sweet talk or gesture is to change my mind about getting you out of my house once and for all and in to see a real doctor –" before she even finished her rant, Nero brought her hand to his mouth and took a healthy bite out of her wrist.

Claudia screamed and slapped him as hard as she could with her other hand, nearly causing it to fracture. "You *STRONZO!*" she spat out, followed by a string of other Italian cuss words.

Nero did not react to anything she said, but his sweating and shaking seemed to cease altogether. More than that, he looked as though he was finally getting out of bed on his own, when seconds ago he appeared to be mere inches from death. As a matter of fact, when he stood up he looked about as strong and healthy as she had ever seen him. But even more terrifying than this miraculous recovery was the look on his face. He stared hungrily at her, wiping her blood off his mouth with his hand and then licking it.

321

This action caused her to gasp, turn tail and run out of the room. She slammed the door behind her, and then headed straight for her son's sickbed. "Nikki, Nikki wake up! Your dad has gone crazy, *pazzo*, so we have to get out of here quick!" Out of breath, she shook the lump under the blankets, but to her alarm there was no body beneath them. Running out of the room, she noticed the door to her ex-husband's room was open, and the room empty. She started walking quietly, afraid for her life but still wanting to save her son by finding wherever he may be.

"Nikki! Nikki, where are you!?" She called his name in as loud of a whisper as she dared. After being more in tune with her surroundings, she heard something from the kitchen. Not knowing which person was in the kitchen, she grabbed a walking stick nearby. Holding it like a baseball bat, she got ready to swing. There was a constant trail of dripping blood from her wrist, which followed behind her. The blood loss was beginning to make her feel woozy, but she needed her son. Finally, she reached the kitchen.

After turning on the light, it took a moment for her eyes to adjust. It was Nikki making the strange noises after all. He was on his hands and knees on the floor, eating her curly haired mutt of a dog. "Nikki? What have you done to poor Fonzie?" As he stood up, she saw that he was changed; strong with blotches throughout his body. Then she felt a presence behind her. Slowly she turned her head to see what it was, but there was no

Forbidden Origins-apostasia

one. Turning her attention back to her son, he was no longer there. Only the bloody, lifeless dog remained on her kitchen floor.

Cody was coming to the end of his rapidly fraying rope. It had been a couple days since he left Shem's place, and he was hungry and tired. He felt terrible about even thinking it, but after being reduced to sleeping on park benches he finally decided to sell the guitar. Thinking back to several conversations he had with Shem, he was given the impression that it was worth quite a lot of money.

Walking into the closest town he could find, he passed what seemed like endless rows of restaurants. The enticing aroma of food tortured his already growling stomach. He thought it probably wouldn't help his sale to look like he was homeless, so he went into one of the fast food places to clean up in the rest room the best that he could.

After putting on his cleanest outfit and washing his face and hair in the sink (earning him some strange looks from a father with a young boy that were in there using the bathroom), he felt like a new person and ready to do some haggling. It didn't take him too long to find a pawn shop on the main street, so he walked in and approached the counter.

"Hello there, what can I do ya for?" was the friendly welcome he received from the middle-aged man behind the counter.

"Uh, hi, I was looking to sell my guitar." Cody picked up Shem's guitar and set it down on the counter-top so the man could inspect it.

Giving it a quick once over, he replied, "Well, she sure is a beauty, I can say that much! Tell you what, I can do as much as $300, but not a penny more."

Cody's heart sank. He thought it was going to be well into the thousands. Shem had told him the day that they first met that this guitar was worth more than his entire store. "Look sir, I don't think you understand. The man that gave me this guitar told me that it was practically priceless. I know he put a lot of work into it and it has to be worth a lot more than just $300."

The man could tell that the young gentleman was very upset by his offer, so he tried to explain it to him. "Listen son, it plays nice and is beautiful, but I don't even see a brand on here. It has clearly been refurbished which can decrease the value, and I need to be able to make a profit when I resell it. So, my offer stands at $300...take it or leave it."

Cody was furious to say the least, so he gruffly responded with, "Thanks anyways." He picked up the guitar off the counter and left the shop. He wasn't about to give up just yet because of

Forbidden Origins-apostasia

what one hick tried telling him. Cody was certain that the guy was probably just trying to rip him off. So he decided to try a couple more pawn shops as well as guitar shops.

But after about three hours and two sore feet later, all of them pretty much had told him the same thing. Several of them admired the interesting artwork that was etched onto the front and back, but they all seemed to agree that since it was not in its original condition, the value had decreased immensely.

Frustrated, he left the fifth shop he had gone into and he sat down on the curb outside to try and figure out what in the world he was going to do. He could sell it for the $300, but that would not get him far. It would provide immediate relief for his hunger and a place to stay for a night or two, but then it would be gone and he would be back to where he started. He hated to part with the guitar for such a small return on Shem's investment. The guitar seemed so important to him. Obviously it was the reverend's bias and admiration of the instrument that misled Cody into overestimating its value. He stared down at the guitar in his hands and studied the beautiful art that Shem had etched on it. His fingers traced the patterns and lines, wondering what inspired Shem to draw them.

All of a sudden he realized that there was a sort of hidden message within the drawing. You really had to be holding it just right and looking at the swirls and shapes at a certain angle, but now that he could see it, Cody wasn't sure how he had missed it before. It almost reminded him of one of those pixelated paintings that you had to stare at for hours before you could see the concealed 'sailboat' or other hidden image within. Putting together the letters and numbers, he saw "Issue # 21". Baffled a little at first on why the heck Shem would put that in his design into the guitar, the more he thought about it the more he thought that it must have something to do with his comics. Opening up his duffel bag, Cody searched through his stack of comic books until he found Issue 21. He had yet to get that far into the *Forbidden Origins* series, so he had not read that one.

After flipping through the first several pages, he got to a part where one of the main characters was trying to decipher an unknown ancient hieroglyph. The more that Cody studied the shapes and symbols that Shem had drawn in the comic, the more confident he was that these same images were also incorporated in the designs on the guitar. In the comic, the hieroglyphs ended up being a map that led the hero to the place he was looking for. Suddenly Cody's worries and fears gave way to excitement and wonder.

"Is this what Shem was trying to tell me just before he died? Was he trying to explain what the message on the guitar meant?" Cody wondered. Staring a little harder at the guitar now, turning it over and also studying the back, he could see that the design could be interpreted as a map to somewhere. There even seemed to be a symbol that looked like an "X", reminding Cody of watching pirate cartoons as a kid where "X" always marked the spot. He realized that it was unlikely that Shem had

Forbidden Origins-apostasia

buried treasure hidden somewhere, but he did feel that Shem had been trying to tell him something important about the guitar when he died. The map may not lead to riches galore or some other such nonsense, but Cody's interest was definitely peaked. The mystery of what it could be and why it was so important to Shem to encrypt a message onto his prized guitar was too alluring to ignore.

Standing up from the curb and brushing the dirt off of himself, Cody found that he wasn't even hungry anymore; at least not for food. Instead he was hungry to solve the mystery of the guitar map, and what it may lead to.

About the Authors

Daniel & Kara Ratcliffe are an inseparable husband and wife team, motivated to deliver new ideas and stories that aren't formed by a cookie cutter ideology. This couple truly loves the audience they are reaching out to and want to make an impact on the lives of others. Their hobbies outside of writing consist of research, teaching, and spending time with their family and friends. They currently live with two treasured pets. A Chihuahua named Dozer and an adopted retired racer; a Greyhound named Lily. Their hope is to extend the family with some babies in the near future.

Visit us at

www.dkratcliffe.com

NOTES

NOTES

NOTES

NOTES

NOTES

NOTES

NOTES

NOTES

NOTES

Made in the USA
Charleston, SC
27 November 2016